Saving Ben

To Alannah —
All my best —
xoxo
Ashley

ASHLEY H. FARLEY

ISBN: 1481960873
ISBN-13: 978-1481960878

For Neal

ASHLEY H. FARLEY

Ashley Farley was born and raised in South Carolina. She currently lives in Richmond, Virginia with her husband and two teenage children. This is her first novel.

Visit Ashley's website and blog at www.ashleyfarley.net

ONE

New Year's Day

I saw them from my upstairs bedroom window. A single set of footprints in the snow, leading to Emma's car in the driveway and then around the house toward the cove. Other than a family of deer munching on the evergreen shrubs out by the road, the only sign of life was a cardinal nestled in the holly tree in front of me, his blood-red feathers a sharp contrast to the white landscape.

I stumbled down the hall and up the stairs to my parents' room. I tapped on the door and peeked in, expecting to find my brother curled up with his more-off-than-on-again girlfriend in our parents' king-size bed.

I shook him. "Ben, Ben, wake up."

He peeked at me through one eye. "Go away, Kitty," he said, pulling the covers up over his head.

"Gladly. But first tell me where Emma is."

An arm appeared from beneath the blanket and patted the empty bed beside him. He scrambled into a sitting position. "What's going on?" he asked, surveying the room.

"I'm not sure, but you'd better come look."

He untangled his body from the sheets and followed me over to the bank of windows that offered a panoramic view of Carter's Creek. "I didn't know it was supposed to snow," he said, holding his hand in front of his eyes to shield them from the glare of the early-morning sun.

2	ASHLEY FARLEY

"It was snowing at midnight. Don't you remember?"

He shook his head, his expression blank. The memory was dim for me as well, but I wasn't ready to admit that just yet.

"Look." I pointed at the footprints leading across the snow-covered lawn and down the hill to the deserted dock.

"Damn." He blinked several times. "Whoever went out on that dock did not come back."

"Duh, Ben. And I'd be willing to bet those footprints belong to Emma."

Ben rubbed his eyes as if to clear the haze of last night's drink. "I can't remember anything that happened after midnight. Did she come to bed when I did?"

Biting back the tears, I shrugged. I had long since exceeded the limits of what most sane people would do to protect their siblings. The experience of a missing girlfriend was just another episode in our continuing drama.

TWO

Sixteen Months Earlier

With barely a glance in the rearview mirror, Ben whipped his Land Cruiser across two lanes of interstate traffic and sped down the exit ramp toward Route 250. He came to a rolling stop at a red light before peeling out in front of a stream of oncoming cars.

"Damnit, Ben." I braced myself against the dashboard. "If you're going to drive like a maniac, pull over and let me out."

"Why are you in such a bad mood today?" His arm shot out toward me, and before I could defend myself, he gave me a noogie, grinding his knuckles on top of my head. "Are you still upset with Mom and Dad for not coming with us?"

"Hardly. What really upsets me is that they trusted their daughter's life to a lunatic. Will you please slow down? I'd rather not die before I've had a chance to spend at least one night as a college student."

Grinning, he flipped me the bird.

"Right back at you, pal."

"Seriously, though, have you ever known our parents to miss out on a social event for our benefit?" When I shook my head, he added, "We've always done fine without them. the only thing that's changed is the venue."

"Exactly. Nothing *has* changed. That's what worries me," I admitted. "In your mind, Ben, there's a fine line between watching my back and being my bodyguard."

"Hold on a minute," he said, lifting his hands off the steering wheel in surrender. "I thought we were talking about Mom and Dad. Why are you attacking *me*?"

"Because you need to back off a little and let me have some fun."

"Since when have I ruined your fun?" he asked.

"Every time a guy comes within a hundred yards of me."

"Oh . . . I see how it is. We're talking about Jack Briscoe again. That guy was a punk, Kitty. You should thank me for saving you from social embarrassment."

"Maybe so. But what about Brad Miller? He's your friend."

"Which is why I didn't want you to go out with him." Ben smiled his gotcha grin at me, but dropped it when he saw I was serious. "Okay, look. Lighten up. I get your point."

"Then I'm counting on you to give me some space. I'm in college now. You need to respect that."

He let out a deep breath of resignation, giving in another fraction of an inch in our long-standing battle over my freedom.

We turned onto Emmet Street and entered the main part of the University of Virginia campus. We stopped at a crossing walk and waited while a mob of people passed in front of us. Most were parents out exploring with their first-year students, helping them locate the bookstore and Alderman Library and the student center at Newcomb Hall. I envied them their perfect families.

I cast a nervous glance at Ben and he winked back at me, reassuring me everything would be okay. Despite my apprehension I wanted to believe him. The past few years had been difficult for me, and while I'd learned to be resilient, the toughness was only as deep as my skin. And even that was fragile like the shell of a bird's egg protecting the soft gooey center that made up my core.

As the last of the herd of people in front of us approached the sidewalk, a woman turned and waited for her daughter to catch up. The daughter towered over her mother by at least four inches, but she was her clone in every other way, dark hair and skinny frame. The woman grabbed the girl's hand and squeezed, her face softening with love for her daughter. I imagined the tearful parting between the two of them, in a few hours, when the mother left to go home alone without her baby girl.

Meanwhile, *my* mother was spending the day on the golf course.

But I didn't need my mother to hold my hand and offer me a guided tour of the university. I already knew my way around. I'd visited Ben several times during the past two years for football games and lacrosse games and once to hear Kenny Chesney at the John Paul Jones Arena.

The University of Virginia had never been my first choice of colleges. My primary objective in looking at schools was to get as far away as possible from my mother and anything that resembled my life in Richmond. Not that my first choice, the University of North Carolina at Chapel Hill, was on the other side of the planet; it was at least in a different state, and the anonymity of existing on a campus with nearly thirty thousand other students appealed to me. Unfortunately, my application to their nursing program didn't appeal to their admissions counselors.

I'd taken my brother's advice and requested to live in Fairfield Hall where he'd lived as a freshman. One of ten dorms available to first-year students in the McCormick Road Residence Area, Fairfield was an antiquated building that made up for in popularity and location what it lacked in modern conveniences. But unlike my brother, instead of living with a friend, or a friend of a friend, I'd taken my chances on the roommate lottery. And it appeared as though I'd hit the jackpot, at least as far as I could tell from a social network page.

I'd friended Emma Stone on Facebook the minute I received my assignment. She appeared to possess the qualities that would make her a good roommate. She was a community volunteer and the salutatorian of her graduating class, she had 587 friends, and she was pretty in a way that rendered Ben clumsy and me speechless the first time we set our eyes on her.

She was in our dorm room, unpacking, wearing a pair of soft-pink Soffe shorts and tennis shoes with a cropped white T-shirt that exposed a good portion of her tanned belly. Her hair was blonde, nearly white from the sun, and her eyes were clear blue like the Caribbean Sea. She had a tiny diamond stud in her nose, so small at first glance I thought it was a blackhead.

"Um . . . hi. I'm Katherine," I managed, grinning and waving like a kindergartner on our first day of school. When Ben stumbled over his own feet and spilled a plastic container of towels and linens across the floor, I added, "And that klutz is my brother Ben."

Emma dumped an armload of clothes on the bed and drew me into a warm embrace. Despite the intense heat in our room, she smelled fresh, like a summer rose garden at dawn. "Welcome to our new home," she said softly in my ear.

"This isn't a home. It's an inferno," I said, pulling away from her before she could get a whiff of my sweaty T-shirt. "Do you have allergies? Because the school will provide an air conditioner if you do."

Emma shook her head. "Does hay fever count?"

Ben, the authority on all things UVA, offered his hand to Emma. "Nope. Allergies, asthma, and migraines are the only legitimate reasons to have an air conditioner."

"Well, fortunately," Emma said, smiling, "or I guess unfortunately in this case, none of those apply to me."

Ben shrugged. "Then it's lucky for y'all that we're in the mountains. It'll start to get cool here at night in a few weeks. In the meantime, take lots of cold showers and stand in front of your fan."

"Naked?" Emma asked, batting her mascaraed eyelashes at him.

A smile crept across Ben's lips. "Now we're talking. Be sure to invite me to the viewing."

"Too bad I forgot to bring a fan," Emma said, winking at me.

"No worries. Kitty brought at least one of everything."

"Kitty?" Emma asked.

I glared at Ben and he backpedaled. "Oh shit, I forgot. Sorry. She doesn't like to be called that."

Emma flashed a sympathetic smile at me. "And who can blame her? I'm a dog person myself."

"It's not that I dislike the name—all of my friends call me that—I just prefer Katherine."

"And I like Katherine," she said. "The name is strong, like a leader. Catherine the Great."

Ben unscrewed the cap from his bottle and swallowed half the Gatorade in one gulp. "Katherine the bitchy boss would be more accurate in my sister's case."

"You're right, big brother. And this bitchy kitty is going to run you up a tree if you don't finish helping me unpack."

Our room was tiny, like a jail cell with cinderblock walls and a tiled floor, but with Emma and Ben sharing the same space, it seemed even smaller. After every load he hauled up to the room, he lingered longer and longer to check his text messages or offer helpful hints for surviving life in the freshman dorm. Emma couldn't take her eyes off his six-pack abs when he pulled his shirttail up to wipe the sweat from his forehead any more than he could keep from staring at her long tanned legs when she bent over to tuck the fitted sheet under her mattress. Their chemistry, thick and funky with their scents, charged the air.

It was close to five o'clock when Ben dropped the minifridge at the foot of my bed and announced, "Thank God, that's the last of it. I hear a cold beer calling my name."

I glanced around the room for my purse. "If you give me a minute, I'll come with you to help you unload your stuff."

Ben waved me off. "Forget about it, Kitty. I'll get some of the guys at the KO house to help me unload."

"Now we're talking." Emma arched her back and pressed her perky breasts front and center. "Cold beer and fraternity boys. What more could one want?"

Ben ogled her breasts in a way that left little doubt about what *he* wanted. "Yep, and we're having a party tonight, if you're interested," he offered. "Great band. Citizen Cope. Everyone's invited."

I grabbed him by the arm and pulled him across the room. "Thanks for the invitation, but if we don't get busy unpacking, we won't make it to *any* party tonight—not yours or any of the other gazillion I've gotten e-mails about." I opened the door and shoved him out. "Bye now."

Emma began folding T-shirts and placing them neatly inside her bottom drawer. "If you ask me, I'd say it's pretty convenient to have a brother in the hottest fraternity on campus. I'm an only child. I'd give anything to have a brother. Any brother really, but especially one who's so adorable. Just think of all the guys he can introduce you to."

"Ha. In Ben's mind there's not a guy in his fraternity, or anywhere on this planet, that is good enough for me."

Emma kicked her drawer shut. "So he's overprotective, is he? I think that's sweet."

"It *is* sweet." In one quick sweep, I raked all the junk piled on my bed to the floor "As long as he can be open-minded if and when I meet a guy I really like."

"Must be nice to have someone care about you like that," she mumbled loud enough for me to hear.

An awkward silence filled the room. "Anyway. Enough about Ben. We need to decide what we're going to do with all this mess."

Emma leaned back against her dresser and crossed her arms, the hint of a smile tugging at the corners of her mouth. "In case you haven't noticed, new roomie, most of this so-called mess is yours."

My eyes followed hers around the room. In addition to the mountain of pillows and comforters I'd just swept to the floor, a stack of hanging clothes was draped over my dresser and my desk was piled high with binders and packages of pens, a printer, my laptop, and my iHome. Emma's side of the room, on the other hand, was empty except for a patchwork quilt on her bed and a digital alarm clock on her desk.

"I guess I got a little carried away. I had a hard time deciding what to bring, so I just brought it all."

Emma let out a little laugh and I joined her.

"I would've brought more stuff too if there'd been enough room in the car," she said. "The guy I rode with drives a Mini Cooper, if you can believe that?"

"Not only do I believe that, I applaud him for saving our planet's natural resources. Where I come from, any car that has fewer than seven seats and gets more than fifteen miles per gallon is considered worthless." I spread my arms wide. "Clearly I have enough to decorate three dorm rooms. Why don't we share?"

Her smile faded a little, enough to make me worry I'd offended her, but she quickly composed herself. "I think that's a great idea," she said, rummaging through my mountain of PB teen accessories.

"But before we do anything, we need to cool it down some in here." I opened the door and placed my box fan in the window to allow for circulation. "That's better. The air is still hot, but at least it's moving."

Emma joined me at the window and together we stared down at the people moving around on the sidewalks below. "I'm not sure any excuse is reason to miss out on your daughter's first day of college. But my father is an English professor. His classes started this morning."

She didn't ask outright, but the question regarding my parents' whereabouts hung in the air between us like the humidity. No way was I going to admit my parents were playing golf. "I didn't realize there was a college in Altoona," I said instead.

She nodded. "Penn State, Altoona."

"Wow. So I'm guessing your father started building your vocabulary at birth. Did you get a perfect score on your SAT?"

"Not quite but almost." Emma's cheeks reddened and she quickly changed the subject. "Just look at them." She pointed at the sidewalk below. "How embarrassing for those poor parents to be hugging and slobbering all over their little darlings."

"You know they're dreading the long journey home to face their empty nests." I jabbed my elbow in her side. "Think of all the pain and heartache we saved our rents."

"Yeah. Besides, mine are old-fashioned. They would never have left me here to live in the same building with men."

I pointed my thumb at my chest. "*My* parents have a special talent for blowing hot air, which is the last thing we need in this hundred-degree heat."

"At least your parents blow something. Mine are as cold as ice-bergs," she said, the bitter tone in her voice contradicting her smile.

"Our parents are the ones who missed out." I draped my arm loosely across my roommate's shoulders. "And if we don't get start-ed on this room, we're going to miss out too—on our first night of college."

For the next two hours, we scattered rugs and hung curtains and strung strands of white icicle lights along the perimeter of the ceiling. We were hot and sweaty and in desperate need of a shower, but by the time we finished, we had transformed our room into a cozy and inviting home.

"Now for the difficult decision." I opened the door to my clos-et. "What does one wear to a fraternity party?"

Emma joined me and together we flipped through my clothes. "Ooh . . . this is pretty." She removed a black sleeveless top with a low-cut ruffled neck. "I'm digging your taste."

"My mother's taste, actually."

"Wait a minute," she said, wide-eyed. "You mean your mother buys your clothes?"

I nodded. "Mainly because I hate to shop and she's compulsive about it. She gets excited about going to Target to buy athletic socks for Ben."

"Sounds like your mother and I would get along just fine. I'd shop all the time if I had the money to buy anything." She went to the mirror, holding the blouse up to her body. "Besides, my parents feel the need to control every aspect of my life. My wardrobe is just another battlefield."

"That bad, huh?" I asked.

She nodded. "But let's not ruin our first day together by talking about them."

I shrugged. "It's your call. But just so you know, if and when you are ready to talk, I'm here for you. Deal?"

Her eyes glistened with unshed tears. "Deal."

I nodded my head at the blouse she was still holding up in front of her. "By the way, you should totally wear that."

When I returned from the shower, I found Emma admiring herself in the mirror wearing the black top with a pair of low-rider white jeans. She had curves in places I was flat, and because she was at least three inches taller than my five foot six, the tank stopped well above the jeans and exposed quite a bit of tanned skin below her bellybutton. If her father was so concerned about his daughter covering her body, where had she gotten the jeans? They certainly weren't mine.

She fixed her crystal eyes on me. "Are you sure you don't mind?" she asked, bouncing around on her bare feet. "I was just trying it on. I still have to shower and everything before I get dressed."

"It looks great. Really." I nodded enthusiastically.

"But you've already been so generous. I would never want to take advantage of you." She was serious and sincere and grateful, so much so I would have lent her anything.

"No worries. I'm happy to share," I said, towel-drying my wet hair.

Emma tilted her head to the side, watching me. "Don't take this the wrong way, but have you ever thought of letting it grow long?" she asked.

I ran my fingers through my cropped locks. "No way. I have too many cowlicks and not enough patience for long hair."

She looked at me from one angle and then another. "Not many people can wear their hair that short, but it works for you. You have that Winona Ryder thing going on."

"Great." I plugged in my hair dryer and turned it on. "How old is she anyway, forty?" I shouted over the noise.

"Maybe, but she's still beautiful," she yelled back at me.

When I was finished drying my hair, Emma came at me with a can of hair spray and her bag of tricks. For what she lacked in clothing, she made up for in makeup. She had one of every tube and stick and compact available at Walgreen's. "Sit still and close your eyes." I felt a tug at my eyelids followed by a flutter across my cheeks and a rubbing along my lips. "Okay, now you can open them." She pulled a handful of silver bangles out of the bottom compartment of her bag and slipped them onto my arm. She held a mirror out to me. "That little girl look is now sexy innocence."

"Me? Sexy? That's a stretch, but thanks." I handed the mirror back to her. "By the way, I met some girls down the hall. They invited us to make the party rounds with them tonight."

"I'll pass," she said. "Big groups are not my style. But you go ahead."

I shook my head. "No way I'm leaving you on our first night as roommates. I just thought it might be fun to get to know some of the other girls from our hall."

"Oh! I do too. Just not tonight." Emma placed her cosmetic case and mirror in her top dresser drawer and turned around to face me. "Let me ask you this. Do you have any interest in joining a sorority?"

"Maybe. I haven't decided yet."

"Well *I* want to, and I don't see how moving around from party to party in a big group, like a pack of dogs on display at the Westminster Kennel Show, will help my chances. Why would anyone want to put themselves in a position of having to stand out in a crowd?"

She pulled the tank top off over her head, and I watched her waltz around the room in naked perfection as she gathered her things for her shower.

Seriously? Emma lost in a crowd? Like that's ever gonna happen.

"Okay, so I can kind of see your point," I said, "but networking is the biggest part of rush. Who knows? One of those girls down the hall might have a sister who can help you get in the sorority you like the most."

She considered this for a minute, and then shrugged it off, sauntering toward the door. "We have three days of orientation ahead of us," she said over her shoulder. "Which is plenty of time for networking. Tonight is all about us. A time for new roommates to bond."

THREE

In the early fall of my eighth-grade year, my mother was seen making out with my best friend's father during a party at the Farmers' house one night. It was Maggie Farmer herself who spotted the lovebirds when she snuck outside to the rose garden for a smoke. According to the rumors that circulated before breakfast the following morning, they were going at each other like teenagers, which was not an easy thing for my tender adolescent ears to hear. Our family lived for weeks in the shadow of my mother's shame, but as typical of most juicy scandals, the gossip had run its course by the time we sat down to Thanksgiving dinner. At least amongst the adults.

The kids weren't nearly as indulgent, especially at my all-girls school where drama was as much a part of the curriculum as algebra. Under normal circumstances, eighth grade is a volatile year for most girls, when some are experimenting with boys and drinking and others are not, when the lines are drawn between *those who do* and *those who don't*. Never mind that we'd all been together since nursery school, only one of my friends stood by my side. Archer Roland, my best friend for life.

I never understood why the others granted their allegiance to Ann Patton instead of to me when her father was as willing a participant in the affair as my mother, but their support boosted her confidence and fueled her anger. All throughout the winter months, Patton and her puppets staged vicious attacks against me. I never knew for certain which puppet was responsible for which prank, except for the most brutal of the assaults. One day in late

January, Ann Patton faked cramps and broke into my gym locker while the rest of us were at swim practice. Not only did she put bleach in my shampoo bottle, which rendered my hair a disgusting shade of puke green, she used my phone to text an up-close-and-personal picture of a girl's private parts, presumably her own, to everyone on my contact list.

The irrational part of me yearned for my mother's touch when I cried myself to sleep at night. I wanted her to acknowledge my suffering as a result of *her* mistake. I wanted her to explain to me how she could've cheated on my father, and I wanted her to apologize for the disgrace she'd brought on our family. But the parents I once knew, the mother and father who'd raised me since birth with love and affection, were lost to me. My mother, immersed in her own pity party, retreated to her room with a pitcher of martinis every afternoon around four; and my father, engrossed in trying to save his marriage for the sake of his family, joined her with a dinner tray every night at six. He spoiled her with boxes of Godiva chocolates and bouquets of exotic orchids; but despite his efforts, the only thing that changed was the sound of their arguments, growing louder as my mother's mood swings became more extreme.

Ben handled the crisis of our mother's affair better than I did, but then again, he was older and more mature, in his tenth-grade year at St. Paul's, the all-boy counterpart to St. Anne's. Unlike mine, Ben's friends not only stood by his side, they followed him around like little Ben wannabes. They played the same sports, dated the same girls, and applied to the same colleges. And because Ben protected me, his friends protected me.

So when I found the three of them waiting for me just inside the front door of their fraternity house that first night, I realized they would ruin my life if I didn't establish some boundaries.

I looped my arm through Emma's. "Meet Spotty Watkins and Reed Randolph, Ben's best friends since birth. Literally. They were born in the same hospital three days apart."

"I was first, of course," Ben said, sticking out his chest. "Then came Spotty, and naturally, Mr. Always-late-to-the-game Reed was last."

Emma turned to Spotty. "Do they call you Spotty because of these?" she asked, tapping the skin along the bridge of her nose.

Spotty's face turned several shades of red. "No, Emma," Reed answered for him. "Spotty is short for Spotswood. He was named after his grandfather and the two before him."

"So, I take it the two of you are Lambda Deltas with Ben?" Emma asked Reed and Spotty who nodded their heads in unison.

I rolled my eyes. "Welcome to Virginia, Emma, where people are born together and die together and spend every day in between either sucking up to one another or stabbing each other in the back."

"Ouch, that hurts," Reed said, rubbing his arm as though someone had pinched him.

Ben waved me away. "Don't listen to her. She's been in a pissy mood all day."

"Of course she has." Spotty wrapped his arm around me and squeezed. "This is an emotional time for her. The start of a new chapter in her life—'Hello Kitty Goes to College.'"

"Awh . . . " Reed pinched my cheek. "Look at you all grown up."

I gave him the once over. "And look at you all tan. Did you actually get a job this summer or did you surf the whole time?"

"I'll have you know I worked as a lifeguard on the beach this summer."

"Some job." I rolled my eyes. "Saving damsels in distress in their thong bikinis."

"Ha! The only woman I saved had no business wearing a bikini."

I nudged Emma and cut my eyes at a group of cute boys across the room.

"No way," Spotty said, stepping in front of me to block my view. "You're here to listen to the band, right? Because if you came over here on the prowl, let me be the first to say that there is no man in this house good enough for you."

I took a deep breath. "Listen up, you two." I pointed my finger first at Spotty and then at Reed. "Y'all need to back off. I've already warned Ben about this earlier today."

Spotty and Reed turned to Ben for help, but he shrugged them off. "I told you she was in a bitchy mood."

"Seriously," I said. "I'm in college now, same as you. And I've earned the right to be here, same as you. As far as I'm concerned, we are on a level playing field. So, you have a choice. We can work out an exchange where you introduce us to some of your more worthy friends, and we do the same for you with our pretty little freshman friends at the bar over there, or I can take my new roommate next door to the DKE house."

The three of them quickly turned their attention to the bar, where four of the prettiest girls from our hall were waiting in line for a beer. Dolled up in little short sundresses, they giggled and flounced around in excitement over being at their first fraternity party. They were peaches, ripe for the picking.

When the guys turned back to me, they were all smiles. "I see no reason for you to have to leave the party." Ben grabbed his friends by the shoulders and turned them toward the bar. "Men, what say we go get everyone a beer while my sister cools off a little?"

"You handled them beautifully," Emma said, turning to me when they were out of earshot. "What a bunch of horny hound dogs. If you want to get a man's attention, talk to his dick."

I burst out laughing. "Exactly."

"Look at them. They're even hitting on the same girl," Emma said, shaking her head in amusement as Ben, Spotty, and Reed made a pass at one of our unsuspecting freshman friends. "Reed can hit on me all day long. I thought you said he was from Richmond?"

"He is."

"Well then, what beach did he work at?"

"Oh right. No. His parents are divorced. His father lives at Virginia Beach now. Reed spends his summers with him down there."

"What about Spotty? He is definitely a cutie, as far as gingers go. His eyes are kind and his smile is sweet."

I nodded. "He's definitely a nice guy. I'm glad to see him happy for a change. He's been a mess for a really long time."

"You mean like drinking too much and stuff?"

"No, more like in a seriously bad mood." I moved closer to her so no one would overhear me. "In high school Spotty was considered the top lacrosse attackman in the state. He was being scouted by Division 1 schools when he tore his ACL, wrestling, of all things, with his brother in their family's backyard. He never regained the speed and agility he needed for D1. Everything else was second best to him."

As the three guys headed back our way, I was glad to see Spotty walking with more pep in his step than I'd seen in several years. He handed me a plastic cup of warm beer. "Here. A peace offering. We talked it over and decided you're right, Kitty. It's time for us to give you some space."

While we waited for the band to start playing, several of Ben's friends stopped to chat, seemingly under the pretense of asking about his summer. But it was obvious they were more interested in meeting Emma. My heart softened a little toward my brother as I watched him interact with his friends. He seemed so happy and relaxed, so well adjusted to his life at UVA. While his constant concern for my safety drove me nuts, I understood he couldn't help himself, that his genetic makeup included this overprotective component of his personality.

Ben is a worrier, has been all his life. When we were young, he worried that our parents would be killed in a plane crash, and that I would get rabies from playing with the wounded stray animals I was always trying to nurse back to health. As his mind and body matured, so did his worries. In high school he worried that *this* girlfriend didn't like him enough, or that *that* girlfriend was cheating on him. He worried he hadn't studied enough for his AP history exam, and he worried his SAT scores wouldn't be good enough for UVA.

Because he had no say in what happened between my parents after the Rose Garden Affair, the only aspect of the situation he could control was keeping me glued together. Ben was the one who rubbed my back at night while I soaked my pillow with tears. He was the one who walked me home after a rough day at school, and he was the one who took me out for ice cream on Friday nights when all the other girls were learning to dance at cotillion or attending sleepovers.

When the music began to play and Emma and I turned toward the band room, Ben grabbed me by the arm. "You've done something different to yourself. You look good." He bent down and whispered in my ear, "Please be careful and remember—don't ever drink anything out of a trash can or take a drink from someone you don't know. The guys around here like to take advantage of girls who drink too much."

"Getting drunk is not my style, Ben. You know that."

"Hey. I watch out for you. It's what I do. I can't just turn that off."

I followed Emma as she made her way to the front of the stage where everyone was dancing as one. We joined in, losing ourselves in the music as our bodies moved to the beat. Emma's fair hair and radiant skin glistened under the strobe light. She was the prettiest girl on the floor, and every boy who tapped her on the shoulder for a dance recognized that. She made it clear to all of them that she was with me. Not in a lesbian kind of way but in a leave-me-alone-I'm-partying-with-my-girlfriend kind of way. That hour and a half was a point in time I wouldn't soon forget. My first taste of real freedom.

When the music stopped and the lights came on, Emma and I joined the long line of girls waiting for their turn in the restroom. We stood quietly, listening to others around us, the older girls who were commenting on the younger girls who were speaking openly of things they should've kept a secret.

By the time I turned my stall over to Emma, the restroom was empty except for one other girl. I snuck a quick glimpse of her reflection in the mirror while I was washing my hands in the sink next to her. I might have considered her unattractive—with hazel eyes, thin lips, and high forehead—if not for her golden hair. It wasn't bleached white-blonde but the color of ginkgo leaves in the autumn.

Our eyes met and she smiled. "You're Ben Langley's little sister aren't you?"

I nodded, surprised. "How'd you know?"

"Your eyes. You have the same deep, soulful eyes."

I felt my face blush and I turned away from her, grabbing a paper towel from the dispenser.

"I've been keeping a file on you, you know?" When she saw my concerned expression, she added, "Relax. I have a file on a lot of incoming freshmen. I'm Honey Mabry." She held out her hand to me. "I'm the president of the Chi Delta sorority. Our mothers were pledge sisters."

"It's nice to meet you." I forced myself to smile. "I'm Katherine Langley, but then you already know that, don't you?"

She covered her mouth and laughed, a tee-hee that sounded more like a sneeze.

Emma came out of the stall and inserted herself between Honey and me. "I'm Emma, Katherine's roommate. Do they call you Honey because of your hair?"

Honey gave Emma a quick head-to-toe inspection before returning her attention to me. "Are you all settled into your room in the dorm?" she asked me.

I've known girls like Honey all my life, girls from wealth and privilege who can spot an outsider from a hundred miles away. They have built-in radar that can alert them to impostors, and girls like Emma show up the brightest. Girls who try too hard. Girls who don't stand a chance in their world.

"Yep. Seems like we've lived there for years." I leaned up against the counter with my back to the sink. "I'm curious too. About your name."

"It's a boring story, really," Honey said, sighing. "But if you must know. When my brother was little, he couldn't pronounce my name, Elizabeth, so he adopted my mother's nickname for me. Honey. It just kind of stuck."

Disappointed, Emma reached over and stroked a lock of Honey's hair in an overly familiar way. "Well your hair *is* very pretty. Exactly the color of honey."

Honey tucked all her hair over to one side and turned her back on Emma. "Anyway, about the file. Our sorority has received a lot of letters written on your behalf, most of them by your mother's friends. Have you given any thought to pledging Chi Delta?"

"Right now our focus is on getting ready for classes. Right, Emma?" I looked at Emma and she smiled, bobbing her head up and down.

"Which is exactly why we defer our rush until January," Honey explained. "College is such a big adjustment. It's better for first-year students to get settled before they have to think about making such an important decision."

"You mean all colleges don't defer their rush?" Emma asked.

Once again Honey ignored Emma, this time to the point of blatant rudeness. "It's against rush regulations for you to come by the house, but I'd love to meet you, Katherine, for coffee one day, or maybe lunch." She removed a small tube of hot-pink lipstick from her shoulder bag and turned toward the mirror. "I understand you've been accepted into the nursing program. We have several nursing students who would love to answer questions or offer guidance on course selections and teachers."

"Thanks. I'll remember that," I said over my shoulder as I turned to leave.

"Wait a minute. Let me give you this." Without so much as a glance in Emma's direction, Honey handed me a card with her initials scripted in pink in the center and her name and cell phone number printed below.

I'd witnessed some horrible snubs in my life, most of them directed at me, but Honey's indifference to Emma was unspeakable. Much to her credit, Emma didn't let it bother her. If anything, she appeared to be even more interested in Greek life than before. As we left the bathroom and made our way through the crowd, she peppered me with questions about the rush process.

"Honestly, Emma, I don't know that much about it. But it's my understanding that, *if* you have a relative who belonged to a sorority or fraternity, then that organization is obligated to give you special consideration."

"And what if you don't have any connections?"

I shrugged. "It doesn't seem fair they would hold that against you. But then again, what do I know?"

While we waited in line for another hot beer, Emma studied the crowd in silence, but once we were back out on the dance floor, her mood lifted and her confidence returned. She raised her arms high above her head and clapped to the beat of the band. The provocative sway of her hips attracted the guys like hummingbirds to nectar. This time she did not deny them. She made her rounds on the dance floor before settling in with a guy who had the build of a football player and the sweet face of a six-year-old boy. When the band played a slow song, the giant wrapped his muscled arms around her and pulled her close, whispering something in her ear that made her laugh. I scanned the crowd, wondering which group he belonged to, hoping there was more where he came from. But no one seemed to be paying any attention to them except the yellow-haired girl, leaning against the wall on the other side of the dance floor. Honey's lip curled up over her top teeth, and I could almost hear her snarl over the loud music. Whether the guy was her boyfriend or merely a love interest, clearly he meant something to Honey. And Emma, whether she'd seen the two of them together earlier or whether she'd simply picked the wrong person to dance with, had made a horrible mistake.

FOUR

I partied more during those first two weeks of college than I ever had in my life. I found it impossible to say no to Emma, whose answer for a hangover was happy hour. She didn't communicate like most college freshman, through texting or Facebook or e-mail, but somehow she managed to know where to find the best parties. I'd always felt alone in a crowd before, but not with Emma. She was a magnet for attention, and standing next to her placed me in the direct line of vision for the cutest boys on campus.

After a few too many Tahiti martinis at the FIJI house one night, we were stumbling across the green on our way back to our room when, out of the blue, Emma blurted, "I'm gonna marry someone rich one day. I mean . . . the kind of rich that'll buy me all the servants I want, maids in black uniforms bringing me champagne and strawberries in bed every morning. I want the cars and the clothes. And I want the plastic surgeon to keep me looking young, when I'm ready for one of course."

Two weeks with Emma and I'd grown accustomed to listening to her ramble. "Give me a break, Emma," I said, hiccupping. "I'm pretty sure you are never *ever* going to need a plastic surgeon. You're so beautiful, you can have any husband you want." I laughed at the irony in my statement. "I mean . . . any man you want. Don't take someone else's husband, for God's sake."

Her heel got stuck in the dirt and she grabbed a hold of me to keep from falling. "Ow! Shit! That hurts."

"Take off your shoes, silly, before you break your ankle."

"Fine." She held on to my shoulder while she slipped off her pumps. "I'm tired. Let's rest a minute?" She relaxed all of her muscles at once and dropped to the ground like a rag doll. "Come on. Sit," she said, pulling me down beside her.

"Ahh, feels sooo good to lie down." I stretched out on the grass beside her, but when the earth started to spin, I sat back up. "Uh-oh. Bad idea. How many of those Mahiti Tartinis did we have anyway?"

Emma burst into laughter. "That's a good one. Mahiti Tartinis."

"You know what I mean." I swatted at her arm but missed. "Whatever you call them things. They were strong." I brought my knees up to my chest and propped my elbows on top.

I was surprised when she pulled a cigarette from her bag. "Since when do you smoke?"

"When I drink sometimes." She offered the pack to me. "Want one?"

"Sure." I took a cigarette and held it between my teeth while she lit it with her little pink lighter. I inhaled deeply, enjoying the taste and the buzz. "Wow. It's been a long time since I had a cigarette."

"What about you, Katherine?" she asked, stuffing the pack of Marlboro Lights back into her bag. "What kind of guy do *you* want to marry?"

"Hmm . . . let's see . . ." I stared up at the dark sky. "The kind who gets up at night to feed our baby a bottle, even though he has to go to work the next day."

"No, dummy. I'm not talking about the kind of father you want for your children. I'm talking about the kind of man you want as your husband."

I took another drag from the cigarette and then flicked it down the sidewalk, watching the sparks fly as the cherry burst apart. "I want to marry a *man*, not a boy, someone who's older than me. Someone who is world-wise and street-smart, but honest and kind, too."

"Oh, how sweet," she said, sarcastically. "But come on, don't you want him to be successful? A doctor or a lawyer, someone who makes a ton of money?"

I shrugged. "Money doesn't matter that much to me."

"Ha! That's because you already have plenty of it."

"Don't get me wrong. Having money definitely comes in handy at times, when you need it, like when your car breaks down or—"

"Or when your computer crashes on the day before you leave for college and your parents can't afford to get it fixed or buy you a new one," she said, chewing on her bottom lip.

I sobered a little as another piece of the puzzle that made up my roommate fell into place. "Why didn't you say something?" I leaned into her a little. "It's not the same as having your own, but we can work out a schedule for you to use mine."

"That'd be great. Thanks," she said, exhaling a thin stream of smoke. "My family is not rich like yours. You already know my father is a professor, but my mother is . . . well . . ."

I could see the tears glistening in Emma's eyes. "Well what?" I grabbed her elbow and squeezed it. "Come on, I'm your roommate. You can tell me anything."

"My mother is a cafeteria worker at a local nursing home." Emma took the final drag off her cigarette and ground it out on the bottom of one of her pumps. "But no one knows about this, so can we please keep it between us?"

"Of course, Emma, but earning an honest living is nothing to be ashamed about."

"It might be honest, but I'd hardly call it a living. Neither of them makes much money and collectively they can barely pay the bills. There's no room for extras like shopping or visits to the salon. Hell, they can barely afford a texting plan for our cell phones. I'm on a full academic scholarship. Otherwise, I wouldn't even be here. So it's easy for you to say money doesn't mean that much to you when you've never been poor."

"I can't argue with that," I said, sucking in my breath as though she'd punched me in the gut. No doubt I was *that* girl, the one who would've run out to the Apple Store and bought a new computer the minute mine crashed.

We were quiet for a minute, both of us lost in thought. "So what *is* important to you, Katherine?" She grabbed a hunk of my hair and yanked on it playfully. "If not the finer things in life?"

"Helping people in crisis. That's why I want to become a nurse."

"Why not a doctor?"

"Because I can't imagine spending the next decade of my life in school. The doctor may be the one who finds the cure, but the nurse is the one who can make or break the patient's recovery. I want to work in the ICU, where the patients and their families are truly in need."

Emma stood and offered me a hand. "You know, Emma, you're a really smart girl," I said when I was on my feet, face-to-face with my roommate. "You don't have to settle for some guy you don't love just because he's wealthy. If you choose the right career, you can make plenty of money on your own."

"Why would I want a career when I can have money without having to work?" She looped her arm through mine and dragged me toward our dorm. "And don't worry. I plan to be plenty in love with the man I marry."

***

Emma and I were so tied up with our new freshman friends, two weeks passed before we saw Ben and Spotty again. It was the Saturday of Labor Day weekend, the first UVA football game of the season. We were all leaving the stadium at the same time, in the middle of the third quarter, not only because our team was losing but because it was steaming hot in the stands.

"How much have you had to drink today?" Ben asked me.

"Nice to see you too," I said, looking first at him and then at Spotty.

"So we're going to play it that way," Ben said, crossing his arms. "Are you having a nice day, Kitty? Is it hot enough for you, Kitty? How much have you had to drink today, Kitty?"

I swatted at him but missed. "Actually, I haven't had anything to drink. It's so hot the thought of it makes me sick. Why do you ask?"

"Because we're going on a road trip and you're driving." Ben hooked one arm through mine and one arm through Emma's and began dragging us toward the gate.

"Ooh, a road trip," Emma said, skipping alongside Ben. "I'm in."

"But we don't even know where he's going," I said to her, and then to Ben, "Exactly where *are* you going?"

"To the river, of course." He quickened his pace. "But we need to hurry if we want to beat the game traffic."

"Wait a minute, damnit." I stopped walking and jerked my arm away from him. "I haven't said I'd go yet. What about Mom and Dad? Are they down there?"

"I just got off the phone with Dad. They're going to a party tonight, but he said they'd see us in the morning."

"Where's Reed? Is he going too?" I held up my hand. "Wait a minute. Let me guess. He's at the beach."

Spotty nodded. "Surfing the waves as we speak."

I looked back and forth between Ben and Spotty as I considered their invitation. "I don't know about this. I have a lot of work to do this weekend."

"And what better place to do it than sitting around the pool or out on the dock," Ben said. "According to Dad, the weather's nice down there, a lot cooler than here."

"Just where is this river, and how long is the driver?" Emma asked.

"The Northern Neck of Virginia, which is on the western side of the Chesapeake Bay. It'll take two and a quarter, probably two and a half with Kitty driving," Ben answered. "And if we leave now, we can make it in time to get pizza from the River Market before it closes."

"Okay, that's it." I stomped my foot. "No fair tempting me with my favorite pizza."

"Think about it, Kitty," Spotty said. "We can spend the whole day tomorrow out in the boat."

Emma clasped her hands together. "Please . . . it sounds like so much fun."

"Alright, already. What choice do I have anyway with the three of y'all ganging up on me like this?"

"Yes!" Ben pumped the air with his fist. "Hurry up and get your stuff. We'll meet you at my car in the lot behind the house in twenty minutes."

By the time I reached the interstate, thirty minutes later, everyone in the car had already surrendered to their afternoon buzzes. Ben slept in the back with his head resting on Spotty's shoulder, and Emma sat in the passenger seat next to me, a thin stream of drool dangling from her mouth onto *my* silk halter top she was wearing.

I cranked the tunes and set the cruise control and allowed my thoughts to drift to the river. My fondest memories traced back to our cottage, not the modernized version my parents created after my grandparents died but the 1920s Arts and Crafts style house in its original form. I appreciated the amenities the renovations offered—new bathrooms and kitchen, central air conditioning—but I missed the creaking boards in the random-width oak floors and the smell of sea grass wafting through the open windows. What I really missed were my grandparents, Herbert and Mabel Langley, a small-town doctor and his country wife. From Memorial Day to Labor Day, Ben and I spent every summer of our youth with Dock and MayMay while our parents were off somewhere, finding themselves on one of their many pre-midlife crisis adventures. Every day we made explorations of our own. If we weren't traveling by boat or picnicking on one of the many area islands, we were working in MayMay's garden, staking tomatoes and picking butterbeans. We set our pots for peeler crabs and dug in the mud for clams. We cast our nets for minnows to use as bait for fishing in the rivers and at the mouth of the bay. Every day we worked like watermen and farmers, and every night we feasted from the land.

All three of my passengers stirred, as if on cue, when I turned on my blinker and made a left-hand turn onto Highway 3. As we headed toward the Rappahannock River Bridge, Ben and Spotty moaned about their hangovers and begged me to stop for more beer, but once we were on top of the bridge, they grew quiet while we watched the orange ball of sun begin to set.

"Emma, if you look to your right," Ben said, "you can see past Stingray Point where the Rappahannock River meets the Chesapeake Bay."

Taking it all in, Emma pointed out my window. "What's down that way?"

"The mouth of our creek, Carter's Creek, is at ten o'clock," Ben explained. "And further past that, on the same side, is the Corrotoman River. On the opposite side, at about seven o'clock, is the little town of Urbanna where the famous Oyster Festival is held every year."

"Yuck," Emma exclaimed, curling her lip. "I've never been a big fan of oysters."

Spotty stared at the back of her head. "That kind of talk is not allowed in this car We were all raised on oysters. Our mothers use to grind them up in a blender and feed them to us in our bottles."

"Ooh, Spotty," I said, catching his eye in the rearview mirror. "That's just gross."

"Oysters *are* gross," Emma said, sticking out her tongue. "They're so slimy, like boogers."

Spotty laughed. "Now who's being gross?"

I winked at Emma. "Give her a break. She's just never had an oyster fried, à la Ben."

"Wait a minute," Emma said, shifting in her seat to face Ben. "You can cook?"

I caught Ben's eye in the rearview mirror and he glared at me. The subject was off limits. Despite the fact that he'd learned all his culinary skills from our grandfather, whom he considered the most masculine of men, in Ben's mind cooking was a sissy task.

"He's a really good cook, actually," I said to Emma. "Our grandfather taught him how to prepare everything from frying soft shell crabs to smoking shark meat. Except lately his cooking has been limited to burgers or steaks on the grill."

"That's because it's no fun to cook it if you're not the one who caught it," Ben said to me in the mirror. "Unlike Dock, Dad's answer to a seafood dinner is buying a dozen crabs, already steamed, from the Yellow Umbrella Seafood Market in Richmond and bringing them down here to eat."

"True," I agreed. "He's neither the cook nor the waterman that Dock was."

"Okay, so who the hell is Dock?" Emma asked.

We all laughed, and for the rest of the way into White Stone to pick up the pizza and then back to the house, we told Emma all about our summers on the creek with our grandparents.

Carter's Creek isn't narrow like a brook or stream, the way most people might think. It's a branch of the Rappahannock, a tributary, more than a quarter of a mile across in some places. Situated up high on a peninsula, our property is surrounded by 270 degrees of water.

The house stands four stories tall with large airy rooms and twelve-foot ceilings. A game room takes up the basement space with a walk-out terraced area that leads to the summer kitchen. The main floor houses the living room, kitchen, and two guest rooms. Ben's and my bedrooms are on the third floor with our parents' on the fourth. At the corner of the house, off the dining room on the main floor, is a large unscreened porch—our tree fort. With wide-open views of the creek in both directions, we spend all our time here, drinking coffee in the morning and eating candlelit suppers in the evening. There's no better place to watch a storm roll in or fireworks on the Fourth of July.

All traces of the sunset had disappeared by the time we settled into the four oversize wicker chairs on the porch, the combination of the humid salty air and the beer and pizza in our bellies making us lazy.

Ben tossed a piece of crust into the empty pizza box on the coffee table in front of us. "Kitty, you're the closest. Why don't you send out a smoke signal?"

I glanced across the creek at the Turners' house. "The lights are on over there, so I'm guessing they're home." I stared back at Ben. "But I'm not moving. I've been driving all day. It's your turn to do something."

"Fair enough," he said, dragging himself from his chair.

I tilted my head back and smiled at him as he passed behind me. "And get me a beer while you're up, will you?"

Thirty seconds later, Van Morrison blasted from the outdoor speakers. Ben let "Moondance" play for a couple of minutes before turning the music off again.

"Somebody please explain," Emma said, looking back and forth between Spotty and me.

"It's a game we play with our friends George and Abigail Turner, who live across the creek," I said. "If either of them is home, they'll respond by playing another song."

"So you mean literally?" Emma asked. "A smoke signal like the American Indians used to use?"

"Exactly." I nodded. "Just like the Indians. Remember, Ben?"

He opened the screen door and tossed me a beer. "Why do we have to bring that up?"

Spotty laughed. "Because who can resist such a great story?" He turned toward Emma. "When Ben was just a Cub Scout, maybe eight or nine, he tried to send out a real smoke signal to the Turners. As only Ben's luck would have it, he picked the driest summer on record in Virginia. The dumbass caught the grass on fire, burned up half of the front yard before his grandmother got to it with her fire extinguisher."

"When we were younger," Ben said through the screen door, "before the fire, we used to signal George and Abby with a flashlight. One long flash was an invitation to come on over."

"And two short flashes meant we were in for the night," I added.

When a sudden blast of "Freebird" permeated the peaceful night, we all cheered, and for the next few minutes, we bounced songs back and forth across the water. Every time Ben changed songs, he raised the volume until it reached an obnoxious level.

"Turn it down, Ben," I yelled, holding my hands over my ears. "You're disturbing the peace."

Ben lowered our volume, and a few seconds later, the music on the other side of the creek died. Not long afterward, we heard the sound of George and Abby's outboard motor heading our way. Ben and I wandered out onto the lawn to greet them on their way up from the dock. As was their ritual, Ben hugged Abby tight, spinning her around and around until she was dizzy.

"Why haven't y'all been down more this summer?" Abby asked, after she and George had greeted everyone and were settled on the wicker love seat, the only available place to sit.

"It's all her fault, Abby." Ben pointed at me. "Kitty's been in the hospital all summer."

"Wait a minute, what?" she asked me, confused.

"I've been *working* in the hospital all summer, Abby, shadowing a doctor in the ER, hoping to get some experience before I started nursing school."

"Speaking of nursing school," George said to me, "I was hoping you'd end up at Chapel Hill with me. What happened?"

Ben shot George a warning look. "Nice of you to bring that up, bro."

"I can handle this, Ben. I'm a big girl now." I shifted in my seat so I could see George. "The truth is, George, UNC was a stretch for me, and my father was a little overconfident about his connections."

"Yeah, right," Ben said under his breath.

"What?" I asked, locking eyes with my brother. I was growing tired of listening to his sarcasm and innuendo every time the subject of UNC came up.

Ben's eyes left mine and drifted to a spider's web in the eaves at the corner of the porch. "I just never understood your infatuation with UNC when it's so obvious you belong at UVA."

I set my beer down on the coffee table and stood up. "What say you and I go inside and get our guests a cold beverage?" I reached for Ben's hand, pulling him to a stand.

"Okay, what gives on the whole UNC deal?" I asked when we were alone in the kitchen. "Every time the subject comes up, you either roll your eyes or throw out some sarcastic remark."

"You're paranoid, Kitty," Ben said, opening the refrigerator and loading up his arms with Natty Lights.

"Was it that much of a joke that I applied to Chapel Hill? Is that it? Did Dad decide not to use his connections to save face from potential embarrassment?"

Ben closed the refrigerator door and faced me. "It's nothing like that. It's . . ." He hesitated, and I thought he was about to come clean. "Look, just don't worry about it. We have thirsty guests to entertain." He turned and headed toward the porch, leaving me to stare at his back.

At least he finally admitted there was something to worry about!

In our absence, George had moved from the love seat to Ben's vacated chair next to Emma. "That's my seat, man. Move," Ben snapped.

"Sorry, dude. I didn't hear you call fives," George said with a self-satisfied smirk on his lips.

"How old are you anyway? I thought we stopped calling fives years ago." Ben passed the beers around and then lowered himself to the arm of Emma's chair, leaning back against her in a territorial kind of way.

With the two of them fighting for her attention, Emma sat up straighter, crossed her legs, and flipped her hair back over her shoulder in flirt mode.

"So, George," Ben said, draping his arm across the back of Emma's chair. "Thank God, your father finally got the marina to rebuild their fuel dock. Those old pumps were an environmental hazard."

"Is your father the mayor?" Emma asked, impressed.

"No. He's the commonwealth's attorney for Lancaster County, but he's pretty important around here."

"As if being important in a town of five hundred means anything," Ben said.

Abby rolled her eyes at me. No matter how large or small the prize, Ben and George had always measured their own success against each other. From battling it out over a board game to comparing the size of a catch. Who could make the biggest cannonball splash, or who could climb the tallest tree? Or in this case, whose father was more important. Until now, the nature of their challenges had always been innocent fun, but a new contest had begun with Emma as the ultimate reward.

"Is that White Stone?" Emma asked, pointing at all the lights on the other side of the creek. "Where we got the pizza earlier?"

"No, that's Irvington, where five hundred of the coolest people in the country live," George said, flipping the bird at Ben. "It's too dark now, but you'll be able to see it tomorrow."

"Don't worry, Emma," Ben said, rubbing her shoulder. "I'll give you the nickel tour of Carter's Creek tomorrow, including the Tide's Inn and the Yacht Club and the haunted boathouse."

"A haunted boathouse? For real?" she asked.

Abby and I locked eyes and smiled at one another, reminded of our first midnight adventure together—the initiation into our secret club. The four of us couldn't have been much older than eight and ten when we snuck out of the house, and used the light from the full moon to guide us as we paddled our canoes up the creek to the haunted boathouse. We pierced our thumbs with a safety pin, swapped blood, and sealed it with spit. My secret code name was Cat, for obvious reasons, and Ben's was Mouse, because he loved to watch old reruns of *Tom and Jerry*. We named Abigail *Yabba-Dabba-Abigail* but called her Yabba for short; and George was Porgie for "Georgie Porgie Puddin' Pie," the nursery rhyme his mother used to read to him over and over again as a child.

"Shh!" George held his finger to his lips. "The legend of the boathouse can only be told on a full moon." He tilted his chair back so he could see the sky. "Nope, not tonight."

"Shut up, Turner. The legend goes—" Ben stopped when he saw Abby and me glaring at him. The story about the old woman who'd lost her waterman husband in a hurricane was legit, but as part of our blood pact, we agreed never to talk about it except under the light of a full moon. "Sorry, Emma," Ben apologized. "Kitty and Abby are the authorities. You're gonna have to wait for the next full moon to hear the story."

"Have *you* heard this legend?" Emma asked Spotty.

"Many times," he said with a nod.

"Ugh. Y'all are killing me." Emma turned to George. "So is this boathouse on this side of the creek or yours?"

"On our side, way up the creek close to the Irvington Bridge." George drained the rest of his beer and set the can down beside him on the floor. "Back in those days, in the early 1920s when the boathouse was built, people only lived on the town side of the creek."

"Really?" Emma asked. "Why is that?"

George flashed her his dazzling smile and I knew he was about to tell her a lie. "They were afraid of the crazies who lived over here. This side of the creek was like the mountains of West Virginia. A bunch of hillbillies who got high every night on moonshine and then had sex with their sisters before splitting their brothers' brains apart with an ax."

"That's bullshit, Turner." Ben crumpled up his beer can and threw it at George.

He caught the can and threw it back at Ben. "Are you trying to deny that this side of the creek is the rural side?"

"Of course not, you dumb fucker. Anyone can see that there's more land and fewer houses on this side. I'm just saying I'd rather own five acres over here than to have to share *your* tiny little hill with the most influential people in the world."

"Enough already." Spotty stood and stretched. "You two sound like a bunch of sissy-girls arguing over who has the biggest slice of birthday cake."

"I agree, Spotty," I said. "We should curl their hair and put ribbons in it."

I moved over to the love seat next to Abby after that, where we held a private party of our own. We caught up on our lives of the past year and talked about our futures, discussing at length where Abby was planning to apply to college. Under the light from the lantern on the wall, I was able to get a closer look at her. Once streaked golden from the sun, her brown hair was now dull and limp around her skeleton face. She appeared to have lost even more weight since I'd seen her briefly two months earlier over the Fourth of July weekend. A couple of years back, Abby had a head-on collision with a hockey stick during field hockey practice one day. The doctors had to wire her broken jaw shut, and as a result of the liquid diet she was forced to eat, she dropped at least twenty pounds. Although we'd never talked about it, I was worried her sudden weight loss had triggered an even bigger problem. Like anorexia.

For the rest of the evening, I ignored Ben and George as much as possible, but I couldn't help but overhear some of their conversation. There seemed to be a point of contention between the two of them in every subject that came up. If they weren't arguing over football, like whether Mike London would be able to pull UVA out of a five-year rut, they were boasting about which one of them was better at wrestling or lacrosse. At one point, I even heard them bickering about who held the record for catching the biggest rockfish. It was tiresome, so much so that Spotty fell asleep sitting straight up in his chair. Emma, on the other hand, stayed perched between Ben and George, loving it every time one of them insulted the other for her benefit. The more she drank, the more she flirted with George, the more Ben sulked.

Shortly before midnight, when Abby insisted George take her home, I dragged Emma off to bed with me. She joined me at my window and together we watched brother and sister board their boat.

"Abby is so shy and quiet," Emma said. "I can't believe she shares the same genetics as George. He is so cute, I want to run my fingers through his chestnut curls and lose myself in his smoky gray eyes."

"The real George is cute. The George you met tonight is an impostor."

"What do you mean?" she asked.

I exhaled a deep breath. "I haven't spent any real time with him in the past year, so maybe he's changed. But *my* George, the George I grew up with, is kind. Maybe a little full of himself, but not braggy and argumentative like he was tonight."

"*Your* George?" she asked, nudging me.

"You know what I mean. My *friend* George." As I stared out the window, watching the bow light of their boat bob up and down as it made its way across the creek, I could feel Emma watching me, waiting for me to tell her more. "I know what you're thinking, Emma, but we really are just friends. As much as I think friendship is the best basis for a solid relationship, he's not the right friend for me."

"I agree," she said without hesitation. "He doesn't really seem like your type."

I studied her face in the dim light streaming from the lamp on my bedside table. Her smug expression made the little hairs on my neck stick up like the fur of a dog in defense mode. Did she think I wasn't pretty enough for him? Or interesting enough?

"Funny thing is," I said, "judging from the way he acted around you tonight, I wouldn't exactly say you bring out the best in him either."

FIVE

I found my mother and Emma in the kitchen the following morning, huddled together over the September issue of *Vogue*.

"Good morning, darling," my mother cooed, running her hand down my cheek. "It's so good to see you. I was just about to whip up some pancakes." She grabbed a mug from the cabinet and held it out to me. "Are you ready for coffee?"

She might've fooled Emma, but I knew my mother was no Betty Crocker.

"Not yet." I waved her away and turned toward Emma. "How long have you been up?"

"For a couple of hours, since around eight. I swam a few laps in the pool." Emma glanced over at my mother and smiled. "And I've been visiting with your parents on the porch."

"Your roommate is charming, Katherine. Just charming," Mom repeated for emphasis, an annoying habit of hers. "Of course if you'd call every now and then, I would've known that already."

"That's just it, Mom. Emma is *so* charming, she keeps me too busy socializing to call you."

"Touché, my dear, touché." Mom grabbed the magazine off the counter and held it up for me to see. "I've discovered that not only is your roommate a lovely little social butterfly she's also a fashionista. She can teach my sweet girl something about style. Which reminds me—" She dropped the magazine on the counter and disappeared down the hall, returning several seconds later with two shopping bags. "I bought you some things at the Farm."

"The Farm?" I asked. "What is that, some kind of tack shop? Did you buy me a pair of riding breeches?"

"Don't be ridiculous. I'm talking about that cute shop you love in White Stone."

"Oh, *that* Farm. I've only been there one time, Mom. To say I love it is a stretch."

Emma took the bags from my mother, set them on the counter, and began digging through them. She removed a long-sleeved gray knit dress from one of the bags and held it up to me. "Doesn't Katherine's hair look nice, Mrs. Langley? It took me a week to talk her into getting highlights."

My mother raised a perfectly shaped eyebrow. "Mrs. Langley?" she asked.

"Oops, sorry. I forgot. Adele," Emma responded.

The bullshit was getting a little too deep for me. My mother had never asked any of my friends to call her by her first name before. In fact the proper way to address an adult was one of the first things she'd taught us when we learned to speak as toddlers.

"Since we're on a first-name basis here, Dell," I said, using my dad's nickname for my mom, "I know you're dying for me to admit it, so I might as well get it out of the way. You were right. My hair is mousy, and I should've highlighted it a long time ago."

"You can call me Mom." She winked at me, an exaggerated batting of her fake eyelashes. "And for the record, I never said your hair was mousy. Every woman should get highlights. Lighter shades around the face brighten the complexion, regardless of hair color."

"What about Spotty?" I asked when he appeared in my line of vision through the french doors. "Do you think highlights would bring out his complexion, make his freckles pop out more?"

My mother placed her hands on her hips. "Stop trying to be difficult, Katherine. I meant every *woman* should lighten her hair. And to answer your question, auburn hair is the exception. What a waste to put such ravishing hair on a man." She ran her hand down the back of her head as if wishing she'd been blessed with such glorious locks.

For as long as I could remember, my mother had worn her rich mahogany hair in a shoulder-length bob. Even during the darkest of her days, she made certain no gray roots were peeking through along her part. She was all about the show. She wore only designer clothes, fitted to perfection on her toned body. Her nails were always polished, her hair always styled, and her face always smooth and tight from laser treatments and Botox. She'd yet to spring for a facelift, but it was on the horizon. She spoke of it often.

"Katherine, look at this," Emma said, holding up a black sequined party dress. "Isn't it pretty?"

I glanced at the dress and then did a double take. My mother had never bought anything so sophisticated for me before. "Maybe for *you*, Emma. I would need to grow a butt and get breast implants to pull that off."

"What're you talking about, honey? You have an adorable little figure. And you will be three inches taller with the shoes I bought you." Mom disappeared around the corner into the hall again and returned with a pair of black pumps with spiked heels.

"Seriously, Mom? You've obviously forgotten what a klutz your daughter is."

Mom took one shoe out of the box and ran her hand across the suede. "Then you'll just have to practice walking in them, because stiletto heels are all the rage."

I turned back around to face Emma who was holding the dress up to her body and looking at her reflection in the oven door. She was literally quivering with excitement. "Go ahead," I said to her. "Try it on."

Emma looked back and forth between Mom and me. Needing no further encouragement than the nod of my mother's head, she took the dress and disappeared upstairs. Emma was clearly more suited to be my mother's daughter than I was. After all, I lacked glamour, I avoided drawing attention to myself, and I'd rather take the SAT again than spend the day shopping.

When my mother's affair with Ann Patton's father was discovered, certain aspects of our past lives became clear. Like when the eye doctor put corrective lenses on me for the first time. I wear contacts now, but back then I was looking at the world through a child's blue-framed glasses. The night in the rose garden was not an isolated incident, a one-time quick little kiss. Theirs was a relation-ship that only public humiliation, not my father, had the power to stop. My mother was much too vain to let the gossipers bring *her* down. She rallied the friends who were not afraid to be seen with a woman scorned, and she marched right on with her tennis matches and her lunch dates.

Her private life, on the other hand, was an entirely different matter. She'd never been much of a drinker before the breakup with Ann Patton's father. Her crushed heart drove her to seek sol-ace from a bottle of gin. And she was a really nasty drunk, a binge drinker, one double martini shy of rehab. When she wasn't roaming the house in a fit of anger, breaking things and insulting anyone who got in her way, she went missing—like on my sixteenth birth-day when my father organized a dinner party for me at the club. He was able to convince my friends that my mother had come down with a sudden bout of the stomach flu, but my friends weren't really the ones who mattered, now were they?

Even though my mother appeared to have stopped the heavy boozing, I wasn't ready to forgive her just yet. I used to worry that harboring so much anger for such a long time would damage my soul, but I'd learned to use her as an example of all the things not to be in life.

I poured myself a bowl of cereal and took it out on the porch to see my dad. "Hey there," I said, kissing him from behind on the bald part of his head.

He looked up from his newspaper and smiled at me. "Sweet-heart! I've missed you."

Ben and I resemble our father, more so than our mother. I wouldn't call him a good-looking man, but he has good genes, and he's in good health. His warm brown eyes draw attention away from his droopy cheeks. He's five foot eight to my mother's five foot nine, although that's never stopped her from wearing super-tall heels.

"Brr," I said, shivering. "It's kind of chilly out here."

"Easy for you to say," Spotty yelled up from the yard where he and Ben were doing stretching exercises. "You haven't just run a marathon with your sadist brother."

"Don't complain, Kitty Cat," Dad said. "This cold front is a welcome relief from the heat and humidity. Here." He tossed his paper on the coffee table and slid over to make room for me on the sofa. "Come and share some of my blanket."

"What time did y'all get home last night?" I asked him when I was all nestled in.

He tucked a stray strand of hair behind my ear. "Truthfully, I'm not sure. Are you checking up on us?" he teased.

I shrugged. "Seems to me like you've adapted pretty quickly to being an empty nester."

Spotty plopped down in a chair across from Dad and me. "They got home about thirty minutes after you went to bed. I know this because I was still awake. The longest night of my young life to date."

Dad and I stared at Spotty, waiting for him to explain.

Spotty used his shirttail to wipe the sweat from his forehead. "Never mind. It's probably best not to go there."

Taking the hint, my dad untangled himself from the blanket. "I think I'll leave the two of you to talk while I go inside for a refill. Katherine, are you ready for some coffee?"

"Sure, Dad, that'd be great. Thanks." When I heard the screen door slam behind me, I said to Spotty, "Okay, What gives?"

He leaned over, propping his elbows on his knees, and whispered so Ben couldn't hear him. "After you went to sleep, Emma came back downstairs to have a nightcap. She was all over Ben like flies on a cow paddy. They were both so drunk. At least he was. I don't know her well enough yet to make that judgment. I hated to deprive Ben of the opportunity to get some leg—"

"Spotty, please! Too much information."

"Fine," he said, laughing. "Anyway, you know what I'm trying to say. I was afraid if I left them alone, and your parents walked in on them—"

"Naked? Yeah. That would've been kind of awkward."

My father cleared his throat to announce his return. He handed me a cup of coffee. "Are you planning to use the boat today?" he asked. "Because if not, your mother and I may go over to Urbanna for lunch. We'd love for you all to join us."

"I thought we decided this last night," Emma said, waltzing onto the porch in the black sequin dress. She balanced herself on her tippy toes and twirled around several times like a ballerina before coming to a wobbly standstill. "Aren't we spending the day with George and his sister? Out in *his* boat?"

"George again?" Ben mumbled, dragging himself up the steps and falling into the nearest chair. "Do we have to?"

"We wouldn't want to hurt his feelings, now would we?" Emma asked, and then executed another spin for Ben's sake.

I watched Ben watching Emma, his eyes huge at the sight of her shapely body in the skimpy dress. He'd been flirting with her since the first day they'd met, but somewhere along the way, he'd crossed the threshold into infatuation. The look on his face was pure lust. In the short amount of time I'd known Emma, I'd already witnessed her hooking up with several different guys. As much as I liked my roommate, I didn't want my brother to get hurt by falling for a girl who wasn't ready for a relationship.

"Too late now," Ben said as he nodded his head toward George and Abigail, who were speeding across the creek in their boat.

I glanced over at Emma. "Don't you think you're a little over-dressed for tubing?"

She giggled. "Then I guess we'd better go change," she said to Spotty and Ben as she glided toward the door.

I wandered over to the railing, watching George navigate his boat alongside our dock. The Turners worked together as a team, quietly and efficiently, like they'd done so many times before, to set the bumpers, tilt the motor, and tie up their boat.

I turned back around to face my father. "Abigail is looking really skinny," I said in a soft voice that wouldn't carry across the water. "I'm really concerned, Dad. She looks like an escapee from Auschwitz."

"I know, honey." He folded his newspaper and set it down beside him. "I saw her parents at a party last night. They are very worried. I was afraid to ask them too many questions, but it sounds as though they are getting her some help."

"At least that's something." I turned back around and yelled to Abby, who was making her way up the hill from the dock. "Wanna come help me pack a picnic while everyone's getting changed?"

She smiled up at me and quickened her pace. Abigail had always seemed younger to me than the fourteen months that separated us. She was still a child in a lot of ways, in her innocence. She was the real deal. Not overly outgoing, but honest and good. It broke my heart to think something was so horribly wrong in her life that made her want to starve herself. When she got to the porch and gave me a quick hug, I made a pact with myself to be a better friend, to stay in touch with her in the hopes she'd open up about what was troubling her.

"So, George, what am I missing out on at Chapel Hill?" I asked when he followed us to the kitchen.

"No point in beating yourself up over this, Kitty. UNC is not all that different from UVA. Think about it. They both have amazing campuses and belong to the ACC. The same fraternities and sororities are popular at both, and business school is kicking my ass at Carolina like it is Ben's at Virginia."

"Maybe you're right. I don't imagine the nursing programs are all that different either."

"Exactly. Now . . . what're we gonna pack for our picnic?" He opened the pantry door and popped the top off a Tupperware container, sniffing the contents. "No way! Are these Blessy's lemon bars?"

Never mind that she's black and has children of her own, Blessy is as much a part of our family as my own mother. In fact, through the years, she was there for me in ways my mother never was. When Mom was off on one of her excursions or sequestered in her bedroom, Blessy took care of Ben and me. She fed us a hearty breakfast every morning and a well-balanced dinner at night. She made certain my father's shirts were ironed and left him sticky notes on the refrigerator to remind him of our sporting events and parent meetings at school. She bandaged our wounds, and when we reached the appropriate age, she talked to us about the birds and the bees.

Blessy's ties with our family began a long time ago when she came to work for my grandparents. I never fully understood the special connection between them, but their relationship was more than just employer to employee. Theirs was a bond so strong my grandfather insisted my father take care of Blessy when she moved to Richmond to be close to a sick relative. Not that my father needed any arm-twisting. Who wouldn't want to have such a formidable woman help raise their children?

I laughed at George when he stuffed a whole lemon bar in his mouth at once. "If you look in the refrigerator, I'll bet there's some of her homemade pimento cheese."

Like a little boy with his presents on Christmas morning, George removed several containers from the refrigerator and lined them up on the counter. "Yum, here's the pimento cheese." He slid the container across the counter toward us and then ripped the lid off the one next to it. "Potato salad in this one, and . . . oh my god, fried chicken. Can we take some for our picnic? Please?"

"Yes George," I said. "If it means that much to you, we can pack all of it."

Abigail covered her mouth to hide her smile. "Do you remember their food-eating contests, Kitty? I still can't believe they once ate a dozen eggs apiece."

George looked up from his containers. "Come on, Yabba. Get your facts straight," he teased. "I'm the one who ate the whole dozen. Ben hurled after only ten."

I snatched the chicken container away from George before he could get his hands on another leg. "Better not let Ben hear you say that or he'll insist on a rematch."

Ben and George kept a tally—in an old composition book hidden under my brother's mattress—of the wins and losses from their contests. Two points for eating the most eggs, and five to the winner of the basketball shootout. Wonder how many points Ben had earned for hooking up with Emma.

Every summer George worked at the Tide's Inn—the grand old hotel located around the bend from us in Irvington—either pumping gas on the fuel dock at the marina or waiting tables around the pool. While we finished making the sandwiches and packing the coolers with bottled water and soft drinks, he entertained us with funny stories from his experiences over the summer.

We were already down on the dock, loading our provisions into the boat, when Spotty, Ben, and Emma finally joined us. "Here, let me give you a hand," George said, holding Emma by the arm as she stepped on board. She was unsteady, but succeeded in wobbling her way to the front seat. When she slipped her T-shirt off over her head, every male pair of eyes zeroed in on her large breasts hanging out of her skimpy black bikini top.

"Emma's never been tubing before," Ben said, dragging the inflatable tube on board. "She wants me to go with her."

Emma shook her head back and forth so fast it made me dizzy to watch her. "I said *maybe*, Ben. I'm not ready yet."

"Yeah. Chillax, man," George said to Ben. "Give her some time to get used to being on the boat."

Spotty untied the line from the dock and jumped on the stern of the boat with me. "I've never known anyone to get seasick before they actually leave the dock," he whispered in my ear.

"I guess we're wakeboarding then. Who's going first?" Ben asked as we were pulling away from the dock.

"Me." George dropped the throttle back to neutral and slipped on his lifejacket. Ben made a move to take the wheel, but George blocked his path. "Abby's driving. She knows how to make the turns the way I like them."

"Whatever, dude." Ben sat back down. "It's not worth arguing about."

George popped right out of the water and immediately began showing off his new tricks, not the simple jumps Ben could do but complicated twists and spins that require a lot of practice. Ben was sitting beside Emma, pretending not to notice, but I could tell he was taking notes on George's fancy moves. When it was his turn, even though he hadn't been on a wakeboard in over a year, he tried to copy one of George's flips. He failed to get enough air off the wake, and like a stone skimming the surface, he skidded across the water on his back.

George was laughing so hard when he pulled the boat up beside Ben he could barely get his words out. "Are you okay, bro? You busted your ass big-time."

Ben stretched his neck and grimaced. "Nothing but a little whiplash. Toss me the tube," Ben said, pushing the wakeboard out of the water to George. "Come on, Emma. It's your turn."

"I'm afraid," Emma said.

It took Ben and George ten minutes to convince Emma she wouldn't get hurt. She finally agreed to go, but only if all three of them got on the tube together. With Emma tucked in the middle between George and Ben, Abby pulled them out into the Rappahannock where there was more room to do doughnuts. Every time the tube went outside of the wake, Emma squealed, and Ben and George, in turn, wrapped their arms around her and pulled her close. They were five-year-old boys again, fighting over the last carton of chocolate milk.

"I can't take it anymore," I yelled to Abby above the sound of the outboard motor. "Make 'em suffer."

Doubt crossed Abby's face for a split second, but then she broke into a big smile, her eyes gleaming with mischief. She cut the boat hard, into the wind. The tube bounced off the wake and soared through the air, sending all three passengers flying in different directions across the water. This time it was *my* turn to laugh, so hard I had to jump in the water and pee as soon as Abby slowed the boat.

Once everyone was back in the boat, towel-dried and settled, we passed out sandwiches and chicken legs and Diet Cokes for lunch.

"So, Katherine, your parents are not at all like you described them," Emma said, cozying up next to George on the bow seat. "I was expecting pompous and disagreeable, but they're good-natured and fun to be around."

George snorted. "Yeah. How many years of marriage counseling did it take?"

I stared at George, appalled that he would say such a thing.

"True, isn't it?" George asked me. "That your father had to train your mother to stay out of the rose bushes."

In one fluid motion, Ben hurled his sandwich overboard, stepped onto the driver's seat where he'd been sitting, and leapt across the windshield toward George. He grabbed him in a choke-hold and wrestled him to the floor of the boat. George's sculpted body was no match for Ben's incredible strength. I clawed at Ben's back while Spotty tried to get a grip on his sweaty body. "Calm down, man," Spotty yelled, wrapping his arms around Ben from behind and hauling him off of George.

"What's the matter, Langley?" George's fists were clenched beside him. "You can't take a joke?"

"Some joke, you prick." Ben managed to get free of Spotty and dove on top of George again. This time it was the piercing sob escaping from Abigail's throat that caught their attention. In unison, George and Ben looked up to see her face covered in tears.

"All right, that's it. Get up." I helped them to their feet. I was tempted to ram my knee into George's crotch, but I knew that would do little to diffuse the situation. "What the hell is wrong with the two of you?"

They stood facing each other, looking around at the floor and the sky and the water, everywhere but at one another or at me.

"Damnit. Look at each other," I demanded. "In the eye. If y'all are gonna act like second-graders, I'm gonna treat you like second-graders."

Slowly, their eyes met.

"Good boys. Now, first of all, George, you were way out of line. You owe both Ben and me an apology."

He hesitated several seconds before mumbling, "Sorry."

"Apology accepted, but if you ever dis my mother again like that, I'm going to supply the gun that Ben shoots you with." I turned to my brother. "And Ben, solving our problems with our fists is not always the right answer."

"But—"

"No buts. I want you to think back ten years to the night we snuck out of our houses, on a full moon and a dare, and entered the woods in search of werewolves. Remember that Abby?" I glanced over at her, relieved to find a thin smile spreading across her lips. "We were scared shitless, but we trusted each other in the way you can only trust your childhood friends. You don't ever get a chance at that kind of friendship again, and the two of you want to waste it on some girl? No offense, Emma," I said without looking her way.

"I'm sorry, Abby." Ben leaned down and kissed her cheek, but when George tried to give him his half-eaten chicken leg as a peace offering, my brother waved him away.

We finished our lunch in silence, soaking up the warm sun as the boat drifted along. The weather couldn't have been any better—blue sky and low humidity—and to be able to enjoy the wide-open expanse of the Rappahannock River, with few boats and no waves, was a bonus.

When Abby and I grew restless, we tossed the tube in the water and climbed on top, declaring we were queens of the mountain. Everyone put forth a heroic effort, but no one could dethrone us. That is, until the three guys ganged up on us and tipped the massive tube over. Everyone had the opportunity to tube after that, and those of us with experience, took a turn on the wakeboard. It was late in the day, close to five o'clock, when we headed back to Carter's Creek to give Emma the promised tour.

We were cruising into our dock when George asked, "What're y'all doing tonight?"

Ben was quick to answer, "Laying low, man. Gonna throw some meat on the grill and then call it an early night." He made a point of not inviting him to dinner, which is why we were all surprised when George showed up at our house two hours later.

We were all showered and dressed and watching Ben fry oysters in the summer kitchen. Before the renovations, the summer kitchen was little more than a one-room storage building with a fireplace, an old stove, and an icebox, as MayMay used to call it. With french doors offering access to the brick terrace, the outbuilding now houses a full-service kitchen with commercial-grade appliances and a small sitting area around the fireplace.

"Here," George said, handing me a packaged rib eye when I opened the door for him. "Emma called and said to bring a steak."

"Oh really? Did she also tell you to bring Abby?" I cut my eyes at Emma, who avoided my gaze.

"Abs is laid out on the sofa, sunburned," George explained.

I rolled my eyes. "Because your sister, the summer goddess, gets sunburned so often."

Ignoring me, George peered over Ben's shoulder. "Are those oysters, man?"

Ben set a row of Ritz crackers on the counter and added a dab of tartar sauce to each. When his oysters were done, he removed the basket from the fryer and then carefully forked one on top of every cracker. "Here, Emma, try this." He turned to her and popped an oyster appetizer into her mouth like a groom feeding his bride a piece of cake on their wedding day.

Spotty opened the refrigerator and tossed me a beer. "Why don't you and I go start the grill?" When we were alone on the terrace, he opened his beer and guzzled down half of it. "I had to get out of there. I can't watch another round of the love triangle."

"For the most part, I really like Emma. Everything was fine between us until—"

"Your brother got in the picture." Spotty pulled the cover off the grill and wheeled it to the edge of the terrace. "I'm warning you, Kitty, I have a horrible feeling about this. I can sense it from a mile away. The two of them are negative chemistry together." Spotty reached beneath the grill to turn on the gas. "Negative chemistry with an explosive reaction." He pushed the starter and the fire caught with a whoosh. "Like that." He turned the knobs to lower the flames and began scraping the grates with a wire brush.

"You know, Spotty, you've always been good at helping Ben deal with his issues. But in this case, I think maybe you're overacting."

"That's because you didn't witness their X-rated performance last night. Haven't you seen the way the two of them look at each other?" We watched through the french doors as Ben fed Emma another oyster. "See what I mean?"

Spotty and I continued to watch the scene unfold inside. Emma picked up an oyster from the tray on the counter and fed it to George. I turned my back on them and walked away. "I have to admit I don't like the way she's playing them off of one another. She's holding a stick of dynamite, waiting to see who will light it first."

"That's not the way I see it at all. Emma is not making a play for both of them. She's using George to make Ben jealous." Spotty closed the grill lid and hung the wire brush on the side. "Speaking of George. I've been down here with y'all a lot over the years, so I feel like I know him well enough to say this. What he said about your parents today took a lot of balls."

"No shit." I took a sip of beer and licked my lips. "I've talked to Abby some about my mother's problems, just as I'm sure Ben has with George, but to bring it up in front of everyone like that was just sick."

Spotty nodded. "I think you and Ben need to watch your backs. I'm not sure George has your best interests at heart."

Ben threw open the French doors and the three lovebirds joined us on the terrace, bringing with them another round of beers and the tray of oysters.

Ben lifted the lid to check on the progress of the grill. He scraped a little more gunk off the grates with the wire brush, closed the lid again, and lowered the flame. "I'm not ready to cook the steaks yet." He downed the rest of his beer and crumpled the can. "The night is still young."

"So much for calling it an early night," I mumbled to Spotty.

"Hey, man, are your parents home?" George asked.

"Nope," Ben answered. "They went to some party over in Weems."

"In that case . . ." George pulled a bag of weed and a pipe out of his back pocket. He loaded the bowl and lit it with a Bic lighter, sucking hard from the pipe before handing it to Emma. After she took several tokes from the pipe, she offered it first to Spotty, who waved it away, and then to Ben.

Ben shook his head. "No thanks."

"Don't be a buzzkill," Emma said, stomping her foot.

Ben ignored her. "Since when did you start smoking weed?" he asked George.

"Since my sister's not here. Come on, dude. Everybody smokes."

"Not everybody." Ben grabbed Spotty's shoulder and squeezed. "There are plenty of athletes who don't want to pollute their bodies with that trash."

"I hate to tell you this, but we're not in high school anymore. Your chances of playing college ball are over," George said, more to Spotty than to Ben, his insult like pouring rubbing alcohol over the open wound of his ruined lacrosse career.

"At least we were once good enough to be considered," Spotty said, with clenched fists. "Which is more than I can say for you."

"Calm down, boys." Emma shoved the pipe toward me. "I know Katherine wants some. She's a party girl, like me."

"No thanks, Emma. I may be a party girl, but I have certain standards. Anyway, I've tried it before. I just don't like the way it makes me feel."

"Look," Ben said, "I don't mind if you smoke it, but just go over there by the fence, away from us."

Emma grabbed George by the hand and led him over to the edge of the property where they could finish their smoke away from our disapproving stares.

A few minutes later, I was exchanging texts with Yabba—not at all surprised to learn that she wasn't sunburned and that George hadn't told her he was coming over here for dinner—when they came stumbling back toward the house. George was dragging Emma along, both of them looking at me and laughing. At first I thought they were just high, but then George came over and kissed the top of my head. "We're friends, right?"

Friends? I looked at him, confused. Was he asking if we were still friends after the things he'd said about my mother, or was he making sure that we were nothing more than friends?

"Of course we're friends," I said to George. "Why do you ask?"

"Well . . . ah . . . Emma may have mentioned that you have a—"

"Crush on you?" I asked and he nodded. "Don't flatter yourself, George. I think maybe the weed is making you delusional."

SIX

Labor Day's rain and fog provided us with the perfect excuse to head back to Charlottesville earlier in the day than we'd originally planned. I dropped my bag off in my room and went straight to the library where I sequestered myself for the rest of the week, away from the distractions of the dorm. It wasn't until late Friday afternoon that Emma and I had our first real conversation. She tracked me down in Phoebe and Carla's room across the hall.

Phoebe was from New Orleans and Carla from Vermont, and that's where the similarities between the two of them ended. Phoebe was a waif, barely passing the five-foot mark, but her silky black hair and dark eyes gave her an exotic look. Carla was big-boned and not necessarily pretty, although she would've been attractive if she brushed her hair and wore something other than baggy T-shirts and gym shorts every once in a while. Both of them were funny, and together, they were a regular stand-up comedy routine.

"Can I speak to you for a minute," Emma asked me, appearing from nowhere in the doorway.

"Sure." I shrugged but made no effort to move.

"Alone." She turned her back on us, leaving me no choice but to follow her across the hall to our room.

"I sense you're upset with me about something." She patted the bed beside her, inviting me to sit. "You've been avoiding me all week."

I lowered myself onto the bed. "I've been in the library all week, Emma, trying to get caught up."

"Well . . . whatever it is you're mad at me about, I'm bringing you a peace offering."

"What kind of peace offering?" I asked, skeptical.

"A date. For the game tomorrow."

As if I couldn't get my own date. "What's his name?"

"Will Chase." She sat up taller and crossed her legs. "I'm going to the game with Will's best friend, Hank McCarthy. The two of them grew up together in Tennessee. They're good ole boys, fun and cute in a rednecky kind of way. So you'll go?"

"I don't know, Emma. I'd planned to study."

She rolled her eyes. "Because everyone studies on Saturday. Please," she begged, sticking her lower lip out in a pout. "His dorm is having a killer party afterwards, one we definitely don't want to miss."

"Oh, all right. I guess one afternoon away from the library won't kill me."

"Goody." She bounced up and down on her bed a couple of times before turning serious again. "By the way, I spoke to my mother this week. Apparently my computer can't be fixed. The ones in the library are so slow . . ."

"I'm sorry. I totally forgot." I grabbed a piece of paper from the printer. "Let's work out a schedule for us to share mine." It made me feel good about myself to be able to share the things Emma didn't have. As long as it wasn't my brother.

When Ben texted me on Sunday afternoon to see if I wanted to play tennis, I suspected him of using me as an excuse to see Emma, until he suggested we meet at the courts instead of offering to come by my room.

"I saw you on the lawn yesterday," he said, popping the top on a new can of balls. "Who's the guy you were with?"

"Emma's date's best friend." I watched Ben's face closely, waiting for his brow to furrow or his eye to twitch. Instead, he surprised me by saying, "Good. I hope you had fun."

I followed Ben out onto the court. "How 'bout you? Did you have a date?"

He nodded. "Maddie Maloney, a friend of Spotty's."

"Did *you* have a good time?" I asked.

He tossed me a tennis ball. "Actually, I did. Enough to ask her out again for next weekend."

Ben was stronger and more agile, a much better tennis player than me, but we played together often. He used our sessions to work on his accuracy and placement while I simply tried to win as many points as possible. We were so hot and sweaty by the time we finished our second set, Ben suggested we get a cold drink.

We crossed Emmet Street and headed up the steps toward Newcomb Hall. "What about George last weekend?" Ben said. "Something's not right with him."

"He's probably just worried about Yabba," I said, shivering at the thought of Abigail's malnourished body.

"No doubt there's plenty to worry about. She looks like shit."

We entered the west side of Newcomb Hall, purchased two vitamin waters from the student center, and then exited the east side to the patio dining area.

"I'm glad you're here, Kitty. At UVA," Ben said when we were seated at an umbrellaed table. "Our paths may not cross daily, but there are certain things I can help you with."

"Uh-oh. Sounds like I should brace myself for a lecture about using a fake ID on the Corner."

"What? You have a fake ID?" He held his hands over his ears. "That's information I definitely do not need to know." When I laughed, he added, "I'm not joking, Kitty. Having a fake ID is a serious offense, as serious as underage possession. You need to be careful."

"Relax. I don't have a fake ID." I stuck my tongue out at him. "What exactly is it you want to help me with?"

He stared at me, his expression both amused and concerned. "For starters, I have a couple of friends in the nursing program who'd be happy to give you some pointers."

"By any chance are they friends of Honey's?" I asked, taking a sip from my vitamin water.

I watched his face as he made the connection. "You mean Chi Delta Honey?" he asked, and I nodded. "Are you kidding me? Has she already been pressuring you about joining her sorority?"

"I wouldn't exactly say she was pressuring me, although she did mention that Mom had gotten some of her friends to write letters for me. I wish Mom hadn't done that, Ben."

He guzzled half of his water and then set his bottle down on the table. "Listen to me, Kitty. In January, when it comes time for you to rush, *if* you even want to go through the process, you choose the house where you feel the most comfortable, where you like the girls the most, regardless of how much pressure you get from Honey or Mom or anyone else."

"Did Dad insist you join KO?" My brother is a two-time legacy of the fraternity.

"What do *you* think? I got it from all sides, including Dock before he died. But I didn't listen to them. I rushed every house, and if there'd been any doubt, I would've pledged somewhere else. Promise me you'll do the same."

"Mom would never forgive me," I mumbled.

He drained the rest of his water and tossed the empty bottle into a nearby recycling bin like a basketball into a hoop. "Since when has that been a problem for you?"

"This is different, Ben, and you know it. We are talking about her sorority, her sisterhood. Being president of Chi Delta was her biggest accomplishment in life." He started to argue with me, but I held my hand up to stop him. "Whatever. This isn't something I have to decide today."

"You're right. You have plenty of time. But I'd like to be able to help you with decisions like these. I wish I'd had someone to guide me through my first year. What do you say we get together more often, maybe even once a week?"

"Who? You and me?" I held my breath, waiting for Ben to suggest we invite Emma to join us the next time.

"No Shrek and Donkey. Of course you and me." He leaned back in his chair. "There are things you need to know, like applying for next-year's housing. Are you aware that you have to turn your application in by the first of November?"

"Already? We're only just getting settled into this year."

He shrugged. "With so many students to place, I guess they have to get started early." He pushed his chair back from the table. "What say we meet at the Virginian for brunch next Sunday?"

***

For the next six weeks, I managed to compartmentalize my life—family, school, social. Emma always had a date for me when one was needed, and many times when one was not. Everywhere we went she was the center of attention. At least amongst the guys. With the exception of Phoebe, Carla, and myself, Emma seemed to have trouble bonding with other females. She made her rounds at parties, introducing herself to all the other girls. But when I encouraged her to join a group from our hall for dinner or a movie, she always declined, although I often wondered if that had more to do with money than anything else. If her parents gave her any allowance, it was minimal. More and more she seemed frustrated over her finances.

Tired of hearing her complain, I asked her, "Why don't you just get a job?"

"And when do you suggest I do that? I'm already working in the library for my financial aid, and my father insists I work for him, for free, during the summers."

"It's none of my business, Emma, but it doesn't seem fair for your father to expect you to work for him without pay. Can't he get another student to intern for him so you can get a job that pays?"

She grew quiet as she often did when something was on her mind. Her silence reminded me of Ben. The invisible wall would go up, and she would retreat inside her castle, alone.

It became our habit, Ben's and mine, to try out a different restaurant every Sunday. When we were pressed for time, we'd walk down to the Corner, but when we were feeling more adventurous, we'd take his car over to the downtown mall. He surprised me on the first Sunday of October by bringing Maddie Maloney along. With shoulder-length black hair and big brown eyes, she was tall and lean, like a model, although her thinness was in disproportion to the amount of food she ate. In the span of an hour, I watched her polish off a chicken caesar wrap, finish what was left of Ben's cheeseburger and french fries, and then split a hot fudge sundae with him for dessert.

Composed and graceful with a true sense of self, Maddie was the kind of girl I would've handpicked for my brother. I thought they had something special going, until I barged into my dorm room two weeks later and found him in a lip-lock with Emma.

"Try knocking next time," Ben said, flustered, as though I'd barged in on him in our bathroom at home.

"Seriously? Last time I checked, this was *my* room."

"Ben was just helping me get an eyelash out of my eye," Emma said, rubbing her eye for added effect. "Guess what, Katherine? Ben just asked me to go with him to the Monster Bash."

Every year the KO's theme for their Halloween party was different. Last year everyone went as mummies, while the year before that, the success of the Twilight Series inspired a vampire theme. This year they'd planned a masquerade ball. The guests were to dress in black tie with scary masks to hide their faces. Emma was determined to go. She'd been obsessing over getting a date for weeks.

I tossed my backpack on my bed and left the room. Ben caught up with me at the bottom of the stairwell. "Why are you so angry?" he asked, grabbing me by the elbow.

"I don't really know why, if you want to know the truth. Only that the thought of you and Emma together makes me angry. She's not right for you," I said, pushing my way through the double doors.

"How can you say that about her?" Ben asked, following me. "She's your roommate."

"And I like her fine as my roommate. I just don't want her going out with my brother." I was walking so fast Ben had to work to keep up with me. "Don't you realize she's manipulating you? All she wants is a date to this party."

"That's cool, because we're just friends. Why shouldn't I take her if she really wants to go?"

When we reached McCormick Road, I stopped and turned to face him. "I thought you were dating Maddie."

Ben shivered, rubbing his arms against the chill, and I realized he was the only one on the street not wearing a jacket. I hadn't been in the room long enough to take mine off, but obviously he had.

"Maddie is going out of town that weekend, to her sister's wedding in DC."

"Really? Well I'm sure she'll be thrilled to learn that her boyfriend has a date with the hottest first-year student on campus while she's gone."

Ben waved at a group of friends across the street and then turned back to me. "Listen, Kitty. I have no intention of screwing things up with Maddie. For the last time, Emma and I are just friends."

"If you say so." I turned left and headed toward the library, calling to him over my shoulder, "Just don't come whining to me when Maddie won't speak to you and Emma breaks your heart."

There wasn't much point of me staying in the library without my backpack, but I ran into some friends who invited me to go with them to Starbucks. Which gave me a chance to calm down a little before I had to face Emma. When I returned to our room, I found her prancing around in the black sequined dress my mother bought for me at the river.

"Please don't be mad, Katherine. I know you think I'm using Ben, but he and I are just friends. He knows how much I want to go to this party."

I couldn't help but smile. She was so predictable. "I should've known. This is all about the dress, isn't it?"

"Well . . ." She chewed on her lower lip. "The dress would look better on me if I didn't have to hide my face behind some disgusting mask."

"Who says you have to wear an ugly mask? You're creative. Can't you come up with something that hides your face in an alluring way?"

"That's it!" She snapped her fingers. "You're a genius, Katherine. I'll go as Batgirl. Your knee-high black boots would be perfect with fishnet tights. That is if you'll let me borrow them." She danced around the room on her toes in excitement. "Surely I can find a Batgirl mask online."

I rummaged through one of my drawers until I found my jewelry case. "What're you looking for?" Emma asked, peering over my shoulder into my pouch.

"Earrings. I have a pair that'd be perfect with your costume."

"Ooh, those are pretty," she said, pointing at my diamond studs. "Are they real?"

I nodded. "They belonged to my grandmother."

"Why don't you ever wear them?"

"They're not exactly the kind of jewelry you wear to biology class. Here." I pulled an earring out of my satchel, a silver medallion on a chain with a black Batman emblem etched in it.

"Are you kidding me? You just happened to have a pair of Batman earrings lying around?"

"I bought them for a costume party a few years ago." I located the mate and handed it to her.

"Thank you, Katherine." She held the earrings up to her ears, admiring herself in the mirror for a minute before setting them down on top of her dresser. "On another subject, Phoebe and Carla asked me today if you and I would be interested in sharing a suite with them next year."

Emma was a master at changing the subject and she'd picked just the right one to get my attention. So with only two weeks left before early applications were due to the housing department—ignoring the nagging concern in my gut and reminding myself that we were compatible as roommates—I committed to living with Emma for another year.

The night of the Monster Bash, I made a point of being out of the room when Ben came to pick Emma up, and I pretended to be asleep when she got home, although I peeked at her when she turned her desk lamp on. She was stumbling around, drunk. Her updo was no longer up, and her lips were swollen and red from kissing.

Friends? Right.

Made of stretchy fabric with no zipper, the dress presented a challenge to Emma as she struggled to pull it over her head. When she was free of it, she hung it in the closet. Then, she put on a pair of flannel pajama bottoms and a T-shirt and switched off the desk lamp.

She nudged me. "Katherine, are you awake? You missed a great party." When I faked being asleep, she whispered, "Too bad for your poor brother. He has no idea what just hit him."

SEVEN

After weeks of begging, I finally convinced Abigail to spend some time with me at UVA. It didn't bother me any that her visit was scheduled at the last minute and had more to do with her parents needing a place to park their troubled daughter for the night while they attended a friend's fiftieth birthday party in Lexington. She arrived just after lunch on the second Saturday in November. Even though she was all bundled up against the cold, her face and neck and the outline of her legs through her jeans told me she'd lost even more weight since Labor Day. Her parents came up to the room with Abby on the pretense of meeting my roommate, but I knew they were scouting out the place to make sure it was safe for their daughter. They didn't hand me a list of special instructions, like making sure Abby got plenty to eat, but the manner in which they turned their daughter over to me—the concerned glances at one another and their hesitancy to leave—reminded me of a new mother trusting her infant child with a babysitter for the first time. These nervous people were not the same parents who once let Abby and me spend our days running wild on the creek. Had things gotten so bad with her eating disorder that her parents were afraid to let her out of their sight?

Abby brought with her a fresh batch of blonde brownies and four fifty-yard-line tickets to Saturday's football game against Duke, a gift from her father's colleague who was unable to use them due to a prior engagement. We texted Ben to bring a friend and come sit with us, but when he didn't respond, Abby was kind enough to invite Emma to tag along. The tickets were ideal, midway up and dead center on the fifty, but the crowd around us was too tame for our taste. When the Cavaliers scored a touchdown within a minute of the half to tie the ballgame, 14–14, we could no longer contain our excitement and joined our peers in the student section on the other side of the stadium.

"Isn't that Ben down there?" Abby pointed at my brother who was sitting seven or eight rows in front of us, flirting and laughing with the girl next to him. "Is that his girlfriend?"

I nodded. "She's pretty, isn't she? Her name is Maddie Maloney. They've been dating for a couple of months now."

Emma removed a flask from her shoulder bag, took a gulp from her Coke, and filled her cup to the brim with bourbon. "Want some?" she asked, holding the flask out to Abby and me.

When I waved her away, Abby followed my lead. Normally I would've accepted, but I didn't want to encourage my anorexic friend to put any unhealthy substances into her feeble body.

"Where'd Emma go?" I asked Abby, five minutes into the second half when I realized Emma was no longer beside Abby. We scanned the crowd until we saw her making her way toward Ben like a torpedo searching through the waters for its target. She wedged herself between Reed and Spotty, who were sitting directly in front of Ben. Pulling her flask out of her bag again, she offered it first to Reed and Spotty before turning around to Ben, as if realizing for the first time that he was there.

I rolled my eyes at Abby. "She's a smooth one, isn't she?"

Abby nodded. "She's trying to make Ben jealous. Just like on Labor Day weekend. What's going on between the two of them?"

I explained to Abby about how Emma had manipulated Ben for a date to the Monster Bash. "Poor Maddie doesn't stand a chance against my roommate. If Emma wants Ben, she'll find a way to have him." Sure enough, halfway through the fourth quarter, Maddie got up and stormed off.

After the game, in an effort to avoid Ben and Emma, I guided Abby out the opposite end of the stadium from the crowd. Temperatures had risen quite a bit during the day, leaving us with a mild and pleasant evening. We took our time in wandering down to the

Corner. Abby's parents had made me promise to take her to the College Inn for a burger—one of their favorite hangouts when they were students at UVA twenty-five years ago. Abby settled into our booth as though she'd been there many times. When our burgers came, I gobbled mine down, but she only nibbled on hers, pinching tiny pieces off her bun without touching the meat.

"Are you just gonna pick at that?" I asked her. "Go ahead. Take a bite. It's really good."

She wiped her mouth with her napkin and then balled it up and threw it on her plate. "Please don't start, Kitty. I already catch enough grief at home."

I'd been trying since Labor Day, via texts and e-mails, to get Abby to open up to me about her problems. So far I'd been unsuccessful. Time for a more direct approach. "Tell me what's bothering you, Abby. Explain to me why it's so hard for you to eat."

"It's just—" she started, but then lowered her head and began picking at a hangnail. "I'm just not hungry. That's all. I ate a big lunch with Mom and Dad on the way here."

"That was hours ago." I grabbed her hand and squeezed it. "Come on, Yabba. You're talking to me Kitty."

"I promise I'll tell you everything, but not now. Not here." She looked back up at me, her gray eyes desperate. "Tonight, I want to have some fun for a change. You've been begging me to come for a visit, so here I am. Show me the college life."

"Fine. I'll drop the subject. For now." I reached for my wallet to pay the check. "What part of college life do you want to see?"

"Greek life," she said without hesitation. "I want to go to a fraternity party."

Which was my worst nightmare. How could I take my friend who weighed less than a hundred pounds and had barely eaten any dinner to a keg party?

"Okay, so I know I promised I'd drop the subject, but—"

She held her hand up. "Don't say it. Please. I hear it all the time from George. No food, no drink."

"Then we'll go see Ben at the KO house." I knew I could count on Mr. Overprotective to help me watch out for Abby. That is *if* he could drag himself away from Emma.

We made our way up University Avenue and climbed the brick steps to the KO house. "I smell weed," Abby said, sniffing. "Everyone is smoking these days. I just don't see the attraction."

I linked arms with her. "Nor do I, Yabba. Nor do I."

As we started up the sidewalk, Ben and Emma stepped out of the bushes and blocked our path. "Kitty, whatzup?" Ben stared at Abigail, confused. "Shit. I may be high, but you look exactly like my friend Abby."

She play-punched him in the arm. "I *am* Abby, silly."

"Yeah, *silly*," I said, punching him in the other arm. "Since when did you start smoking weed, Mr. Serious Athlete-that-you-are?"

Ben pointed at Emma. "Since she gave me this humongous bud." He laughed hysterically until he realized he was the only one laughing. Straightening himself, he asked me, "Why didn't you tell me Abby was here?"

"We sent you a text to come sit with us at the game," Abby explained. "Didn't you get it?"

Ben whipped out his cell phone and began scrolling through his texts. "Damnit. I totally missed it."

"Wait a minute," I said to Emma. "You didn't tell him Abby was here?"

"Seriously?" Ben stumbled toward Emma. "*You* knew about this?"

Emma caught Ben and pushed him off of her. "I guess it just slipped my mind." She glared at me. "What're you doing here, anyway? Your friend doesn't exactly strike me as the fraternity-party type."

"My friend?" I said to Emma. "You spent the weekend with her over Labor Day, and you went to the game today on her fifty-yard-line ticket. I would think by now you know her well enough to call her by name."

Emma placed her hand on her hip. "A-BI-GAIL," she said, emphasizing every syllable in Abby's name for emphasis, "doesn't seem like the fraternity-party type to me."

"According to who? You?" I asked. "Didn't someone ever tell you it's politically incorrect to social profile?"

"I'm sure she's smart enough to get into UVA. But look at her." Emma held her hands out toward Abigail. "She's not sorority material. She's earthy. I'd pick her for one of the clubs. Science or Marine Biology maybe."

Ben and I both looked over at Abigail in time to see her eyes fill with tears.

"That's enough, Emma," Ben said, his voice sober. "I'm with Kitty on this. You don't know Abby well enough to make that assumption." He wrapped his arm around Abby's shoulders and pulled her to him. "Come inside. I want you to meet some of my friends."

Abigail took a deep breath and smiled up at him. "That's okay, Ben. We weren't planning to stay here long, anyway."

I moved a little closer to Abby. "We just ran into Honey on the Corner. She invited us to go for ice cream with some of her friends. Emma may not think Abby is sorority material, but Honey sure does," I said, enjoying the hell out of the look of envy on Emma's face.

"Come on, Ben. Let's go." Emma grabbed him by the elbow and began dragging him up the sidewalk toward the fraternity house.

I took Abigail's hand and led her in the opposite direction, across University and through the maze of sidewalks to the heart of campus. We walked in silence, composing ourselves, Abigail fighting back the tears while I tried to calm the rage. In less than four hours, Emma had ruined Ben's relationship with Maddie, convinced him to smoke weed after all these years of standing firm against it, and made a game out of tearing Abby's confidence to shreds. I'd never known Emma to be so blatantly cruel to anyone before. Whether she was showing off for Ben or whether she felt threatened by my relationship with Abby. Who knows? Maybe she was just being mean because she could.

Lucky me! I'd just signed a contract to room with her for another year.

"So, this is the Academical Village?" Abby asked when we were standing in the center of the grassy expanse known as the Lawn.

"Isn't it amazing? And to think Thomas Jefferson designed it himself all those years ago. The Rotunda is the focal point at that end." I pointed north toward the enormous domed structure. "And these buildings on either side of the grassy area are known as the Lawn rooms. Can you believe it's considered a privilege to live here? Only fourth-year students can apply, the smartest of the class, and these people stand in line to live in a room with no air conditioning or heat."

"What do you mean there's no heat?" Abigail asked.

"I mean there's no heat. Each room has its own fireplace. Notice the wood stacked alongside the walkways?"

"Okay. That's pretty cool. I've been to Charlottesville several times with my parents for football games, but to think I might one day be a student here puts everything in a different perspective."

Lost in our own thoughts, we made a couple of laps around the Lawn and then stopped at the Rotunda where we took a seat on the cold granite steps, leaning back-to-back like we used to do when we were kids.

"Funny thing, Abby. I can totally see you living here, on the Lawn, wilderness woman that you are, building your fires at night and hiking it over to the outhouse to use the facilities."

"Ha. You must have me confused with someone else."

"Come on. As smart as you are? Don't sell yourself short."

"I'm glad you think so—because according to your roommate, I'm not even fit to be in a sorority."

"Believe me, Emma is no expert on Greek life. You, Abby, have a much better chance of getting into a sorority than she does." Sitting back-to-back, I couldn't see her face, but I could tell by Abby's breathing pattern—catch, hold for several seconds, release—she was paying close attention to everything I said. "Not only are you a legacy, your parents have plenty of connections with women who'd be thrilled to write letters for whichever sorority you choose." I knew Abby's parents well enough to know they'd do anything to make her happy, to get her to start eating again.

I shifted on the step so I could see her face. "No matter where you decide to go, what school you attend, you're going to have a blast. Trust me on this. You know I wanted to go to Chapel Hill, but I'm having the best time ever, even with a bitch for a roommate."

Her eyes lit up with hope and I knew she desperately wanted to believe me.

"If you decide you want to rush a sorority, the process is fair and you'll find the right house for you."

"Sounds like you've already made your decision about sororities."

"Me? No way. I'm taking Ben's advice and keeping an open mind until I go through rush."

"But what about this Honey person? Sounds like the two of you are tight."

I looked away from her, ashamed of myself for being dishonest with my closest friend. "I'm sorry, Abby. I shouldn't have lied earlier. I was just trying to get back at Emma. She's convinced Chi Delta is perfect for her. Funny thing is, Honey, their president, keeps blowing her off."

"What would your mother say if you decided to pledge a sorority other than Chi Delta?"

"I hope she'd be supportive. Wishful thinking, huh?" I leaned against Abigail, pushing on her until she toppled over. Stretched out on the steps, we stared out across the lawn and up at the stars. "I'm feeling all mushy and sentimental right now, but I can think of at least ten corny clichés that describe how I feel. The world is our oyster, Yabba. Life is what we make of it. *If* you come to UVA and *if* you decide pledging a sorority is not for you, there are over seven hundred clubs to choose from. Besides, who's to say you can't do it all?"

"*What* clubs?" she asked. "Science and Marine Biology?"

"If that's something you're interested in, then yes. But they also have a group that goes hiking on the Blue Ridge Parkway every weekend," I said, hoping to appeal to her sense of adventure.

"Now, that's way cool. Tell me more."

I moved closer to her, and we snuggled together like we were six again and camping out in our sleeping bags on the porch at the river. We talked for a long time about all the opportunities available to students at UVA and about college in general.

"I know you don't want to talk about what's going on in your life, but believe it or not, I understand a little about how you feel. I had my own issues in high school, and I couldn't wait to get away from them. Hang on Yabba. College is liberating, and you're almost there. Just stay focused on the process of applying to schools and try to block out all the other bad stuff."

I reached for her hand, and wishing I could channel some courage through my touch, I squeezed it. Despite the sick feeling in my gut that suggested otherwise, I wanted to believe the things I'd said might offer her some encouragement, enough to make a difference.

EIGHT

Ben was ultimately the one responsible for inviting Emma to spend Thanksgiving with us at the river. He mentioned it to her, and then she mentioned it to me; and in a moment of weakness, one I'd live to regret, I agreed. According to Emma, she had neither a ride home to Altoona nor the hundred bucks for a train ticket. She declined my offer to loan her money by insisting she was indebted to me enough already.

We were planning a short trip anyway, with one night in Richmond on the way to spend Thanksgiving at the river. Since it was the Cavaliers' turn to travel to Blacksburg for the rival game of the season, all three of us wanted to be back on campus by late Friday afternoon in order to watch the game on super screens at the John Paul Jones Arena midday Saturday.

Among the big parties in Richmond that Wednesday night, Kit Matthews was hosting a reunion at her parents' house for our high school classmates. Although Archer was the only person I really wanted to see, I was pleasantly surprised that the mood of the group, as a whole, was entirely different than it'd been in May at graduation. The talk was of campus life, as diverse as the University of Alabama was from Yale. People who hadn't paid any attention to me in years were suddenly interested in every aspect of my life at UVA. Even Ann Patton approached me like we were old friends.

As if one polite conversation could erase the past six years.

"Katherine, it's so good to see you," Ann Patton said, kissing the air beside my cheek. "I met your roommate a few minutes ago, outside on the patio beside the keg. She seems like a great girl. Y'all must be having so much fun at UVA."

I leaned into her. "And we're not the only ones. I saw your father at the football game a few weeks ago," I lied. "Funny thing, though. He was *not* with your mother. How does the saying go? Once a cheater, always a cheater?"

Archer, who was standing next to me at the time, burst into laughter, and she was still laughing three hours later when she pulled her Jeep into our driveway alongside Spotty's 4Runner.

"Come on, Arch," I said to her. "It's not *that* funny."

"It's hilarious, but more than that, it's about damn time. I'm proud of you, Kitty."

I unbuckled my seatbelt. "Then come inside with me, and I'll let you be the one to tell Ben and Spotty what happened."

She shook her head. "I can't. It's almost midnight."

Emma leaned over the back of Archer's seat. "You mean you still have a curfew?"

"Not a curfew. An early-morning flight out to visit my Gram in Florida," Archer said to Emma. Then she turned to me. "What about your parents, Kitty? Are they here?"

"They're already at the river. Please," I begged. "I won't get to see you again until Christmas."

"All right, then." She turned off the car and grabbed her purse. "But only for a few minutes."

The guys were at the back of the house, zoned out in front of the television in our family room. Spotty and Reed sat at opposite ends of the sofa while Ben sprawled out in a chair with a bottle of scotch and a tumbler on the table next to him.

"Hey, Ben," Archer said, tousling his hair.

He looked past Archer and me at Emma. "Where have y'all been?"

"Across the river, at Kit Matthews's house," Archer said, plopping down on the sofa between Spotty and Reed. I squeezed in next to her, leaving Emma the only available chair across from Ben.

"Damn, Arch, I almost didn't recognize you," Spotty said, tugging on a strand of her hair. "You look hot."

And she did. In the months since I'd seen her, Archer had managed to tame her unruly strawberry-blonde locks into a shiny mane, and like me, she'd begun to use a little makeup and spend more than a millisecond picking out her clothes.

Beneath the freckles, her face beamed bright red. "Coming from you, Spotty, I'll take that as a compliment."

He was unable to take his eyes off her. "I'm surprised you haven't come to see us in Charlottesville. You know Lexington is only an hour away."

"And how would I have gotten there? Walked?" she teased.

"Duh. Aren't freshmen allowed to have cars at W and L?"

She nodded her head. "But for whatever reason, my parents wouldn't let me take mine."

"Have y'all been here all night?" I asked Ben. "There are parties all over town."

"We've been babysitting your brother," Reed said. "He's not much in the party mood."

Ben poured three fingers of scotch in his glass and swallowed it in one gulp. "Who says I'm not in a party mood?" he slurred, slamming the glass on the table.

"You might want to lay off the Glenlivet," I said to Ben. "Mom wants us to get to the river early in the morning so you can fry the turkey."

Reed threw a pillow at Ben. "Sounds like Bobby Flay needs to get his beauty sleep."

Ben glared at him. "Shut up, you prick." He glanced over at Emma and saw her covering her mouth to hide her smile. His face flushed and his eyes narrowed. "What'd *you* think is so funny? Should we tell everyone about *your* hobby? About that thing you do with your tongue when you suck my—"

"Okay, Ben, that's enough." I moved to the edge of my seat, ready to pounce on him if necessary.

"Don't worry about it, Katherine. I can handle this." Emma got up from her chair and walked over to Ben, swaying her hips back and forth in exaggerated motion. She walked her fingers up Ben's chest and wrapped her arm around his neck from behind, whispering something in his ear that made him smile. Then, in a big show of it, she licked his neck from his collarbone to his ear. When she was finished with her performance, she sauntered down the hall toward the stairs, leaving the rest of us gaping at her back.

"Shit! Looks like the party's over." Spotty got up and the rest of us followed him from the room, leaving Ben alone to brood.

I walked Archer to her car, and we hugged good-bye. "I haven't seen Ben in such a foul mood in a long time," she whispered to me.

I pulled away from her, removing a strand of her hair from my mouth. "I can't figure out what's going on between him and Emma. He's obviously really into her, but she only pays attention to him when it's convenient for her."

"He's lucky to have you to keep a close eye on him," she said, pinching my cheek.

Archer was no stranger to Ben's OCD issues, and she knew how much I worried about him. Certain elements of this situation were reason to be concerned. That Archer felt the same way only made me worry more.

By the time I'd finished locking up and dragging Ben up the stairs to his room, Emma was already in my bed with the lights out. I crawled in beside her, fully dressed, and went right to sleep. But when I woke up an hour later to pee, Emma was gone. I tiptoed down the hall to Ben's room, cupping my ear against his closed door.

Seriously? I didn't know much about sex, but I knew enough to question whether a man in such an inebriated state as Ben could offer that kind of pleasure to a woman. I returned to my room, where I tossed and turned for a while before I finally surrendered to the bed spins.

I was still alone in my bed when my phone alarm woke me at eight o'clock. I cracked Ben's door and peeped inside his room. Emma was not there, or anywhere else in the house I discovered after a quick search. I was on my way back to Ben's room, to wake him up, when I heard the sound of water running in my parents' bathroom. I tiptoed down the hall to their room and yanked open the door to their bathroom. Dressed in my mother's cashmere robe, Emma was leaning over the spa tub, watching the last of my mom's favorite bubble bath—the expensive Lavender Foaming Bath that Ben and I always gave her for her birthday and Christmas—flow down the drain.

Our eyes locked and we stared at one another.

"It's a good look for me, don't you think?" she asked, waving her hand around the room. "The robe, the man, the house. Just think, little Kitty, one day I might be your sister-in-law."

"Over my dead body."

She stood to face me. "And just what're you gonna do about it?"

I turned my back on her and headed toward the door. "For starters, I'm going to tell Ben about your little bubble bath. He knows how private my mother is about her space."

"Oh really? Whose idea do you think it was?"

I stopped dead in my tracks. The Ben I knew would never have allowed his girlfriend access to my mother's bedroom. I turned back around to face her. "I want you to stop seeing Ben. I don't think you're the steady influence he needs."

She walked toward me. "I'm sorry you feel that way, but there's not a whole hell of a lot you can do about it now, is there?"

She was right, of course. There wasn't anything I *could* do about it, but even if I couldn't prevent it, I had no intention of promoting a relationship between the two of them.

"Funny thing is, Emma, I won't have to do *anything* about it." I wandered over to my mother's sink and studied my reflection in her mirror. "It might take some time, but he'll get tired of you. It's always that way with Ben." My eyes met Emma's in the mirror and I winked at her before leaving her to pick her jaw up off the tiled floor.

I pounded on Ben's door several times, and because it felt good to hit something, I beat on it some more. "Get up, Ben. I'm going to take a shower, and when I'm finished getting dressed, I'm leaving for the river. If you're not up and ready by then, I'll take my own car."

Thirty minutes later, I found Emma and Ben waiting for me, leaning against the back of his car, drinking coffee and nibbling on the same muffin. I was tempted to take my own car anyway, but the sight of my brother so vulnerable to Emma's charm caused me to reconsider. His eyes were bloodshot and he was clearly hungover, but the adoration on his face as he pinched off a piece of muffin and fed it to her was too obvious to miss. After all the years he'd taken such good care of me, the tide had finally turned and it was now my responsibility to look out for him. The only way I knew how to do that was to stay close and hope a committed relationship might actually work for them.

I held my hand out to Ben for the keys. "I'm driving, since I'm guessing you're still legally drunk."

He slapped the keys in the palm of my hand and crawled into the backseat. The trip to the river was very much like the one I'd made on Labor Day weekend with me driving while my passengers slept. When we got to the house, Emma presented my mother with a bottle of her favorite wine. She claimed I was the one who told her what to buy. But I only knew three things about the wine she loved—it was expensive, it was Italian, and my father bought it by the case from the Commonwealth Club.

"You're very sweet, Emma," my mother said, taking the bottle from her. "This wine is not easy to find."

"No ma'am, Mrs. Langley . . . um . . . I mean Adele. The wine shop I went to in Charlottesville knew exactly what I was looking for."

Mom nodded her head in approval. "I'll have to drop by the next time I'm in Charlottesville shopping."

"Really, Mom?" I said. "Be sure to drop by and see Ben and me as well."

"Katherine." My mother shot me a warning look. "Do you remember the name of the wine shop, dear?" she asked Emma.

Emma stared up at the ceiling as if she might find the name written there. "You know, I can't remember, but I'd be happy to look it up for you."

"Thank you, Emma," Mom said, kissing her on the cheek. She handed the bottle of wine to me. "Be a dear, Katherine, and stick it in the ice maker to chill."

For the next hour, everyone was preoccupied with dinner preparations. The men were out in the summer kitchen cooking the turkey while the women worked in the main kitchen, buttering rolls and rotating casserole dishes in and out of the oven. Emma and Mom jumped from one conversation to another—food and fashion and holiday gift giving. I ignored them as much as I could, even when we all sat down to eat.

I'd once considered Thanksgiving my favorite holiday. The simplicity of preparing a meal together and then sitting down at the big table to offer our thanks and celebrate our loved ones appealed to me. It hadn't been the same for me since my grandparents passed, but on this particular day, I could barely bring myself to make nice.

When the table was cleared and the dishes put away, Ben hit the sofa with the remote. He was snoring, five minutes later, when the rest of us left to go on a boat ride.

As is often the case in November in Virginia, it was a mild day, sunny with temperatures in the lower sixties, but we still needed a fleece to protect ourselves against the wind and the dampness from the water.

Breathing in big gulps of air, I asked my dad, "What is it about the salt air that's so calming?" We were standing together on the dock as he lowered the boat into the water from the lift.

"It's one of God's many mysterious gifts." He handed me the line to hold while he boarded the boat. "So many aspects of nature restore the soul, but for me, being on the water is the most cleansing." He started the motor and we all climbed on board, Mom and Emma settling into the bow seats up front while I climbed onto the pedestal seat beside Dad behind the wheel.

"What're you looking at?" he asked me as we circled around to the front of our dock.

"The Turners'. Their house looks so deserted. Don't they usually have all their family in for Thanksgiving?"

Dad nodded. "Enough to field two football teams. Normally they'd be out on the lawn by now." Both his tone and his expression were sad and reminiscent.

Dread seized my stomach and spread throughout the rest of my body. "Abby came and visited me a couple of weeks ago, but she hasn't responded to any of my texts or calls since then. What do you know that you're not saying?"

Dad shifted toward me, resting his arm on the back of the seat. "I wanted to wait until after we'd finished eating to tell you this."

"Tell me what?" I asked in full alarm mode, every hair on my body standing to attention.

"I don't have all the details yet, but it's my understanding Abigail's parents have taken her for treatment at a facility in Maryland that specializes in anorexia."

"What?" I jerked my head around, looking back up at their house, wanting more than anything to see Abigail running down the hill. "That can't be right. We talked a little about her disease, and she politely told me to mind my own business, but I had no idea she was in such bad shape."

"That's the biggest part of her problem. She refuses to open up to anyone. Not her parents or her friends or the therapists." He squeezed my shoulder. "They can't help her, honey, if she won't help herself."

"This can't be happening." I put my feet up on the console, propped my elbows on my knees, and rested my head in my hands. "Can people die from anorexia, Daddy?"

"I wouldn't worry about that just yet, sweetheart. That's for extreme cases, for people who don't seek the help they need."

"Does Ben know?" When Dad shook his head, I said, "Then let me be the one to tell him. We need to try and get in touch with George."

On this special day of thanksgiving, it was hard for me to feel grateful with my friend suffering and my brother being tortured by a devil in Barbie disguise. With the windshield blocking us, I couldn't hear what Emma and Mom were saying as they huddled together against the wind. They were so captivated by one another that we could've driven them out to the bay and left them stranded on a bell buoy and neither one of them would've noticed.

As much as I wanted to confide in my mother about my recent discoveries, she was way too enamored with Emma to believe she was anything less than perfect. And she never would've believed I found Emma floating in a cloud of *her* lavender bubbles. My mother had a long history of accepting another person's word over mine. Like the time last summer when she insisted I fly with her to Maine to visit some of her old college friends. On the second night at the Claytons', their daughter, Ellie, who was the same age as me, insisted I go with her to a party at a friend's house. The scene was unlike any I'd ever experienced. Lines of cocaine were laid out on the dining room table and two girls were practically having sex on the sofa in the middle of the crowd. Ellie left me to fend for myself for more than two hours while she disappeared upstairs with her boyfriend. Being the sober one, I insisted I drive home. When Ellie puked all over her parents' oriental rug, just inside the front door, the Claytons maintained that nothing like that had ever happened before. Never mind I swore on my grandmother's grave I hadn't had a drop of alcohol, instead of defending me, my mother accused me of being the instigator. No way the beautiful and popular Ellie could've been telling a lie.

We rode up and down the creek, in and out of the coves, and around by the Tide's Inn. We were gone for more than an hour. When we got back to the dock, Emma grabbed me by the arm and began dragging me toward the house.

"Guess what, Katherine?"

"No telling." I prepared myself for the jolt from the news to follow.

"Your mother's going to write a letter for me."

I cut my eyes at her. "That's funny. I thought all college students knew how to write."

"No, silly. I'm talking about the sorority. She's going to write a letter of recommendation for me for the Chi Delta house."

I walked faster, out ahead of her, making her work harder to keep up. "She writes letters for lots of people, Emma," I said over my shoulder. "It doesn't really mean anything. If I were you, I wouldn't get my hopes up."

"Yeah, but she promised to talk to some of her friends about writing letters for me as well."

I shrugged. "If that's what you want, I hope it works out."

With Emma following close behind, I entered the game room and started up the stairs. "Are you going to stay mad at me all day?" she asked, tugging on the hood of my sweatshirt.

I yanked my hood out of her hands. "Here's a news flash for you, Emma. The world doesn't revolve around you. For your information, my dad just gave me some bad news about Abigail." I climbed the rest of the way up the stairs and waited for her to join me at the top. "Besides, I'm tired. I had a hard time going to sleep last night after I heard you and my brother having sex down the hall."

Her lips curled into a smirk. "Why don't you just admit it? You're jealous."

"Jealous of who, you?"

"The sooner you can admit your obsession with your brother is unhealthy, the sooner you can get some help."

I burst into laughter. "Only your sick and twisted mind could make a normal sibling relationship sound like incest. But then again, I wouldn't expect someone like you, an only child, to understand a sister's love for her brother."

***

We spent the rest of the afternoon watching football and eating leftovers. By ten o'clock, everyone was ready for bed. Ben insisted on going fishing with Dad the next morning, which delayed our departure for Charlottesville. But seeing the excitement on my brother's face over the citation-sized rockfish he caught was worth the extra time I had to spend with Emma. It was almost two o'clock before we sat down with Mom and Dad at Willaby's for a burger on our way out of town.

We were just passing the Richmond airport when, in working on my study guide for exams, I realized I'd left my English lit book on the table beside my bed on Wednesday night. Moaning and groaning about having to make a pit stop, Ben exited the interstate onto the downtown expressway toward Cary Street.

"It's a five-minute detour, asshole. You have no right to complain. I've been waiting around for you all day."

As fast as my short legs would take me, I jumped out of the car and ran up the front steps to the house and then all the way upstairs to my room. On the way back down I stopped in the kitchen to get a snack, a peace offering, for Ben. I grabbed a recycling tote from the pantry and stuffed a bag of Smartfood and three strawberry Nutri-Grain bars inside. When I opened the door to the beverage refrigerator in search of a Diet Coke, I noticed a bottle of my mother's wine lying flat on the bottom shelf. I ran my finger across the map of Italy on the label, from Venice down and around the boot back up to Rome. I was lining three cans of Diet Coke up on the counter, when it hit me.

"Wait a minute," I said out loud to myself. Emma told my mother she'd gotten the wine from Charlottesville, but that didn't make any sense. I'd searched through Emma's things for my black tank top on Wednesday night, when we were getting dressed to go out, but the wine wasn't in her bag then. I'm certain I would've remembered seeing a loose bottle rolling around in the car. There was only one possible scenario.

I raced to the mudroom and down the uncarpeted steps. Our basement was strictly utilitarian with a small laundry room and a wine closet my father designed and built himself over a decade ago. Three walls were fitted with cubbyholes that held one variety or another of expensive wine—my father's collections. There were several cases lined up against the wall. I leaned down and flipped back the top on the box closest to me. Every section was full of my mother's fancy wine. Except one.

NINE

Ben and I drove home from Charlottesville in the pouring snow for the Christmas Break. Exhausted and mentally drained from exams, all I wanted to do was crawl in my bed. I stayed there for twenty-four hours straight, craving mindless activity. When I wasn't sleeping, I watched movies on my laptop and stalked people on Facebook and ate whatever junk food my father delivered to my room on a tray. Other than a trip to the Homestead with Archer's family for New Year's, I had nothing scheduled during the next three weeks. Three weeks of having my room all to myself. Twenty-one days of not having to share a bathroom or my computer. Over five hundred hours without Emma.

Archer came over late in the afternoon of my second day in isolation and dragged me out of bed and over to Kit Matthews's house. We got smashed on Cosmopolitans, which landed me right back in bed the next day with a hangover. After that, Archer and I made a pact to stay sober for the rest of the break. We went to the movies and out to dinner. And we shopped ad nauseam. In addition to the many things Archer had learned during her first semester at Washington and Lee, she'd discovered how perfect her long, lean frame was for the latest fashions. When we weren't exploring the many boutiques in Carytown for more items to add to Archer's Christmas wish list, we were brainstorming for the ultimate gift for me to give Ben. Like a one-way ticket to Alaska for Emma or a specially formulated deterrent to keep her off of him—such as the one our gardener uses to protect my mother's roses from the deer.

"Have you seen Emma's Facebook page?" Archer asked me. It was two days before Christmas and she lay sprawled out on my bed, surfing the web, while I wrapped presents down on the floor. She swung her legs over the side of my bed and sat up, her strawberry-blonde hair sticking out from her head with static electricity. "Your roommate has over sixteen hundred friends and only a small percentage of them are female. What's up with that?" she asked, turning the computer around so I could see it.

I shrugged. "She loves men. What can I say?"

Archer's jaw went slack. "And one of those men is Ben. She all but admitted to you that she's digging for gold and this house and *your* brother are her mines."

I ignored her gaze and focused on cutting a length of wrapping paper. "So maybe I overreacted."

"Since when? All you've done since you got home for the break is complain, Emma this and Emma that."

"I'll admit I was really angry with her after everything that happened over Thanksgiving, but I've been thinking about it a lot the past couple of days. It's Christmas, Arch, time for forgiveness. Maybe Emma can't help herself."

"You mean she can't *stop* helping herself, helping herself to your stuff. What the heck, Kitty? She stole a bottle of wine from your dad's stash and gave it to your mother as a gift. How did she even know about the cellar if she wasn't sneaking around your house when you were otherwise preoccupied? When would that have been, anyway? You were here for less than twenty-four hours. While you were taking a shower or sleeping? Don't you find that the least bit creepy?"

I finished tying a red satin bow around the present and tossed it aside. "Emma is enamored with all this," I said, waving my hand in the air. "She doesn't have the kinds of things you and I have. Maybe she just wanted to know what it was like to soak in a spa tub full of lavender bubbles. And maybe she just wanted to make a good impression on my mother and couldn't afford to buy her some flowers or a tin of cheese biscuits."

"OMG, you really are too nice for your own good," Archer said, kicking her leg out at me. "At least you already have one semester behind you. Only one more of living with psycho-bitch to go."

I coughed to clear my throat. "Not exactly."

She lowered her chin and looked at me from beneath her furrowed brow. "I'm afraid to ask what *not exactly* means." When I didn't answer her, she nudged my arm. "You're not seriously considering living with Emma again? Are you nuts?"

I set my scissors down and climbed up on the bed beside Archer. "What was I supposed to do? I had to turn in my residency application in order to get housing. Anyway, it'll be different having Carla and Phoebe as suitemates."

Archer continued to glare at me, waiting for an explanation she could accept. I looked away from her. "I have until February to make a change request."

"Ugh!" She threw herself back on the bed. "Why wait until February?"

"To see what happens when we go back to school after the break. I'm hoping Emma will be bored with Ben by then."

"And if not?"

I lay back and rolled over on my side, facing Archer. "Then I might have to stick it out, just so I can keep a close eye on Ben."

"Really? And who's going to watch out for *you*, Kitty? I have a bad feeling about this. And you know how I am about these feelings."

"Oh, yeah. I know all about your freaky feelings," I teased, poking her in the side. It was easier to make light of the situation than to admit that Archer's intuition, her so-called feelings, were premonitions that almost always came true. "I'll be careful. I promise."

***

Every year for as long as I could remember, my parents insisted Ben and I go with them to Max and Loraine Robinsons' house out in Goochland on Christmas Eve. The Robinsons aren't close friends of my parents. They don't drop by for drinks or go to the club together for dinner. In fact my parents never socialize with the Robinsons at all except for this one party every year.

Ben and I were probably six and eight the first time we were invited for Christmas Eve. The parties were small affairs back then, with a dozen or so adults crammed around the mahogany table in the dining room for an elaborate dinner that lasted until way past time for Santa to come. The Christmas Eve party had metamorphosed since those early days. The dinner was now a large cocktail buffet with trays of meats and cheeses and seafood spread out on the dining room table for the guests to enjoy at will. A pianist played Christmas carols at the baby grand in the corner of the living room while a gang of children chased each other in and out and around the crowd.

Ben and I were standing off by ourselves in a corner of the dining room, nibbling on beef tenderloin and boiled shrimp. "You better put that away," I said to him when he pulled his cell phone from his blazer pocket and began texting. "You know how Dad is about us using our cell phones during social functions."

"Would it make any difference if the text was from George?"

I paused in mid chew. "George Turner?" I asked with a mouthful of turkey.

"No, George Bush," Ben said, giving me a noogie. "Of course I'm talking about George Turner."

I swatted his hand away. "In that case, don't leave me hanging. What'd he say?"

Ben read the text to me. "Abby seems better this week. She even ate a bowl of coffee ice cream this morning."

Ben and I locked eyes and together we were taken back ten years. Instead of Popsicles or Nutty Buddy cones or Push-Ups, our mother always kept coffee ice cream in the freezer. All of us hated the taste of coffee except Abby who polished off the carton every time.

I grabbed Ben by the arm. "I have an idea. Follow me." I led him back to the Robinsons' family room, which was empty except for a kid who was watching *Home Alone* on the gigantic-screen television. "Take a picture of me blowing Abby a kiss and text it to George," I said, standing in front of the Christmas tree.

"No way you get to do this alone." Ben surveyed the room. "Hey, kid, can you peel your eyes away from Macaulay Culkin long enough to take our picture?" The boy was so young Ben had to show him how to take the picture with his iPhone. "How old are you, anyway?" Ben asked.

"Six," he answered, holding the phone up in front of his face.

Ben and I puckered our lips while the boy took the picture. When he handed the camera back to Ben, he crinkled his nose in distaste. "Y'all are weird."

Ben burst out laughing. "Maybe so, big man, but everyone's a little weird at Christmastime, aren't they? I mean, think about it. Don't you think it's weird that we will all be waiting up tonight for a fat man in a red suit to come sliding down the chimney?"

"I don't believe in Santa Claus," the boy said, sounding very sure of himself for a six-year old.

"You're kidding? Why not?" Ben asked.

The boy climbed back up on the sofa. "Because my brother said there was no such thing as Santa Claus. And he's ten, so he ought to know."

"That old, huh? You know, you shouldn't believe everything someone tells you just because they say so." Ben pointed toward the television. "Take Macaulay Culkin, for example. He believes in his heart that his parents will come home and save him from those really bad dudes, right?"

The boy nodded.

"So, what if Macaulay's brother was there in the house with him? Do you think his brother could convince Macaulay that their parents weren't coming back?"

The boy stared at Ben, thinking it over. He reached for the remote and turned the volume up. "My parents told me never to talk to strangers," he shouted over the television sound.

"Leave the poor kid alone, Ben. Let's go outside." I turned the bolt on the french doors and stepped out onto the terrace. "The Robinsons put the same colored lights in the trees every year, but I never get tired of looking at them."

Ben stretched out on the chaise lounge. "Why is it that those big colored lights are so familiar to me when all I can remember us having on our tree are the little white ones."

I felt the cushion on the chaise next to Ben to make sure it was dry before I sat down. "Because we used to put colored lights on our tree when we were little. Although, now that you mention it, I don't actually remember the colored lights either. I've only seen them in pictures."

Ben placed his hands behind his head. "I don't understand this whole anorexia thing. How could someone who used to be so chubby, who used to like to eat so much, end up so thin?"

I shrugged. "It all started when she broke her jaw and lost all that weight. My guess is, she liked being thin and was worried about gaining it back."

"It doesn't seem fair for someone so kind to have to suffer. Yabba is such a good girl."

I nodded. "She has the strongest morals of anyone I know. And she shoots from the hip. Maddie is like that." I kicked off my heels and leaned back against the cushion. "What happened to y'all, anyway? I thought the two of you were really into one another."

"I like Maddie a lot. A whole lot, even. She just doesn't excite me the way Emma does."

I turned my head to the side so I could see him. "Are you and Emma a couple now?"

Ben furrowed his brow. "Depends on your definition of a couple."

"I'm not talking about friends with benefits. I'm asking if the two of you are in a relationship together. You know, seeing each other exclusively?"

"Why is it that every time you start talking about Emma, your voice gets all squeaky? What exactly is your problem with her? I thought she was your friend."

"Just because she's my friend doesn't mean I want her in a relationship with my brother. Do you have any idea how many date requests she gets every day?"

Ben's body tensed and his face reddened. "That's all in the past. We've been talking some heavy shit on the phone over the break. By the time school starts again, we'll be . . . how did you put it? Exclusive." He reached over and squeezed my hand. "Don't worry, Kitty. Everything will be fine."

"I hope you're right on this, Ben. But if you get in over your head, which is a very real possibility, remember, I've got your back."

TEN

"Guess what, Katherine?" Emma said, dumping her suitcase on the floor and plopping onto her bed. "I got back together with my old boyfriend over the break."

"Really?" I closed my laptop and leaned back in my desk chair. "I'm pretty sure you never mentioned him before."

"I told you about him. You just weren't listening. Peter and I dated our whole senior year. We were even voted the best-looking couple. He was the captain of the wrestling team and the football team. He has these enormous muscles."

"If he's so great, why in the world did you ever break up with him?"

"Because he decided to go to school all the way down in Florida, at Flagler. We didn't think we could make a long-distance relationship work, but when we saw each other over the break, we realized we'd made a mistake." Her eyes clouded over as she stared off into space. "It's like we fell in love all over again."

I wanted to excuse myself to go vomit, but I needed some answers first. "Peter sounds like a great guy and all, but what about Ben?"

"What about him?" she asked, jerking her head back to earth.

"Hello . . ." I leaned over in my chair, waving my hand in front of her face. "Ben is under the impression the two of you are in a relationship."

"Why would he think that?" She swung her legs over the side of the bed and sat up, stretching her arms behind her head.

"Hmm . . . let's see." I tapped my chin with my finger. "It might have something to do with all the time you spent on the phone with one another over the break."

"I don't know what you're talking about, Kitty." The tone in which she used my nickname was both snarky and condescending. "Ben and I are just friends."

Emma's unreadable expression—her soft smile and the matter-of-fact set of her jaw—scared the hell out of me. She was either lying or she'd innocently misled Ben. "He feels differently about you, Emma, and as a favor to me, as well as to Ben, I'd appreciate it if you'd come clean with him about Peter."

"Since when are *your* brother's delusions *my* problem?" she asked, removing her toiletries bag from her suitcase and disappearing down the hall.

And just who are you to call Ben delusional when you're the obvious whack job?

I picked up the ceramic mug full of pens from my desk and hurled it at the wall over Emma's bed. The three-week break from my roommate had given me the opportunity to put things in perspective and look at the situation with a fresh pair of eyes. As much as I'd been trying to give her the benefit of the doubt, it was clear Emma had some deep-seated emotional issues that made me fear for my brother.

While I was too preoccupied to worry much about Emma and Ben during the two weeks that followed, the process of sorority rush, of acquainting myself with the sixteen different sororities, at least gave me the opportunity to stay close to Emma. As far as I could tell, she had no communication with Ben whatsoever. He didn't come flying through the door in a rampage over having learned about Peter nor did she disappear for unaccounted hours to be with him at his fraternity.

Being on display every night and having to meet new people at every turn are not my favorite things to do. By the time we got through to the third round, I was exhausted and had to rely on Emma's enthusiasm to pull me through.

Ben's advice about finding the right sorority that suited me played over and over in my mind. I tried for my mother's sake, but unlike Emma, I just couldn't warm up to the Chi Deltas the way I did to the Tri Betas down the street. I was torn between an allegiance to my mother and an allegiance to myself. Every night I felt more and more guilty watching as Emma shamelessly spread it on thick to every Chi Delta she met. She wanted to be one of them, and she made it clear she'd do anything to make that happen.

Somehow I made it through to the final night, the night before we were to submit our pledge cards, but I still wasn't sure if pledging a sorority was something I even wanted to do.

"Are you waiting for someone?" Honey Mabry asked me when she saw me standing alone in the front hall of the Chi Delta house.

I nodded. "Emma. We were supposed to meet here about thirty minutes ago. Have you seen her?"

Honey glanced around to make certain no one could overhear her, even though we were the only two people in the room. "Then I'm guessing she didn't tell you."

"Tell me what?" A chill of imminent doom traveled my spine. "Did something happen to her?"

A group of rushees came barreling through the front door, bringing with them a blast of cold air. Honey grabbed me by the elbow. "Come in here for a minute." She dragged me into the adjoining room, the formal room they called the parlor, and closed the door behind her. "Because of your mother's history with this sorority, we gave Emma every consideration we could. Unfortunately, it wasn't enough. I hated to have to do it."

My stomach did a somersault followed by a backflip. "What exactly did you have to do?"

"First of all, please understand this is standard procedure for us when we have concerns." Honey saw the impatient look on my face. "Okay . . . well, we did a background check on Emma."

It took a minute for my brain to register what she was saying. "Hold on. Did you just say you conducted a background check? I thought Emma was rushing a sorority, not applying for a job in the CIA?"

"You're so funny, Katherine." Honey managed to fake a laugh. "It wasn't *really* a background check. Only our version of one. In this case a cousin of a friend of mine who lives in Altoona and went to high school with Emma. You should be thanking me right about now. I saved your family a lot of embarrassment. If word had gotten out that your roommate's father is in jail—"

"In jail? What're you talking about?" I asked, trying to keep my voice steady despite the goose pimples breaking out all over my body.

Honey's face was smug as she announced, "Emma's father is serving five to ten for possession of heroin with intent to distribute."

"There must be some mistake," I blurted. "Her father is an English professor at Penn State Altoona." As the words crossed my lips, it occurred to me that Honey might actually be right. Emma had lied about many things. Why wouldn't she lie about her father's occupation?

"Oh . . . he used to work there alright. As a custodian, dealing drugs to students out of his cleaning closet." Recognizing my dismay, she softened a little and nodded toward the sofa. "Shall we sit for a minute?"

"No thanks. I'm fine."

"All right, then." She straightened her back and flung her hair over her shoulders. "Has Emma ever told you how she spends her summers?"

I shook my head, even though I'd heard Emma complain many times about not getting paid for helping her father in his office at the university. Another lie. She couldn't possibly have been working for him if he was locked away in prison.

"She works as a nurse's aid at the retirement where her mother is a cafeteria worker. You roommate changes bed pans."

I already knew part of this to be true, so the rest of it came as no big surprise. "So what? I admire her for working to put herself through college, so she can have a better life."

"Look, Katherine. Her summer job isn't the issue here. Emma lied, which doesn't cut it at an institution that was founded on its honor code."

I was shaking with anger, not only at Emma for putting me in this position but also at Honey for being so smug. I wanted to smack the smirk off Honey's face and poke her twinkling eyes out. "Is the honor code the only thing you're worried about? Seems to me it might tarnish the sacred reputation of this great sisterhood to have the daughter of a jailbird as a member."

"We've always protected our own, Katherine, all the way back to when your mother was a sister here. I'm pretty sure *she* wouldn't want her alumni friends to know about this."

"Is that a threat?"

Honey shrugged. "I mean, the idea that your mother would recommend such an undesirable for membership . . ."

"But how could she have known?"

Honey stared at me, hard, her eyes full of hate. "Maybe her daughter should've figured that out for her."

I knew if I didn't get out of that room soon, I might seriously hurt her. I turned to leave, but when my hand reached for the door-knob, she grabbed my arm to stop me.

"Because your mother was once the president of this sorority, we're obligated to take you," she said as if I were some kind of stray animal. "You're a good girl, Katherine—a little misguided but I think your heart is in the right place. We can get past this."

"I wouldn't belong to this sorority if it were the only one on campus." I swung the parlor door open, grabbed my coat from the foyer, and stormed out of the Chi Delta house into the bitter winter night.

Ignoring the sleet stinging my face, I marched down the street to the Tri Beta house. As subtly as I could and as quickly as I could, I let them know their sorority would be first on my bid card. With tears blinding my eyes, I slowly made my way back to my dorm by taking baby steps in the crunchy grass to avoid the slippery sidewalk.

Fortunately for her, Emma was not in the room when I got there. I locked the door behind me, flung myself on my bed, and buried my face in my pillow. I sobbed and screamed and pounded my fist in a full-fledged temper tantrum. After a long time, maybe twenty or thirty minutes, I rolled over on my back. I was calmer and focused, but still mad as hell, mostly at myself. The thing that hurt the most was the truth in what Honey had said. I was the one responsible for bringing Emma into our home, and for months, I'd watched her manipulate my family. Because she had everything in common with my mother that I lacked, it was easier to listen to the two of them talk than to have to make conversation with my mother myself.

What the hell else is she hiding?

I reached for my computer. I doubted Emma realized that, as system administrator, I could change her password and sign onto her user account anytime I wanted. Under normal circumstances, I would never have violated her privacy, but these were not normal circumstances.

I went straight to her Facebook account where I discovered she had quite the following. The number of friend requests and pleas for dates was substantial. Out of her whole list of friends, there was only one boy I didn't recognize as a student at UVA. His name was Peter. Peter Packham. Despite his nice dimples, I had to wonder what kind of parents, with a last name like that, would name their kid Peter.

Her inbox was full of love messages from Ben, the most recent received at 6:05 p.m. that evening, inviting her to come over and hang out with him.

I changed into jeans and a sweatshirt before heading back out into the winter night. The sleet had turned to snow, but because I was wearing my gumshoes, I was able to run all the way to Ben's fraternity house. I burst through the front door and dashed up the stairs, only vaguely aware of the loud music coming from the back room. I pounded on Ben's door repeatedly. I was about to give up and look elsewhere when he answered.

"What're you doing here?" he asked, his face flushed and his eyes glassy.

"Looking for Emma," I said, standing on my tiptoes so I could see past him. "Is she here?"

He placed both hands on the doorjamb, filling the doorway with his body, blocking my view of his room. "Now is not a good time."

"Move," I said, grabbing a hunk of skin under his arm and pinching him as hard as I could.

"Ow!" He jerked his arm back. "Damnit, that hurt."

"Sorry," I said as I scooted past him.

Ben's was the largest of the single rooms in the fraternity house. In addition to his bed and desk, he had enough space for a small This End Up sofa and matching chair. Emma was sitting dead center in the middle of the sofa, wearing my new purple dress, the one I'd wanted to wear earlier but couldn't find.

Ben squeezed past me, and without bothering to offer me a seat, he sank down to his chair.

"I went to the Chi Delta house looking for you," I said to Emma. "I thought the plan was for us to meet over there at nine."

"Rush is over for me." Her eyes darted around the room until they came to rest on Ben. "I told him everything."

"You told him about Peter?"

"Yes, Katherine," she snarled. "I told him about Peter. Are you happy now?"

"And you're okay with this?" I asked my brother. "I mean, two weeks ago she announced to me that she was in love with her ex-boyfriend, yet here she is with you. Fourteen days is not a long time, Ben. I hope her love for you is more lasting."

Ben ran his hands through his hair. "This is really none of your business, Kitty."

"It is my business, Ben. You're my brother and she's playing with you like a wind-up Kewpie doll."

Without realizing the irony in his actions, he stood and began pacing in circles in the small space between his chair and me.

"Stop talking about me like I'm not here," Emma screamed.

"Okay, fine. Then I have a question for you." I turned toward her. "Why is it that Ben deserves to hear the truth about your father but I had to hear it from Honey?"

"Because she didn't think you'd be very accepting of her situation," Ben interjected. "I tried to tell her she was wrong about you, Kitty, that you are not a judgmental person, but I'm not so sure anymore."

"You've been trying to keep us apart from the beginning," Emma mumbled, playing the poor, pitiful victim.

I looked back and forth between the two of them. Ben hung his head and watched his feet as he paced, while Emma bit her lower lip to keep from smiling, clearly enjoying herself. She'd picked the most vulnerable person on campus to be her ally, the one guy who was truly in love with her.

"That's because I had this sick feeling a relationship between the two of you might end in disaster. Turns out I was right. You *are* a liar and a manipulator."

Ben stopped pacing and looked up at me. "Wait a minute. If you think she manipulated me, you're wrong. I was a willing participant."

"What about Mom? She was also a willing participant in having her friends write letters on Emma's behalf. She's going to be pissed when she finds out Emma disgraced her."

"If I were you, I wouldn't waste my time worrying about how Mom feels." Ben pointed his finger at me. "Mom's the manipulator. She manipulated you right into coming to UVA and you were too stupid to realize it."

"So now we're getting somewhere." I turned to him. "You've been hiding something about my application to UNC and I want to know what it is." I grabbed his arm. "Tell me."

Ben jerked his arm away. "You want to know the truth? Okay, here it is. Dad had plenty of contacts to help you get in UNC. He just never used any of them. Mom wanted you to be a Chi Delta at UVA, and you know how she always gets her way."

"You're lying," I screamed, pushing him backward. He stumbled into the chair behind him, knocking the chair out of the way enough for me to see what was hidden underneath.

"So you're doing drugs now?" I reached for the mirror before Ben could get to it. He tried to grab it away from me, but I turned my back on him, lifting the mirror to my lips and blowing the white powder all over the room.

"What the fuck? Have you lost your mind?" Ben's whole body quivered in his effort to control himself. I'd seen him this mad before, just never at me.

"You can thank me tomorrow." I wiped the mirror with my sleeve and handed him the rolled-up dollar bill. "See. This is all her fault." I pointed at Emma. "Like father, like daughter."

Emma smirked. "Maybe so, little Kitty Cat. My dad might not have been successful, but he wasn't stupid. After all, where'd you think I got my brains? College life is full of pressures, and there's nothing wrong with a little numbing agent to kill the pain. Why not take advantage of the opportunity and earn a little money in the process?"

I ignored Emma and pleaded with my brother, "She's a bad influence on you, Ben. I mean, come on. Drugs? That's not who you are."

"You don't really know a thing about who I am. We're in college, Kitty. We're supposed to experiment with drugs."

"I'm sorry, but I'm not going to stand by and watch her drag you down."

"Fine, then leave." He opened the door. "Emma's been right about you all along. You *are* naïve. Time to grow the fuck up, Katherine." Coming from Ben, the use of my given name was the worst kind of insult. I was no longer his little sister. I was a stranger to him.

I held the mirror up in front of Ben's face so he could see himself. "If this is what grown-up looks like, then no thanks." I turned around and tossed the mirror on the sofa beside Emma, catching a glimpse of her smug expression.

"*You* will get what's coming to you," I said to her, and then to Ben, "And *you* know where to find me when you come to your senses."

ELEVEN

After I left Ben's room, I roamed aimlessly around campus, on the sidewalks over by the dorms and back and forth across the lawn, anywhere I felt safe alone at that time of night. I was numb to the cold. I was numb to the pain in my chest.

When Ben and I were little, sometime around the ages of five and seven, we ran away from home—if you can call wandering two blocks to the country club running away. We'd learned so much in kindergarten about the importance of dialing 911 in an emergency, we wanted to test the system to see if it really worked. Funny thing, though, we never considered what might happen if the police actually showed up. After the policeman gave us a lecture about not wasting taxpayer dollars, Blessy sent us to our rooms to await our parents' wrath.

We stuffed our backpacks with pajamas and a bag of pizza-flavored Goldfish and snuck out the back door, wandering through the neighbors' yards and up Iris Lane to the club. The woman behind the snack counter served us a double-dip chocolate cone with a smile, right before she called our house and ratted us out. Ben and I made a pact that day, promising we'd always be there for one another when one of us felt sad or needed help. It was an agreement to which we'd always remained true. Until now.

Whether it was thirty minutes or two hours, I trudged through the snow until my eyelashes were frozen. I went back to my dorm room, crawled into bed in my flannel pajamas, and called Archer.

Her voice was reassuring. "This is just something Ben has to work through on his own. Go ahead and pledge Tri Beta. It will not only help take your mind off of your problems with your brother, it'll give you your own piece of UVA you won't have to share with Emma."

I inhaled a deep breath. "Pledging a sorority is a big decision. If only I had some time to think about it, considering everything that happened tonight."

"What's there to think about?"

"I feel like a part of me is only doing this to get back at my mother."

"Of course it is. For the past six years, your motto has been Make Mom Pay. So set that aside, and look at the real issue. You like the girls at Tri Beta the best, right?"

"True, but . . ."

"But what? Come on, Kitty. What is it that you're not saying?"

"I like the Tri Beta girls here, but what if I transfer to UNC?" I blurted, feeling an immediate release in just saying the words. I'd unlocked the cage door and set my feelings free, ones I'd been suppressing for a long time for fear of rejection.

"Wait a sec." Archer groaned, and I could tell she was struggling to sit up in bed. "Are you seriously considering that?"

"Honestly, I didn't realize it until just now, but I guess I am."

"Then do it! And don't worry about the sorority thing. My sister's roommate is a Tri Beta at UNC."

"I love Becca! Okay . . . so that makes me feel a whole lot better."

"You need to *stop* worrying about pledging Tri Beta and *start* figuring out how you're going to get back at that Honey bitch."

"That, my friend, has already been taken care of."

"Shut up! What'd you do?"

"After I left Ben's room, I found her pretty little pink convertible Volkswagen in the parking garage and let all the air out of her tires."

We laughed so hard that by the time we hung up five minutes later, I felt calm enough to sleep.

Emma didn't come back to our room that night, or the next, or even the night after that. But when I returned from dinner Monday evening, her suitcase was gone from her closet along with most of her clothes. The only things missing of mine were my Virginia sweatshirt and a worn flannel tunic I liked to wear to class with leggings and Uggs. She'd never borrowed either before. She didn't take them because she wanted them; she took them because they were my favorites. I removed my diamond stud earrings from my jewelry case, slipped them into a small leather satchel, and hid them in my tennis racquet case along with my sunscreen and a travel package of tissues.

***

Mom and Dad hounded me with phone calls during the next two weeks, but I ignored them, even Blessy when she left a message scolding me for being so disrespectful to my parents. Then, on Wednesday morning during the last week of January, I returned to my room from my nine o'clock English class to find my parents waiting for me. The visit was so unexpected my immediate thought was that something had happened to Abigail.

"We didn't mean to alarm you," my father reassured me. "From what we hear, Abigail is doing well in her treatment in Baltimore."

"That poor, sweet child should not have to suffer so much." My mother dabbed at her dry eyes with my father's linen handkerchief. "But Katherine, by refusing to return any of our calls, you left us no choice but to come up here and see what was going on for ourselves."

My father nodded his agreement. "I think your mother deserves an explanation. Don't you?" he asked me.

I dumped my backpack on my bed and turned around to face them. "As much as I deserve an explanation about my application to UNC." He looked surprised, and I added, "That's right, Dad. I know all about how you chose not to use your connections to help me get in to the college of my dreams."

My father dropped to the bed, as if suddenly burdened by a ton of bricks. "Who told you?" he asked. Before I could respond, he said, "Of course, Ben. Let me ex—"

"No, let me," my mother interrupted him. "I'm the one responsible for that, not your father. I wanted you to experience what I experienced during the happiest time in my life. Was it so wrong of me to want my only daughter to follow in my footsteps?" She brought her hand to my face and ran her fingers along my cheek. "I wanted us to share the wonderful sisterhood of Chi Delta."

My mother was so sincere and humble, I almost felt sorry for her. Almost. "I'm pretty sure Chi Delta has a chapter at UNC," I said, brushing her hand away from my face.

Her face scrunched up in thought, as though she'd never considered it before. "That would not have been the same and you know it. Honey said—"

"Wait a minute." I took a step back, away from my mother. "You talked to Honey? What did you do, call her?"

"As a matter of fact, *she* called *me*. Honey is very disappointed that things worked out the way they did." Mom stepped toward me, regaining the lost territory between us, and wrapped her arm around my shoulders. "It's a big decision, and I'm sure you were feeling overwhelmed when you made it. Honey is in a position to change this if—"

"That's not going to happen, Mom." I ducked out from beneath her arm. "This wonderful sisterhood you keep talking about isn't so wonderful anymore, the way it was when you were president."

"What do you mean?"

I didn't have the energy to explain something to my mother she'd never understand. In her mind, people aspired to be like Honey, shallow and self-important. I was curious, though, to know how much Honey had told her about Emma's situation.

"What did she tell you about Emma?" I asked, scrutinizing my mother's face for her reaction.

Her eyes narrowed and she smiled a tight smile. "The numbers aren't in Emma's favor this year. According to Honey, they have too many legacies that they're obligated to accept."

I wasn't surprised Honey had spared my mother's feelings. After all, Mom is a respected alumna who gives a hefty sum to their annual giving campaign every year. What surprised me, though, was that my mother believed Honey's lies.

"Oh really? So Honey encouraged her to try again next semester?" I asked.

"Katherine, you have to understand that these girls are threatened by Emma, by her beauty. It makes some women feel bad about themselves to have a person like Emma around, a person who has it all."

I stared, openmouthed, at my mother. It was as clear as the smug expression on her face that she actually believed this. I had no intention of adding to her self-righteousness by being the one to tell her that her protégé was dating her son.

"She has it all except enough decency to be honest with those who support her," I said under my breath.

"I beg your pardon?" she asked.

"Never mind, Mother. I have another class in thirty minutes." I removed my English anthology book from my backpack and replaced it with my biology book from my desk. I actually had the rest of the afternoon free, but my parents didn't know that. "If only you'd called first, I could've warned you not to come. I have back-to-back classes all day."

My father stood and smoothed the wrinkles out of his khakis. "Can we at least take you to lunch? We can walk around campus and wait for you until your class is over."

"I don't have time for lunch. Or anything left to say." Slinging my backpack over my shoulder, I started toward the door but turned back around. "Actually, there is something you need to know. From now on I'm making my own decisions. For your information, I'm very happy with my choice to pledge Tri Beta, and I have no intention of changing sororities. As far as schools go, it's too late to do anything about it now, but next fall I may apply for a transfer to UNC for my junior year. This time I won't be asking for your help."

My parents stopped calling after that, although I did receive a handwritten letter from my father apologizing for his part in sabotaging my application to Chapel Hill. He explained how he was only trying to make my mother happy. But that much I already knew.

I didn't see Ben again until mid-February when Phoebe and I found ourselves seated ten rows back from him at a Hoos basketball game. Spotty and Reed sat to Ben's right while Emma occupied the seat to his left. She was feeding him popcorn and rubbing his arm and laying her head on his shoulder. She was the picture of an attentive girlfriend until a dark-hair hottie sat down in the empty seat next to her. For the rest of the first half, she was so busy flirting with the Channing Tatum look-alike, she ignored my brother completely. Ben stormed off at the beginning of halftime. And when he didn't return by the middle of the third quarter, Emma left as well, presumably to go look for him.

I ran into Spotty and Reed after the game, while I was waiting for Phoebe outside the ladies' restroom. "What the heck is up with Ben and Emma?" I asked them. "Their little scene was more entertaining than the game."

Spotty and I had been in constant communication with one another since my argument with Ben. Even though we agreed there wasn't much we could do to help him, staying in touch was at least something.

"That's what I've been trying to tell you, Kitty," Spotty said. "It's always like that between them."

"Yep. Better than the *Jerry Springer Show*," Reed added.

"Great." I rolled my eyes. "Must be a boatload of fun to be around. How do y'all stand it?"

"It's the worst kind of pain in the ass you can imagine," Reed said, disgusted. "She's the thing that won't leave. Every time Prima Donna Emma wants to take a shower, your brother has to clear everyone out of the bathroom. You can imagine how well that goes over in a house full of men."

"Doesn't your fraternity have rules about girlfriends living in the house?" I asked.

Spotty nodded. "But there are special considerations in this situation," he mumbled.

"What considerations?" I asked, and when he hesitated, I added, "Come clean, Spotty. This is important."

"This isn't easy to say, which is why I haven't told you until now." Spotty leaned in to me so he wouldn't be overheard. "Ben is unstable, Kitty. Several key people have talked to him about the situation, but he won't listen. He's irrational when it comes to Emma. We are all walking on eggshells for fear of upsetting him."

I blinked back tears. "Is he really that bad off?"

Spotty's green eyes were cloudy with worry. "The worst I've ever seen him. He's in it deep, drugs and all."

Phoebe appeared suddenly and the four of us started toward the exit. I grabbed Spotty by the elbow, holding him back a couple of steps.

"I went to see one of the school's psychiatrists," I said, confiding in him what I hadn't told anyone else.

"Seriously?" he asked. "I never knew anyone who actually did that."

"Shows you how desperate I am to help my brother."

"You can't, though, can you? That's what the shrink told you, isn't it? You can't help Ben until he's ready to help himself."

I nodded. "And according to Elise Withers that won't happen until he hits rock bottom."

Spotty grabbed my shoulder and squeezed. "And you better hang on tight, because I'm afraid it's going to be a bumpy ride."

Ten days later I encountered Ben and Emma in a compromising situation, maybe not rock bottom but definitely a new all-time low.

It was the end of an unseasonably warm week, and with spring break on everyone's mind, the Corner was packed. Even more so in the Island Cafe, thanks to their tropical ambience and two-for-one pitchers of draft beer. I was gathered in a booth with a group of my

Tri Beta pledge sisters. We were working on our third round, enjoying a rare break from our duties at the sorority house.

"I'm going to the bathroom. Will you order a cheeseburger for me when the waitress comes back?" I asked Janie, my pledge sister sitting next to me.

I had to fight my way through the frenzied crowd to get to the restroom at the back of the tiny restaurant. There were only two stalls, one of them already occupied. As I squatted to do my business, I heard muffled giggles and the whole metal stall shook as if someone had fallen. Curious, I leaned down and looked under the partition where I saw four feet instead of two. A pair of wedged heels with pink-painted nails peeking through the toe hole, opposite two big hairy feet in Rainbow flip-flops.

I flushed the toilet, twice for effect, and got the hell out of there as soon as I could wash my hands. But instead of going back to the table, I hovered near the door and waited, out of curiosity, for the couple to exit the restroom. Several minutes later, when they finally emerged, Ben and Emma were all smiles as they adjusted their clothing. I caught my brother's eye and glanced down at his shoes, raising an eyebrow in question. He smiled at me at first, as though happy to see me, and then it hit him. He looked down at my feet and back up at me. For a split second I saw sorrow and regret in his face, and then he winked at me, mocking me.

Ben was raised to be a gentleman. He understood he was to wait for women to be seated before he sat down at a table, and he knew to open car doors and watch his profanity in mixed company. The Ben I knew was not the kind of person to stoop so low as to have sex in the stall of a public restroom, a *women's* public restroom no less. Emma made him do things he'd never considered before. She had complete control over him, like a psychiatrist leading her patient around in a hypnotic state, and it terrified me to think of what the doctor might have in mind for her next session with him.

TWELVE

After spending seven amazing days with Archer's family in the Turks and Caicos, I returned to school from spring break reenergized and ready to finish the semester in a big way. My enthusiasm lasted exactly one day.

On Tuesday afternoon, the second day back in classes, Reed and Spotty tracked me down in the amphitheatre where I was studying, stretched out under the warm mid-March sun.

Their expressions were somber as they sat down on either side of me.

"Uh-oh," I said, closing my anatomy book. "I don't like the looks on your faces. What gives?"

"We've just returned from the spring break from hell with your brother and his girl-thing," Reed said.

I leaned back against the stone step. "Start at the beginning and tell me everything."

My brother had been planning this trip to Key West with Spotty and Reed and a group of their fraternity brothers since Christmas, but Emma was never part of the package. She showed up with Ben, with her bags packed, as the convoy was pulling out of the parking lot. "There's an empty seat in the car, why not?" Ben argued. He promised they'd get their own room, but he never thought to call ahead and check availability. One night of sleeping in the same room with the lovebirds was enough for Spotty and Reed. After that, they slept on the floor of whosoever room they happened to be partying with when it was time to go to bed.

"Ben promised to pay us back," Reed said, "but I doubt we'll ever see the money."

"He's broke, Kitty," Spotty added. "His credit card was declined when he tried to buy gas on the way home."

I shook my head. "That's hard to believe. Dad gave us extra allowance for spring break. What did he blow it on?"

"Any and every thing Emma wanted," Reed said. "A bikini with very little fabric comes to mind. And some jewelry. I mean, seriously? How many bracelets can a person wear at once?"

"Were they doing drugs?"

Spotty and Reed exchanged a quick look. "Probably, although they never did anything in front of us," Spotty said. "Their relationship is not healthy. What worries us the most is the constant fighting."

Reed shook his head in disgust. "They got kicked out of a restaurant one night for disturbing the other customers, and hotel security had to quiet them down several times."

"Not to mention Ben almost got arrested for starting a barroom brawl," Spotty added.

"Really?" I tucked my chin to my chest and looked at them from under my eyebrows. "What was the fight about?"

"He was jealous over the way some guy was looking at Emma," Reed explained.

Spotty shifted in his seat so he could see my face. "Reed and I have been thinking about calling your parents, Kitty, but we wanted to talk to you first."

"Ooh, I don't know if that's such a good idea. For whatever reason, my mother's crazy about Emma. I'm not sure she'd believe anything you tell her."

"What about your dad?" Reed asked.

"My father is all about not upsetting my mother. But I'm pretty sure the two of you already know that," I said, looking pointedly at each of them in turn. "Anyway, it's not like Ben's gonna break up with Emma just because my parents ask him to."

"Do you have a better idea?" Reed asked. "We have to do something before he falls off the cliff of no return."

I stood and began pacing back and forth along the edge of the knee wall in front of Spotty and Reed. "We need to separate them, because there's no way we'll get through to Ben while Emma is living in his room." I stopped pacing and faced Reed and Spotty. "And I have an idea that just might work."

I was optimistic when Ben responded immediately to my text and accepted my invitation to meet the following morning after our first class. When I saw him standing in line to order at Bodo's Bagels, I hardly recognized him. He'd lost weight, his hair hung limp and greasy in his face, and his clothes were wrinkled and dirty. If I'd spotted him on a street corner, I might've mistaken him for a bum. Or a drug addict.

I handed him a ten-dollar bill. "There's only one table left outside. I'll grab it, if you'll order a sesame bagel with strawberry cream cheese on the side for me."

When he joined me at the table ten minutes later, the first words out of Ben's mouth were: "Do you think you might be able to loan me some money? Since Archer's parents always pay for everything, you gotta have some of your spring break money left."

"Really?" I stared at my brother who'd become a stranger to me. "We haven't spoken to one another since January and all you can do is ask to borrow money from me? Whatever happened to the brother who was so interested in helping me adjust to college life?"

He shrugged and took a bite of his bagel. "Turns out your roommate needed the help more," he said when he finished chewing. "After all, you got the sorority bid and she didn't. Are you going to lend me the money or not?"

"Don't give me this bullshit, Ben. Emma would've gotten a bid *somewhere* if she'd turned in her card. Besides, you know as well as I do her parents would not have been able to pay the fees. Or I should say her mother, since her father's not earning any money in jail." He glared at me, and for spite I added, "Unless, of course, you were planning to pay for those like you pay for everything else."

"Shh," Ben said, glancing around at the surrounding tables. "Keep your voice down."

"*You* are asking *me* to keep my voice down? After you nearly got kicked out of your hotel in Key West for arguing with your girlfriend." Right away I realized I'd gone too far. I'd jeopardized the confidential conversation I'd had with Spotty and Reed.

"Who told you that?" he asked in mid chew.

"Several people, as a matter of fact. Apparently, what happens in Key West doesn't stay in Key West."

"Emma was right about you," he said, his lip curled in disgust. "You *have* changed."

My appetite suddenly gone, I threw my bagel in the basket and wadded up the waxed paper. "You should look in the mirror," I said, biting my lip to hold back the tears.

"Okay, look. Don't cry." He grabbed my hand and squeezed it hard. "Have you heard anything from Abby or George?"

I shook my head. "You?"

"Nope. I'm sure you've seen the shrine on her Facebook page."

I nodded. "I hope it helps her to know how much everyone cares."

Ben stared off toward campus, his face masked with concern. But after several long minutes, his expression hardened and he returned his attention to me. "So, are you going to lend me the money or not?"

"I thought I already made that clear." I stood to leave. "FYI—and you might want to pass this along to your girlfriend—I submitted a request for a roommate change."

"You did what?" Ben said, raising his voice, no longer concerned whether the people around us heard our conversation. "You can't drop a bomb like that and then leave. Sit back down."

"Why are you so surprised?" I asked, lowering myself to the chair. "I don't like being alone, Ben. *My* roommate is living with you, not me."

He leaned toward me. "And just who are you planning to room with?" he asked as though no one on the planet would ever consider being my roommate.

"A friend of Carla's who's transferring here from Tulane."

He pounded the table with his fist. "What about Emma? When were you planning to tell her?"

"I haven't *seen* her to tell her, Ben. Anyway, it's not like it makes any difference who she lives with. She doesn't need a roommate. She just needs an address to give to her parents—or her mother, rather, in case she ever comes for a visit. I mean, Emma can't exactly entertain her in your room at the fraternity house, now can she?"

He glared at me for a long minute, as if waiting for me to change my mind, and then he gathered his trash and walked away.

The truth is, I would've told Emma sooner if I thought there was any hope the transfer would go through. Campus housing was too tight for the administration to care whether I got along with my roommate or not. All I wanted to do was scare her into moving back in with me, away from Ben. And it worked perfectly, because when I returned from my bio lab late that afternoon, I found her curled up on her bed, facing the wall, her suitcase unopened on the floor beside her.

"Hey there." I managed to sound cheerful despite the sick feeling in my stomach. I was paying the price for helping Ben by living with someone I despised.

Emma rolled over, and I could see from her swollen eyes she'd been crying, a strategy meant to summon my sympathy.

"I take it this means you're moving back in?" I asked and she nodded. "Good. It's lonely without a roommate."

She sat up in her bed and swung her legs over the side. "You're not mad at me?"

Mad? I wanted to pull every hair out of her head and rip her nails from her hands and feet. She'd taken my brother, a kind and generous person, and turned him into a self-centered bastard. "Why would I be mad?" I asked, forcing my lips to smile.

She sniffled. "Ben said you made a request for a roommate change. Do you think it's fair for you not to tell me?"

"About as fair as me having to live alone while you're shacking up with my brother," I snapped. The blonde bitch brought out the worst in me. I would have to try harder if I was going to make it work. "Seriously, Emma, this situation isn't working for me, and I can't see how it's working for you either, having to share a bathroom with all those stinky boys."

"OMG," she said, pinching her nose. "They smell like sour milk."

I held out my hand to her. "Listen, if we can try and work things out, maybe I won't have to make the change."

"I'd like that." Taking my hand, she smiled at me, although I was mindful of the smirk playing along her lips.

"Is that yours?" I asked, nodding at the new MacBook Air on her desk.

She bobbed her head up and down. "Ben bought it for me."

No wonder he's broke! He must have cleaned out his savings account. Ben was Emma's sugar daddy. She was taking advantage of him, and he was letting her walk all over him. Silently, I vowed to put an end to it.

The weeks ahead were challenging, but I was armed and ready to defend myself against Emma's manipulation. I learned to read her face so I could tell when she was lying, or when she wanted something, or even on the rare occasion when she was being sincere. Much to her credit, she honored her commitment by spending every night, even the weekends, in our room. According to Spotty, who was having lots of time alone with Ben, our plan was working, although we were taking painfully slow baby steps.

Literally, I bounced up and down with joy when Ben agreed to go with Spotty and Reed to Virginia Beach for the long Easter weekend. Relieved to have a few days away from Emma, I accepted a last-minute invitation to go with Archer to her family's cottage on Smith Mountain Lake. I didn't see Ben again until our first day back at school when I found him leaning against the wall, his head hung low, outside my chemistry class.

"It's Abigail, isn't it?"

THIRTEEN

Ben opened his arms and I went to him, feeling his body tremble beneath mine as we hugged. We were oblivious to the mob of students moving past us as they rushed between classes. We were on our own island, surrounded only by our grief.

When the bell rang and the halls quieted down, I asked, "When?"

His voice caught in his throat and he took a deep breath. "At daybreak on Easter morning, if you can believe that."

I wiped my nose on his shirt and pulled away from him. "When's the funeral?"

"Tomorrow morning at eleven. Mom and Dad are at the river waiting for us. We need to get your stuff." He put his arm around my shoulders and began guiding me toward the exit. "My bag is already in the car."

We walked in silence on the way back to my room. Words were of no use to any of us now. It was too soon for expressions of sympathy to ease the pain of the ones left behind, and it was too late for words of wisdom and motivational speeches to inspire Abby. We'd all tried to help her—doctors and family and friends—but we'd all failed.

Emma greeted us at the door, slobbering Ben with kisses. "I'm going with you," she said in her determined way.

"That's not a good idea, Em," he said, his arms dangling by his side while she clung to him. "I need to spend this time with Kitty. Alone."

To give them some privacy, and to get the hell out of the line of fire of the missile Emma was certain to launch at any minute, I busied myself in my closet. I tried not to listen to them, but I couldn't help but overhear their mumbled conversation. Emma whined and begged, but Ben remained firm.

I neatly folded my gray knit dress and placed it in my bag, tossing in some underwear and a pair of jeans on top. "I'm going to the bathroom for my toiletries and then I'll meet you downstairs," I said to Ben as I hurried from the room.

Ben and I didn't speak again until we were an hour outside of Charlottesville. Our grief erased the tension of the past months and took us back to a time when it wasn't a big deal for Abigail to eat three slices of chocolate fudge pie.

"She saved my life, you know," I said, breaking our silence. "Too bad I couldn't return the favor."

Ben glanced over at me and then focused back on the road. "I'd forgotten all about that."

When I was ten, maybe eleven, Abigail and I were sailing, past the point where we were allowed to go, when the wind changed and filled the sail from the opposite direction. The boom hit me in the head and knocked me unconscious and out of the boat in one swoop. Despite the constant nagging from my parents, my stubborn preadolescent self wasn't wearing a life jacket. If Abigail hadn't jumped in to rescue me, I would've immediately drowned.

"She treaded water, holding me afloat with those strong legs of hers until help came."

Ben smiled sadly at the memory. "Most people mistook her shyness for weakness when she was really the opposite. Do you remember that day when we were fishing for flounder by the bridge and George got his hook stuck in my arm?"

I ran my finger along the scar on Ben's forearm. "It was gross watching Abigail work it out, but she did it slow and easy, just like a surgeon."

"Yep. And then there was the time she and George got in a fight over who was going to carry the wakeboard up the hill to their house." Laughing, Ben slammed his palm against the steering wheel. "She beat his ass good."

I joined him in laughter. "Remember the steak? Like, who walks around with a raw piece of meat on their eye?"

It seemed disloyal to be laughing, but in our own way, we were honoring Abigail as much as we were easing our pain.

When our fit of laughter ended, the sober reality returned. "If she was so strong, Ben, why'd she do it? Why'd she starve herself to death?"

"I don't know," he said, shaking his head. "I'm hoping George can tell us something that'll help us understand."

Our parents left a note asking us to join them at the Turners' house to pay our respects. While neither of us had the energy for a crowd, Ben and I very much wanted to see George. It didn't take us long to choose the first song. Abby's favorite. Springsteen. "Born to Run." George responded right away with "Independence Day," and from there we moved on to more of her classic-rock favorites.

When I noticed specks of light coming from the Turners' yard, I grabbed the binoculars from inside. It was so dark I had a hard time making out the faces of the people standing on the lawn, but every one of them was holding a lit candle toward the sky.

"Here." I handed the binoculars to Ben. "You need to see this for yourself."

He adjusted the binoculars to fit his face. "Holy shit. Her very own candlelight vigil. I hope Yabba can see this from heaven."

Ben and I gathered every candle we could find from inside and lined them up on the porch railing. It took a few minutes of fighting against the breeze but we finally got all of them lit. When the crowd started singing, we joined in, our voices ringing out our farewell tribute across the water. "Viva La Vida." An appropriate, bittersweet tune to end on.

Thirty minutes later we heard George start his motor and make his way across the creek. By the time we got down to the dock, George had tied up and was waiting for us, sitting on the side of his boat with his feet dangling in the water.

"Isn't that water cold?" I asked him.

He swung his legs around to the inside of the boat. "I can't feel it," he said, looking up at me with a sad smile. "Like the rest of my body, my feet are numb."

The tide was so low Ben and I had to sit on the edge of the dock and slide off into the boat. We wrapped our arms around George in a group hug. None of us tried to hide our tears as we clung to one another. An eternity later, reluctantly, George pulled away and suggested we take a ride out to the bridge.

It was a beautiful evening despite the chill in the air. When we reached the bridge, George killed the motor and moved to the front of the boat, stretching out on the seat across from Ben and me. We stared up at the stars and listened to the sound of the cars overhead while we drifted. We were each lost in our own thoughts, acutely aware of the void created by Abigail's absence.

In our younger days Abby and I would occasionally spend time on our own, sailing or catching butterflies, while the boys were off fishing or spying on the Herrington twins around the bend. But for the most part, we'd done everything as a foursome. Three just didn't feel right. Three felt lonely.

"Talk to us, George," I said when I could endure the silence no more. "We've been so worried."

George looked bewildered, as if he'd just woken from a nightmare to find himself floating in the boat with us. In a way, he had. "I'm not sure where to start," he mumbled.

"Abigail seemed fine, all things considered, when she spent the weekend with me in early November. But by the time we came down here for Thanksgiving, she was in the hospital. Can you tell us what happened after that?"

George sat up and wrapped his arms around his knees. "Mom refused to leave Abigail's side, not once during the whole four months. Dad got up there almost every weekend, but because Baltimore is a six-hour drive from Chapel Hill, I only managed about every third. Sundays were the hardest, having to leave, not knowing what condition she'd be in the next time I saw her. I had no idea it would ever come to this. It wasn't my decision to keep the two of you out of the loop. Or Yabba's either, really. My parents were just trying to protect her."

"Protect her from whom?" I asked.

He hesitated a minute before he admitted, "From people obsessing over how much she was or wasn't eating." I sensed from the anger in George's voice his parents were worried about more than a little gossip.

"Go on," Ben said.

"You know, she talked about the two of you all the time," George said, smiling at Ben and me. "Especially at the end when she was too weak to do anything except listen to me tell her stories from our summers past.

"Her health went back and forth. One minute she'd go downhill, and then she'd rally, and we'd think she was getting better. But in February, around Valentine's Day, she stopped eating altogether. You have no idea how much it sucked to watch her waste away like that during those last few weeks." George pressed his forehead against his arms, staring down into the dark hole between his legs.

I moved over next to George, nudging him to make room for me. "Do you know what caused her to stop eating?" I asked, rubbing his back.

"She never told you?" He sounded surprised.

I shook my head. "I tried to get her to talk many times. . ."

"She was just so damn proud." George shoved his balled fist in his mouth to stifle a sob. "It's all those girls' fault. Those fucking bitches." George rolled over on his side and broke down, crying uncontrollably.

Heartbroken at the sound of his sobs echoing out across the river, I curled up to his back, spooning him, holding his trembling body tight. I wanted him to explain about the bitches, but to push him to continue would have been cruel.

It seemed like hours before George sat up again. He pulled a wad of tissues from his pocket and blew his nose. "Yabba would be horrified if she knew I'd cried in front of y'all—especially you, Ben."

"That's where you're wrong, man. Once, when we were little and I stubbed the hell out of my big toe on the pool deck, Abby told me that real men aren't afraid to cry."

I smiled. "According to Yabba, real men aren't afraid of a lot of things, like wearing pink or taking a girl flowers."

"And now she'll never know *her* real man." George's eyes filled with tears again. "That's the tragedy, isn't it, in someone dying young? All the people they'll never meet, the children they'll never parent, the successes they'll never enjoy. Abby will never get to fulfill her dream of exploring the Great Barrier Reef."

"Wrong again, bro," Ben said. "That's where she is now, except she won't need scuba gear and oxygen tanks. She's swimming with the fishes."

We talked for a few minutes about all the discoveries Yabba would make in the magnificent world of the beyond. And for the rest of the evening after that, we spoke only of happy memories, our private farewell to her. Even though she was physically absent, I felt her spirit in solid force, more than I had in months.

It was late, almost midnight, by the time we pulled up to our dock. I had one foot out of the boat when George said, "My parents and I would like for the two of you to sit with us at the funeral tomorrow."

I stepped back down into the boat and faced him. "That's very kind of you, George, but I'm sure you have plenty of family who need those seats."

"That's sort of the point, Kitty. You and Ben *are* family."

"But what about Yabba's other friends?" Ben asked.

"None of them meant as much to her as the two of you," George said, looking back and forth between Ben and me. "Trust me. It's what Yabba wanted. She told me so."

Ben climbed from the boat and headed toward the house without saying good-bye. Halfway up the dock, we watched him stop and pull his shirttail up to wipe his eyes.

"We're honored, George, really." I hugged him close, feeling his body relax as he released months of built-up stress. He'd been strong for Abby, and now he would need to be strong for his parents. His life had changed forever, and I knew it would be a long time before his world made sense to him again. "We're here for you, Porgie. Anytime you need us."

Fourteen

Hearing Ben's muffled sobs, I tiptoed next door to his room and crawled in bed with him. I placed one earbud of my iPod in each of our ears and selected the playlist I liked to listen to on nights I couldn't sleep. The sound of his breathing changed after a few minutes, and I assumed he was asleep, but when I made a move to leave, he grabbed a handful of my T-shirt, pulling me back.

"Don't go," he whispered. "I don't think I can handle being alone right now."

I curled back up to him.

He sniffled and reached for the tissue box on his bedside table. "I feel like an idiot, blubbering like a baby."

"There's nothing to be ashamed of, Ben. In fact you should feel proud. You were always so good to Yabba. Most guys find their friends' little sisters annoying, but not you. Whatever was wrong in her life, you were one of the bright spots."

"You've got it all wrong, Kitty. She was the bright spot in *my* life. She was so innocent and pure, a reminder of the goodness in a world full of hate." He rolled over to face me. "I did a little research on anorexia and I can kinda relate to how Abby must've been feeling."

"What do you mean?" I'd done my own share of googling, and I was curious about Ben's perspective, since anorexia is often linked with obsessive-compulsive disorder.

"When you think about it, your body is the only thing you have total control over. That's one of the reasons I've been such a die-hard weightlifter and athlete."

"Forgive me for saying this, Ben. But if that's true, what does it mean that you haven't exercised in months?"

"Touché, Kitty. I'm big enough to admit it. Emma has been in control of me lately. But hey, I'm a twenty-one-year-old man with certain needs, if you know what I mean."

"I prefer not to think about it."

He let out a deep breath. "By the way, I *have* been exercising again. A lot, actually."

"I noticed. Keep it up." My brother looked a lot better than he did when I'd seen him a month earlier, but while his body was taking shape again, his face still appeared haggard, which was worrisome considering his recent history of drug use.

"Other than Emma and Abby, what else feels out of your control?" I asked.

"Basically my whole life." He rolled over on his back. "Why am I even majoring in business when you're the one with the math brain? I'll be lucky if I pass two classes this semester."

"That doesn't sound good."

He nodded. "And I'm broke, as you already know. But that's my own fault. All of it is my fault. I let things slide a little and now I'm one step ahead of an avalanche."

I sat up and propped several pillows behind my back. "Let's break it down so it doesn't seem so overwhelming. Why *are* you majoring in business?"

He shrugged. "It seemed like the right thing to do at the time."

"That's a lame answer if ever I heard one. You need to follow your heart, find your passion. It's not too late for you to change."

He raised an eyebrow at me. "Look at you with your grown-up wisdom."

"Well here's some more advice. You have to be confident in your own skin before you can make someone else happy. And whether you believe me or not, I'm not just talking about Emma."

Ben propped himself up on one elbow. "Don't you dare say I told you so, but I'm kind of glad Emma moved back in with you. It feels good to be on a schedule again. Don't get me wrong, she really turns me—"

"Please," I said, holding my hand out. "Too much information."

"Okay, fine," he said, stuffing the earbud back in his ear. "As much as I've missed being able to talk to you, that's all the seriousness I can handle for one night." He rolled over and was snoring within minutes.

I drifted off to sleep not long afterward, and when I woke again, light was creeping in through the blinds, casting vertical shadows on the ceiling. It took me a minute to remember where I was and to realize Ben was no longer sleeping next to me.

I found him on the porch wrapped in a blanket on the love seat. He was staring, through swollen eyes, across the creek at Abby's house, as if willing her to appear on the hill and wave for him to come over for a visit. I moved one of the wicker lounge chairs close to him and tucked my feet up underneath his blanket.

The pink sky of daybreak gave way to the sun, and to my utter amazement, the wildlife came alive around us. Many years ago, our grandfather had an osprey platform built on our property line up close to the beach. Every spring the same male and female osprey returned to their nest, and every summer we could see the little heads of their offspring bobbing up and down. I watched the male osprey circle overhead with his wings spread wide. He carried a stick in his beak, dipping it in the water before flying it back up and tucking it amongst the others in his nest. Unfazed by all this activity, the blue heron on the beach below stuck out his long neck toward the water in search of food while the sparrows dove in and around the eaves of the porch.

Moved by the beauty of my surroundings, my thoughts turned to my grandfather. I prayed to Dock to give me guidance, to show me how I could help my brother.

If you are strong for Ben, he will be strong too.

Beneath the blanket, I pinched Ben's leg with my toes. "I'm honored George asked us to sit with his family today, but it's gonna make things that much harder for you and me. We have to be strong for him, Ben. We can't let him down."

Ben nodded. He understood that I was telling him in a polite way to pull himself together.

As the sun continued to rise, we watched the sky change from pink to orange to yellow.

"Isn't it beautiful?" I asked Ben. "I don't think I'll ever be able to see the sun rise, or watch a school of porpoises swim, or witness any other wonder of nature without thinking about Abigail."

He laid his head on the arm of the sofa. "Yabba was a child of the earth. Her parents should have named her Summer, because that's when she came to life, when freckles appeared across her nose and the bottoms of her feet grew hard and black from running around barefoot."

I was moved by his eloquence in describing Abby. "Ben, I've given it a lot of thought," I said, even though I'd only just that moment made up my mind. "I've decided to lend you the money,"

He bolted upright. "Really?" he asked, his hair sticking up on top of his head like he'd been riding around in the boat all day.

I nodded. "But you have to pay me back. I'm gonna take it out of my savings."

"No worries. I already have two jobs lined up for the summer."

"The weight room and . . ."

"Bartending. Actually, I'm starting out as an assistant to the bartender at City Limits."

I was more than a little worried about him being in the bar scene environment, but I didn't want to discount his efforts. "You should make nice to the chef. Maybe you could show him how to add a little zing to a hamburger."

A twinkle appeared in his bloodshot eyes. "I hadn't thought of that, but maybe."

"How many classes did you say you are behind in?"

He lay his head back down. "Just two, really. Why?"

"Like I said earlier, it's not too late for you to change your major. You might have to go an extra semester or two, but wouldn't it be worth it? To major in something that interests you."

"Whatever, Kitty. I really don't want to think about this right now." He pulled the blanket all the way up over his head, hiding from me.

"Fine, I'll shut up—after I say this one last thing. You have a week left before exams. If you study, I mean really study, do you think you can pass your classes?"

The blanket moved up and down as he nodded his head underneath.

"Then do it! Because you might be able to apply those business credits to a new major, if you decide to change. Especially if it was something like restaurant management."

He pulled the blanket off his head. "Seriously, Kitty? I hate to tell you this, but I don't think they have restaurant management at UVA."

"Okay then, after you get your business degree from UVA, you can go to cooking school. Combined, you'll have all the skills you need to open your own restaurant."

He sat up and untangled himself from the blanket. "Come on. We need to get some sleep. The only thing you've said since you came out here that makes any sense, other than the part about you loaning me money, is that we have to be strong for George today."

FIFTEEN

I'd spoken to my father on the phone a couple of times, but I hadn't talked to my mother at all since our fallout over the sorority ordeal back in January. Instead of "How are your classes going?" or "I've missed seeing you," the first thing she said to me was, "You're planning to wear *that* to the funeral?" about the gray knit dress I'd chosen in my haste to leave Charlottesville.

"What's wrong with it?" I peered at her over the rim of my coffee mug. "You're the one who bought if for me, remember?"

"And I liked it then, before it was washed a few thousand times. Here," she said, handing me a garment bag. "I picked this up for you yesterday."

I didn't have the strength to argue with her, so I took the bag and headed upstairs to change. Naturally, the dress was perfect: a tailored black-linen sheath. A big-girl dress for a grown-up occasion. I dumped the contents of my jewelry pouch onto my bed and searched through the pile until I found my grandmother's diamond studs and the single strand of pearls my father had given me for my sixteenth birthday. I wanted to look nice for Yabba. To say good-bye.

The only funeral I'd ever attended was my grandfather's, which in no way prepared me for the scene inside the Irvington Presbyterian Church. Then again, he died of a massive stroke at age eighty, not anorexia at age seventeen. His friends had come to celebrate his life's accomplishments, but these people were here in grief, to mourn the tragic loss of life. As I walked with the usher toward the front, I noticed the families gathered together on either side of the aisle. Passing tissues and clucking tongues, the mothers whispered words of pity across the pews while their husbands bowed their heads and thanked the Lord their own daughters were healthy and alive. Teenage boys wiggled in their seats like kindergartners while their girlfriends and sisters, sitting next to them, cried openly. The pain on these girls' faces was so raw, so intense, I found it hard to believe any of them were the bitches George had mentioned the night before. But if not them, then who?

My mother often described Mrs. Turner as homely, a term most people consider derogatory. The British, however, define homely as "simple and pleasant in a way that makes you feel comfortable and at home." In my opinion it was a flattering, fitting description for Abigail's mother. Over the years, she'd doctored my many scrapes and stings, but as much as I wanted to pay her back, a Band-Aid or an ice pack was no cure for a broken heart. Mr. Turner was a patient man, having developed most of that patience teaching me to water-ski. I was six, maybe seven, when he spent an entire weekend driving the boat around in circles, encouraging me to try again every time I wanted to quit. Abigail's parents did everything together. They liked to garden and to fish and to spend their weekends immersed in some sort of home improvement project. Today, together, they would bury their daughter.

I hugged Mrs. Turner first and then her husband. Knowing there was nothing I could say to ease their pain, I told them what was in my heart. "Abigail was not only my first friend, she was my truest friend." I choked back a sob. "I already miss her terribly."

Ben didn't manage as well in paying his condolences, but Abigail's father handled him gently, patting him on the back and ushering him further down the pew toward George.

As George made his way to the pulpit to offer the eulogy, I tried to grasp why his parents would have requested something so unimaginable of their son. But he delivered it flawlessly. When he finished, there was not a dry eye in the church nor a doubt in anyone's mind about how much he loved his sister. He made his way back to our pew, bowed his head, and proceeded to fall apart.

I moved closer to him and grabbed his hand. He sobbed so hard, he rocked the pew, and his father and I had to rub and pat and whisper to him until he eventually calmed down.

After the brief service, the family, which included Ben and me, followed the pallbearers out of the church and waited while they loaded Abigail's mahogany casket into the long black hearse. Ben and I declined George's offer to ride to the cemetery with his family by explaining we needed to spend some time with our own parents.

I regretted the decision as soon as I slid into the backseat of my father's Mercedes.

"Such a shame," my mother said, clucking her tongue. "Poor darling didn't stand a chance."

"What's that supposed to mean?" I asked her.

Mom turned around in her seat so she could see me. "Abigail was always so . . . well . . . she was just so shy and weak, pitiful really. I can still remember her plump little legs trying to keep up. She was never a match for you."

"I'll tell you what's pitiful," I hissed, sending particles of spit through the air toward my mother's face. "It's pitiful that you didn't know her any better than to call her weak when she was one of the strongest people I know—."

"Especially considering all the time she spent in our house," Ben said, his face flushed with anger.

"Ben's right. What does that say about you as a person, Mother? That you never knew how determined and intelligent and resourceful Abby was."

My mother cocked an eyebrow at me. "If that's so, then explain to me why she died the way she did. Even with the best doctors in the country, all that determination and resourcefulness couldn't help her overcome an eating disorder?"

My brick wall of resolve began to crumble, and like a wave over a dam, all the pent-up anger came rushing over the top. I'd been holding it in for too long. Five years too long.

I waited until Dad drove into the parking lot of the cemetery before I said, "Anorexia is not a choice, Mom. It's a disease. Abby died because of people like you, people who had so little faith in her. Shame on you. She looked up to you and you didn't even know it. She admired you." When I saw the surprised look on my mother's face, I added, "That's right. She thought you were the coolest, hippest mom ever, and you couldn't even be bothered to offer her a little support."

"What do you mean? I supported her," my mother said, straightening her shoulders.

"Oh really? How? Did you send her a card or some flowers? Did you call her mother or her father periodically to check up on her?" My mother's silence spoke for her. "Abby was a sensitive girl. I'm sure she knew how you really felt about her."

"That's enough, Katherine," my father said.

I stared at the back of his head. As much as I wanted to unleash on him, I knew it wouldn't change anything. He would always take her side. "No it's not, Dad. It's not nearly enough." I returned my attention to my mother, realizing I was crossing a line but forging ahead anyway. "What would you know about pain and suffering? You do whatever you want, whenever you want, without giving any consideration for how your actions affect other people. Well here's a news flash for you, Mom. Someone or something caused Abigail so much pain she starved herself to death, as much pain as you've caused Ben and me over the years with your nasty indiscretion and subsequent drunkenness."

The Rose Garden Affair was a ubiquitous presence in our lives, like the invisible dust particles in the air, and even though Ben and I had talked about it all the time, neither of us had ever dared to speak of it to our parents.

I jumped from the car, slamming the door behind me, and made my way to the front row of folding chairs where George was saving a seat for Ben and me, two feet away from Yabba's beautiful wooden box. My head was throbbing with unshed tears, but I couldn't cry. For George's sake, I wouldn't cry. I made it through the short ceremony by reminding myself over and over that Abby's soul was not in the coffin with her body. She was off somewhere, enjoying her day, either soaring with the eagles or swimming with the dolphins. She was a part of nature now—the petals on the flowers, the leaves in the trees, the waves in the rivers and oceans. She was the beating of my heart. She was free. And as I caught sight of my mother and father in the crowd, I wanted nothing more than to fly off into forever with her.

SIXTEEN

I apologized to my mother. Although truthfully, my apology had more to do with alleviating my own guilt than any real feelings of remorse or regret. I wasn't sorry for unburdening myself, for saying what I'd wanted to say to her for so many years. I was only sorry that nothing had changed. I'd hoped that broaching the issue of my mother's affair would have led our family to talk things out like in a good old-fashioned therapy session. But my parents continued to dance around the issue like they'd always done.

My apology did little to lessen her anger toward me. Never mind that she'd been way out of line in the things she'd said about Abby. In my mother's eyes, I was the one at fault. And she loved to play the role of victim. Every comment out of her mouth carried a poor-pitiful-me tone.

I signed on for another summer in the emergency room at the New Community Hospital, not only because the experience would be invaluable for nursing school but because the twelve-hour rotating shifts would get me out of the house as much as possible.

Sensing the urgency to separate my mother and me, my father surprised her with an eight-week trip to Europe, which included a ten-day cruise on the Mediterranean.

Typical of my parents to flee from crisis.

They departed from the Richmond International Airport on the second Sunday in June, leaving Blessy in charge, although she wasn't actually staying in the house with us. We didn't need a babysitter. My dad insisted she was there to keep the refrigerator stocked and to cook a healthy meal for us every few days. But Ben and I knew the real reason my parents wanted Blessy on standby was to prevent us from having any wild parties or to straighten us out if we got in trouble.

Because of our work schedules, Ben and I rarely saw one another except in passing, in the kitchen for a glass of milk before bedtime or on our way to the bathroom during the night. He appeared tan and fit on the surface, but his smile didn't quite reach his eyes and his voice carried a bitter undertone. And although I knew his surly moods had a lot to do with his grief over losing Abigail, I suspected his funk also had something to do with Emma, who was nannying her eight and ten-year-old cousins in Texas for the summer.

***

I'd seldom known a Fourth of July that didn't include a ride in the Irvington Parade in Abigail's father's 1966 Mustang convertible or a trip to the Tides Inn to watch the fireworks display from the deck of the *Miss Anne*—the 127-foot vintage yacht whose cruises were as much a tradition on Carter's Creek as the boat parade was at Christmas. But, instead of being at the river, surrounded by all the things that reminded me of the friend I'd lost, I was stuck in Richmond. Even though I was looking forward to the party Archer's parents were hosting that night, I still missed Abigail, more than all the other days since she'd died.

And I wasn't the only one suffering.

I was waiting impatiently at the bottom of the stairs for Ben when he came rushing down. "Here," he said, handing me his wadded-up bowtie. "Can you help me with this?"

I glanced down at the tie in my hand and back up at him. "Seriously? Like I know how to tie a bowtie?" I teased.

"Goddamn it, Kitty, can't you at least try?"

"Not if you're going to talk to me like that." I balled up the tie and tossed it at him as I turned to walk away.

He grabbed my arm. "I'm sorry. It's been a bad day for me." Ben's face was full of pain and his eyes brimmed with tears.

"You're not the only one who misses her, Ben." I stooped down and picked up the tie. "You think it's bad for us. Imagine how George feels." As I was turning up his collar, I caught a whiff of the scotch on his breath. "Have you been drinking already?"

"So what if I have." He smacked my hand away from his neck. "Forget the tie. Let's just go."

A nagging little voice, the one I knew I should listen to but hardly ever did, warned me that this was not a good omen. I wanted to barricade myself in my room and pretend it was any day other than the Fourth of July; but as much as Ben needed a chauffeur, he also needed someone to keep him from embarrassing himself.

The Rolands live several miles out River Road where stately homes are sited high above the James River. Archer's parents were using the holiday to throw a belated graduation party for their oldest daughter, Lizzie, who'd graduated from Chapel Hill in May. Not that the Rolands ever needed a reason to celebrate. Their parties were famous, and this one, with a band and professional fireworks display, promised to deliver.

"Time to put on our happy faces and pretend we're having a good time," I said to Ben as we drove up the winding driveway.

"Take a drink, Kitty," he said, his first words to me since we got in the car. "It'll help your mood."

"Right. And who will drive us home if I do?" I got out of the car and walked around to his side, opening the door for him.

He pulled me in for a quick hug. "I can always get a ride home if you want to spend the night with Archer," he said in a soft tone.

"This is not a getting-drunk kind of party, Ben. I have no intention of making a fool of myself in front of Archer's parents. And I hope you won't either. I will drive us home, when we're both ready to go. Deal?" I asked, and we shook on it.

Ben and I made our way around to the back of the house where we were immediately swallowed up and separated by the crowd. Under an enormous tent to my right, the Voltage Brothers were already on stage, blasting R & B tunes across the group of dancers on the floor in front of them and out across the lawn. When I caught a glimpse of Archer to my left, I followed the tiki torches through the terrace toward the pool.

"Geez, Archer," I said, hugging her, "this party is like a wedding reception on steroids. What're your parents gonna do for an encore when Lizzie gets married?"

She shrugged. "Who knows? Horse-drawn carriages or a flotilla of boats cruising down the river? But whatever the theme, you've gotta wear that dress. It looks killer on you."

My dress was not the wedding kind of dress, but it was perfect for the Fourth of July with its varying shades of blue and white. Archer's was prettier and dressier, strapless and hot pink, a stark but attractive contrast to her strawberry-blonde hair.

"You look pretty hot yourself, and I'm not the only one who thinks so."

"What're you talking about?" She spun around, searching the crowd.

"Duh." I nodded my head toward Spotty, who was standing across the pool pretending to talk to her father but his eyes were glued on her. "What gives? What have you not been telling me?"

"Well . . . we *have* been seeing a lot of each other lately—you know like hanging out and stuff." Her green eyes grew wide like cat's eye marbles. She leaned in and whispered to me, "There's a super cute guy headed our way. I want to introduce you to him." Before I could object, she stepped out in front of the guy to block his path. "Thompson, I want you to meet my friend Katherine."

He turned toward me and held out his hand. His brown hair was golden from the sun and his eyes were deep-ocean blue. "Kather-ine," he said, pronouncing my name in the exaggerated syllables of a lazy Southern accent. "My favorite aunt is Katherine."

I stuck my hand out to shake. "Nice to meet you . . . uh . . . What did you say your first name is?"

He chuckled. "Thompson *is* my first name. I'm Thompson Mc-Cray." He squeezed my hand again and then released it.

"Katherine is in nursing school at UVA," Archer said to him, and then turned to me. "And Thompson is starting medical school there in the fall."

"Really? Then why are you moving to Charlottesville in July?" I asked, shocked at my own rudeness. "I'm sorry. I don't mean to be so blunt."

"No worries." His lips spread into a smile that produced the most adorable dimple on the left side of his mouth. "I graduated from UNC in May, which is obviously how I know Lizzie, but I stayed behind in Chapel Hill to wrap up a research project. There's not much point in going home to Atlanta for only a couple of months. I need to find an apartment. Then I guess I'll get a job until school starts."

Spotty appeared behind Archer and whispered in her ear in a manner that left little doubt in my mind something was going on between them. Without even a glance in our direction, the two of them headed off toward the band tent.

I felt awkward being alone with this cute stranger. "Have you ever heard this band before?"

He nodded. "Several times in fact. Would you like to dance?" When I hesitated, he asked, "Are you here with somebody?"

I coughed to clear my throat. "No, but—"

"Then what are we waiting for?" He grabbed my arm, leading me through the crowd and onto the dance floor. He smiled that naughty-boy smile I was growing fond of. "Since I don't know anyone here, it's your duty to entertain me," he shouted above the music.

"You don't expect me to believe that, do you?" I yelled in response. "Half of Lizzie's sorority is out here on the dance floor with us."

He leaned over and whispered in my ear, "That may be so, but what are parties for if not for making new friends?" He blew on my neck, a puff of warm breath that sent shivers to parts of my body I didn't know existed.

We danced until the band took a break and the firework's display began. "Are you ready for a drink?" he asked as we pushed our way to the edge of the crowd for better firework viewing.

"Yes, please. A bottled water."

"Water?" he asked, surprised. "Are you sure you don't want something a little stronger? Maybe a beer?"

I nodded. "I'm the designated driver. My brother is the one on the other side of the terrace holding up the tree." I pointed through the crowd at Ben. Thompson and I watched Ben grab a glass of champagne from the tray of a passing waiter and down it in one gulp.

"Looks as though you may be on borrowed time," Thompson said, winking at me.

I managed a weak smile. I wanted to lock Ben in the Rolands' laundry closet in their basement, away from the bar, until I was ready to go home. Leave it to me to meet the most amazing guy on the same night I had to babysit my drunk brother.

The Rolands had spared no expense in providing a brilliant fireworks show, one vibrant explosion of color after another above the cries of delight from the crowd below. Afterward, when Spotty and Archer were nowhere to be found, Thompson led me to a quiet table on the other side of the pool where we talked for a long time, a little about his family—his sisters and the mother he clearly adored—but mostly about medicine. I had no doubt his gentle manner would assure him success as a doctor. "Pediatrics," he told me, and I wasn't surprised. I'd been around enough ER doctors to know he was perfect for the job.

When something caught Thompson's attention behind me, I followed his gaze. Ben was drunk. He stumbled from one group of people to the next on the lawn over by the band, making a complete nuisance of himself.

Thompson ran his finger lightly down my cheek. "It kills me to say this, but I think you need to get your passenger home. Come on." He stood and pulled me to my feet. "I'll help you get him to the car."

"Come on, Ben. It's time to go home." I tried to take him by the arm but he snatched it away from me.

"Go ahead, then," he said, searching the crowd. "I'll get a ride with Spotty."

"Spotty is spending the night out here," I lied.

"Then I'll get a ride with someone else." He turned his back on me and started to walk away.

"You're not going to let your sister drive home by herself, now are you?" Thompson said to my brother's retreating back.

Ben spun around, and, noticing Thompson for the first time, he stumbled back toward us. "And just who the hell are you?"

"Ben, meet Thompson McCray," I said. "He's a friend of Lizzie's from Chapel Hill. He came up for the party."

Ben's eyes narrowed as he tried to focus on Thompson's face. "Forget it, dude." He shoved Thompson out of the way and began dragging me toward the car. "No way you're gonna use *my* sister as your one-night slam piece," he called over his shoulder.

Thompson followed at a safe distance so as not to draw Ben's attention. Once Ben was situated in the passenger seat, Thompson led me around to my side of the car. "Katherine, we've only just met—and this is really none of my business—but please know, I mean this in the most concerned way. I've witnessed a lot during the past four years of being in a fraternity. I think your brother is *on* something, something more than just alcohol."

Tears filled my eyes and I looked away.

He lifted my chin toward him. "This isn't news to you, is it?"

As much as I liked this guy, I wasn't ready to betray my brother to a virtual stranger. "I've gotta get him home," I said, reaching for the door handle. "Can I give you a ride somewhere?"

"No, but thanks. I'm staying here tonight. Will you at least text me so I'll know you made it home safely?"

Nodding, I handed him my phone so he could enter his number. He kissed me then, gently brushing his lips against mine. I wanted him to wrap his arms around me, to press his body to mine and bury his handsome face in my neck. I was imagining a night alone with Thompson, locked away in my bedroom at home, when Ben blew the horn and put an end to my fantasy.

"You didn't have to embarrass me by dragging me out of there like that," Ben said as soon as we were heading down the driveway.

"Embarrass you, hell. You should be thanking me for saving you from yourself. I only hope Archer's parents didn't see you stumbling around."

"You are such a bitch." He untied his tie, and sticking his finger between his collar and his neck, he yanked the top button off his shirt. He thought it was the funniest thing ever when the button ricocheted off the front windshield and pinged the side of my head.

We didn't speak again until we were in our driveway and I was texting Thompson to let him know I'd made it home safely. Ben snatched my phone away and tried to focus his eyes on the screen. "Who're you talking to, your new lover boy? That guy makes me sick."

"You don't even know him." Grabbing my phone back and throwing it into my bag, I stormed from the car and rushed up the stairs.

Ben was right behind me, and then on top of me, breathing down my neck as I unlocked the door. "I know plenty of guys like that douche, so slick with their preppy Southern manners."

"Just mind your own business," I shouted at him when we were inside.

"Like you mind yours?" He shoved me and I stumbled backward, catching myself on the arm of the settee. "You have been in my shit since I started dating Emma, and I'm sick of it."

"Grow a backbone, Ben. Why are you letting that psycho-bitch control you all the way from Texas?"

Like a lion assaulting his prey, Ben came after me and pushed me against the wall. I was no match for his incredible strength. He pinned my shoulder to the wall with his left hand and clutched my throat with his right. He lifted me higher and higher against the wall until my feet left the ground. He was in my face, his breath a sour mixture of alcohol and vomit. His bloodshot eyes were full of rage, and I could see traces of a white substance around both nostrils. He squeezed harder, cutting off all the air to my windpipe. I was so terrified, I lost control of my bladder—which was probably what saved my life. Hearing my tinkle hit the hardwood floor brought Ben out of his frenzy and back to reality.

"Oh god, I'm so sorry, Kitty." He relaxed his grip and eased me down to the floor, but instead of letting me go, he pressed his body against mine so I couldn't move. We stared at each other with tears streaming down our faces.

So this is what it feels like to hit rock bottom.

When I felt his body go limp, I pushed Ben off me with all my might and bolted for the stairs. He dove after me, trying to tackle me, but he missed and landed on the bottom step. I locked my bedroom door and shoved my desk chair underneath the knob. I raked everything off the top of my dresser and slid it in front of the door, adding a club chair and a blanket chest for good measure. I searched the room for my handbag, but when I couldn't find it, I realized I'd probably dropped it downstairs during the shuffle. With no cell phone to call for help, I opened the window and stared at the row of holly bushes below. There was no escape. No porch roof to break my fall or tree branch to climb out on. I thought about screaming my head off for help—the Coopers lived next door, but then I remembered they were visiting their daughter and her new baby girl in California. The only signs of life in the dark night, a dog barking several streets over and the sound of firecrackers popping in the distance, did little to diminish my fear.

After changing out of my wet clothes and into a pair of sweats and a T-shirt, I crawled way back in my closet, using my old prom dresses to shield me from view. The house was so quiet I could hear the second hand on my watch ticking, but then the sound of shattering glass pierced the silence.

I heard Ben's footsteps, pounding up the stairs and down the hall toward my room. "Come on, Kitty, let me in," he said, banging on my door. "Please . . . I just want to talk to you. I'm sorry. I didn't mean to hurt you."

When I didn't respond, he moved down the hall, opening and closing doors. I shut my eyes and counted until I reached a hundred. I was beginning to relax a little when he was at my door again, this time tapping lightly.

"You don't understand. I've had such a bad day. I lost my job, and I had this great big fight with Emma."

As if any excuse was reason to scare me to the point of peeing in my pants.

When his voice finally tapered off, I yanked an old terrycloth robe from a hanger and balled it up, using it as a pillow. I closed my eyes, but I didn't sleep. Not for hours. Not until I saw daylight peeking underneath the door.

I must have dozed then, because the next sound I heard was Blessy's voice in the hall. "Are you the one that broke your mama's vase? Because if you are, you're gonna be in big trouble when she gets home. Where's your sister? And why are you sleeping out here instead of in your bed?" I couldn't make out the mumbling that followed, but then Blessy tapped on my door. "Come on now, baby, open up so we can get to the bottom of whatever's the matter."

After struggling to move the furniture out of the way, I opened the door and rushed into her arms, nearly knocking her down. Over her shoulder, I could see Ben watching us with his head hung low. I reached my foot out and kicked the door shut in his face.

She had to pry me away so she could examine my body. "Good Lord in heaven, what happened to your neck?"

I caught my reflection in the mirror behind her. Five purple bruises in the shape of Ben's fingers marked my throat. "What did he tell you?" I asked, covering the bruises with my hand.

She led me over to the bed. "Only that he let his temper get out of control. What's going on here, Kitty Cat?"

I lay down and rolled over on my side with my back to Blessy. Now that she was here, I felt safe and all I wanted to do was sleep. "He *is* out of control. I'm scared *for* him as much as I am scared *of* him. He's doing drugs, Blessy."

She drew in a big breath of air and released it slowly. "Start at the beginning."

And so I left nothing out. I told her everything that'd happened since Emma came into our lives nearly a year ago. I also admitted that I thought Ben was having a hard time dealing with Abigail's death and that he'd mentioned something about losing his job.

When I was finished talking, Blessy went to the door and yelled down the hall to Ben, "Get yourself cleaned up, young man. You're going with me to run some errands." Leaving the door open, she began straightening my room.

"I guess maybe I should go and stay with Archer for a while," I said, swinging my feet over the side of the bed. As much as I didn't want to be within a fifty-mile radius of Ben, the thought of leaving my house and facing my friends was an even less attractive option.

"If you'd feel better at Archer's, then that's where you need to be, but I'm gonna get some of my things so I can stay here for a while. Ben needs a heavy hand right now, and it's a good thing your parents are gone, because I'm gonna give it to him." She picked my soiled dress up off the floor, holding it in the air and pinching her nose.

I turned my head away so she couldn't see my tears.

"Aw, baby." Blessy came to me and rubbed circles on my back. "Leave everything to me. I'm gonna get our Ben back, good as new." She brushed my hair off my forehead. "Do you have to go to work today?"

I shook my head. "Not until tomorrow."

How would I ever be strong enough to leave my house again, let alone go back to work? The bruises would fade from purple to green to yellow, and eventually disappear, but the scars on my heart were permanent. Within a couple of weeks, I'd be as good as new on the outside, but my insides were damaged goods for life.

"Okay, then. Why don't you crawl under the covers and go back to sleep." She pulled my duvet back and waited while I nestled in. "Ben and I will be gone for most of the morning, but when I get back I'll fix you a grilled cheese just the way you like it, piled high with bacon and tomatoes."

When I heard the front door slam, I hurried down the hall to my parents' room and watched them climb into Blessy's ancient Ford Taurus. I hated for her to have to leave her family and stay with us, but her children were grown, and we needed her help.

Once they were safely out of the driveway, I ransacked Ben's room. In the bottom drawer of his dresser, hidden in a stack of ratty T-shirts, I found a plastic baggie of pot. Feeling like the poster mom for War Against Drugs, I flushed the marijuana down the toilet and placed the empty baggie back where I found it.

His iPhone was on his bedside table. Dead. I plugged it into his charger and waited for it to power up. Just as I'd suspected, Emma was jerking Ben around. She was almost pornographic in her come-ons to him in one text, and then she'd tell him she wanted to date other people in the next. Ben, in turn, was pathetic, in his attempt to appease her. He promised he'd fly out to Texas to see her, but when that wasn't enough, he offered to marry her. In the most recent entry, she broke up with Ben, claiming she was in love with one of the golf pros at her uncle's country club. The time and date on that text—July 4, 5:08 p.m.

SEVENTEEN

The loud pounding on the door and ringing of the doorbell woke me from a deep sleep. I glanced at the clock on my bedside table. It was almost noon.

Must be Blessy and Ben.

I staggered down the steps and whipped open the front door. "Did you forget your—" I was stunned into silence. It wasn't Blessy or Ben, but Thompson, poised with his fist in the air preparing to knock again.

Like a missile on its target, he zeroed right in on my bruises. "What happened to your neck?"

I drew my hand to my throat.

"Did your brother do that to you?" When Thompson moved toward me, I closed the door tighter between us. "You can't stay here alone with him. When are your parents coming home from Europe?"

Of all the things Thompson and I had talked about at the party, the subject of my parents never came up. He would have learned of their trip from Archer. I imagined the breakfast scene in the Rolands' kitchen—with everyone gathered around the island and shoveling down pancakes as fast as Archer's mom could take them off the griddle. In her curious but nonchalant way, Archer would ask Thompson, "Did you have fun with Katherine last night? I never got to say good-bye to her. Did she leave early?" And Thompson would nod his handsome head and explain that I had to drive Ben home. Which would lead to the discussion about how drunk

Ben had been and poor me for having to take care of him while my parents were away.

"Blessy's here now." When his brow furrowed in confusion, I added, "She's our nanny."

A smile crept across his lips. "Aren't you a little old to have a nanny?"

"You know what I mean. Blessy is like a mother to us. She knows how to take care of my brother."

"And who's going to take care of *you*?" He tilted his head to the side and softened his smile. "I'd like to help, if you'd let me. I'm a good listener. Can I take you to lunch so we can talk?"

As much as I wanted to drive off in his Land Rover with him, I couldn't let myself get any closer. It wasn't right to share our family's problems with someone I barely knew. "I'm sorry, Thompson. Now is not a good time for me. Last night was fun. Let's just leave it at that."

His shoulders slumped. "Okay, but only for now. I don't give up that easily. I'll give you some time to sort things out, but in a week or so, when you're feeling a little better, I'd like to drive over from Charlottesville and take you to dinner."

Somehow I managed a slight smile. "We'll see."

"We *will* see. I'll be checking on you periodically, but in the meantime, you have my number if you need anything." He ran his fingers over my bruises and then leaned down and kissed my cheek.

After watching Thompson drive away, I closed the door behind me and slumped to the marble floor.

Damn you, Ben. I've been bogged down in your twisted relationship with Emma for the past God-only-knows-how-many months, and then I meet someone I find attractive and intelligent and kind, someone with the potential for a serious relationship, and I have to make him go away in order to protect you.

I had no idea where Blessy and Ben went that day, but they were gone an awful long time, way past lunch and well into the afternoon. When they returned, I immediately sensed a new bond between them. As much as it was killing me not to be a part of their

secret, it was an enormous relief to have Blessy around to take care
of Ben.

Living in the same house with my brother was torture. Every
time I closed my eyes to sleep, I saw the anger in his face and felt
his fingers around my throat. Unable to endure the shame in his
eyes when he stared at the five purple bruises on my neck, I avoided
him in the kitchen and hallways. I longed to flee, to run to the
safety of Archer's house; but she and Spotty had gone public with
their relationship, and I wanted nothing to do with love. I even
ignored Thompson's calls and texts. Living in the shadow of my
parents' dysfunctional marriage had made me wary of the notion
of everlasting love, but it was watching Ben being tormented by
Emma that destroyed my last shred of hope of ever having a healthy
relationship.

I had no clue how to move on with my life, so I immersed
myself in the only thing left that made sense to me. After two days
of moping around the house, I went back to work. I wore a cotton
turtleneck under my scrubs to hide the bruises, and I stayed at the
hospital for three days straight, working double shifts and taking
naps whenever I could find an empty stretcher and a few minutes
to myself. To be needed in the understaffed ER went a long way
toward restoring some of my sense of self.

When I finally returned home, around dinnertime on the
fourth day, I found Blessy and Ben in the kitchen making homemade marinara sauce. They were using Hanover tomatoes and fresh
basil, and it smelled so unbelievable I didn't resist when Blessy insisted we all sit down at the kitchen table together to eat.

It was the first real food I'd had in days, and I was concentrat-
ing more on stuffing my face than on Ben's explanation about losing his job at City Limits. He was saying something about them
needing to cut back on staffing because their business was slow.
But he caught my attention—and I looked up in surprise—when
he mentioned he'd gotten an internship at Traveler's, the five-star
restaurant recently opened in a converted warehouse in Shockoe
Bottom.

"How'd that happen?" I asked. "I mean, you don't just walk into Traveler's and apply for a job."

"Reed's father is one of the original investors in Traveler's," Ben said, his eyes shining with excitement. "He arranged the interview with Nick Nixon for me."

As much as I wanted to share his enthusiasm, especially since I'd been bugging him all year to consider a career as a chef, I came up empty.

"Did you know Nixon learned to cook the same way as me?" Ben asked.

I shook my head, unable to speak. I hadn't seen Ben that fired up since he scored the winning touchdown against Benedictine his senior year in high school. How could this be the same person who tried to cut off my air supply with his bare hands less than a week ago?

"He spent the summers with his grandparents at their farm in Charles City," Ben continued. "Just like us, they cooked all the meat they hunted and all the fish they caught. They even had a little vegetable garden. Do you remember ours?"

He waited for my answer like a little boy eager for an ice cream cone, but I couldn't summon any enthusiasm. Doing so would've been letting him off the hook. It infuriated me that he could be so happy when I was so miserable. I wanted him to suffer, same as me.

"In my experience, an internship means no pay," I said, glaring at him. "Don't forget you still owe me money. A lot of it in fact."

Ben's whole body slumped, head and shoulders and torso. I'd accomplished my objective. I'd caused him pain. Funny how it didn't make me feel any better. And to see the disappointed look on Blessy's face only made matters worse.

"Where're you going?" she asked me when I pushed back from the table.

"I'm not hungry," I mumbled, dumping my plate in the sink and running up the back stairs to my room.

She followed me and closed the door behind us. "What's gotten into you, Katherine? I didn't spend all this time pumping that boy up just for you to tear him down again."

My guilt alone was difficult enough to bear, but being on the receiving end of Blessy's wrath brought on an outpouring of tears.

She sat down beside me on the bed and wrapped her big arms around me. "Poor Kitty Cat," she whispered. "Shame on me. Here I am always counting on you to be the strong one."

Her kindness only made me cry harder.

"But you *are* strong." She lifted my chin so she could see my face. "You've traveled down more rocky roads than some people do in a lifetime. But those tough times have given you confidence. That's not to say you don't have feelings like the rest of us. Ben knows he scared you. Hell, he scared himself."

"Seriously?" I asked, sniffling.

She nodded. "What happened here the other night was more than just a wake-up call for him. He views it as a sign from God."

I studied her face. "He admitted that to you?"

"In those very words." She wrapped her big hands around mine and squeezed. "It's obvious you still need a little more healing time. But while you're straightening things out for yourself, be aware of how hard Ben's working to make it up to you."

I scooted off the other side of the bed and stood, staring out of the window in silence for several long minutes. "What if he can't make it up to me, Blessy? What if my wounds won't mend?"

"No one's expecting you to forget what happened here the other night, but I can promise you the memory will grow blurry as soon as you're able to forgive."

I turned around to face her. "That's pretty profound."

"That's the truth," she said. "It's not so much what happens to us in life; it's the good grace we show in reacting to those experiences. It's within your power to rise above this, just like you've done in the past with your mother."

I thought a lot about forgiveness and trust during the sweltering weeks that followed, when I retreated to the windowless tombs of the emergency room where the air conditioning was kept low enough to cure meat. To prevent my patients from questioning my age or credentials, I learned to approach them with confidence and compassion. All they really needed from me was someone to hold their hand and answer their many questions. Their trust in me lasted as long as their belief in my promises. If their pain didn't subside in a reasonable amount of time or the doctor took too long to get in to see them, they were quick to drop my hand and send for my supervisor.

The kids were the easiest. Their favor could be earned for the price of a SpongeBob Band-Aid or a Dixie cup full of ginger ale. With their broken arms and croupy coughs, their faces pinched in pain, they reminded me of Ben and me when we were little, those long-ago days when we believed so easily and trusted so freely—before our mother destroyed our innocence.

I'd never forgiven my mother her betrayal, mainly because she'd never asked me to. But I saw how much my trust and forgiveness meant to Ben. As the days blended together and grew into weeks, I softened toward him a little, especially when he left the money he owed me with a sweet note and three chocolate truffles he'd made on my bed. He was working hard to get his life together. Regardless of what time he got home from the restaurant at night, he was up every morning at seven for his five-mile run before reporting for duty in the weight room. According to him, he was back to his high-school weights, both the amount he was lifting and the amount on his scales. Work was also going well for him at Traveler's where he'd been promoted from dishwasher to an assistant pastry chef. As for Emma, I didn't ask, and he never mentioned her name.

On the first Sunday afternoon in August, our parents made a sudden reappearance in our lives, loaded down with leather goods from Italy, a wallet for Ben and a pair of soft boots for me. Over pizza, they showed us pictures of all the places they'd visited and all the friends they'd made. Never once did they inquire about how we'd spent our time while they were away.

The next morning when Blessy got to work, she summoned my parents into my father's study where they stayed for more than an hour. Placing a glass against the wood-paneled door, I tried to hear what they were saying, but the only thing I could make out was that Blessy was the one who was doing all the talking. Whatever she told them, however detailed her account was of the happenings at home in their absence, she got through to them. They came out of that meeting stunned, with cloudy eyes and trembling hands. My father left right away for a last-minute lunch meeting at the Commonwealth Club while my mother wandered around the house in a semi-state of delirium, looking at Ben and me as though she recognized us but couldn't quite place us. Late in the afternoon, I discovered her in the family room surrounded by old photo albums, either searching for the years she'd lost or reacquainting herself with the children she'd forgotten.

Mom went to bed that night in a comatose state and woke up the next morning a new person. Or an old person, really—the mother I remembered before I went to kindergarten. She made blueberry pancakes and freshly squeezed orange juice for breakfast, and sat with us while we ate.

"I owe both of you an apology," she said, a real tear trickling down her cheek. "I've made a lot of mistakes in my life, but the biggest one was assuming that the two of you would come to me when you had a problem and needed guidance. When you never did, I assumed everything was fine." She rose from the table and searched in the junk drawer for a pocket-size pack of tissues, then wiped her eyes and blew her nose. "If you'll let me, I'd like to try and make it up to you."

Ben and I both shrugged, unable to make sense of our mother's overnight transformation.

"According to my calendar, you still have a couple of weeks before you head back to school. Do you think we can manage a long weekend at the river? Just the four of us."

It took some juggling and compromising but we finally agreed on four days and three nights during the third weekend in August. It was the only vacation Ben and I had taken all summer, and once the plans were made, we were excited at the prospect of a change of scenery and a break from the demands of our jobs. As soon as we got to the river on Thursday afternoon, we jumped in the boat and sped across the creek to the Turners'.

I almost didn't recognize Mrs. Turner when she answered the door. The plump, rosy-cheeked woman I'd always known had grown old over the summer. Her hair hung in gray limp strands around her face; and even though it was four o'clock in the afternoon, she was wearing an old flannel robe with faded blue flowers, the once-white background now yellowed with age. When she pulled the robe tighter around her, I noticed her waist was thinner, nearly three dress sizes if I had to guess.

"Ben, Katherine," she said, holding the door open a little wider. "It's so nice to see you. We've missed you this summer."

Ben and I took turns leaning in to kiss her cheek, apologizing for not getting down to see her sooner.

"Is George home?" I asked.

"No, dear, he's out of town." She stepped onto the porch and spread her arms wide. "There's a nice breeze today. Would you like to join me on the porch for a glass of lemonade?"

Ben and I nodded our heads with enthusiasm. Mrs. Turner made the best homemade lemonade in the Northern Neck—freshly squeezed with a mountain of sugar and real floating lemon slices—and she never served it without her oatmeal raisin cookies.

She smiled. "Well then, why don't you make yourselves at home out front on the porch and I'll be with you in a few minutes."

We wandered around the side of the house to the porch where we could see up and down the creek for a mile in each direction. We waited in silence, side by side in metal rocking chairs, a thousand memories on our minds. Curling up in their hammock and listening to the rain ping against the porche's tin roof was once my favorite lazy-day pastime.

Mrs. Turner joined us fifteen minutes later, dressed in a pair of white shorts and pale pink top with her hair pulled back in a clip at the nape of her neck.

"How long will George be gone?" Ben asked her.

"At least another week, possibly two." She lifted the crystal pitcher from her tray and poured three glasses of lemonade. "I'm hesitant to tell you this, but I think George would want you to know. His father and I . . . well . . . we had to send him away for professional help. He's having a hard time dealing with Abigail's death."

I looked over at Ben, whose face was pinched in anguish. All summer long we'd been focused on our own problems—Ben with Emma and me with Ben—while our good friend was suffering. "That explains why he's been ignoring our calls," I said.

Mrs. Turner nodded. "He's not allowed to have his phone."

"I'm so sorry we didn't try harder to get in touch," I said, close to tears. "We should've realized things were bad for him."

Mrs. Turner stirred her lemonade with her finger and stared into her glass, as if it were a crystal ball with the answers she needed to put her family back together again. "There's nothing anyone could've done. He's just so angry, and his drinking got way out of control."

I could feel Ben's eyes on me, and I knew he was thinking about his own alcohol abuse and anger management problem.

Mrs. Turner looked away from us and stared across the water at a group of kids sailing their Sunfish back and forth across the creek. "It's so hard for him to have to see those girls around town all the time," she mumbled, more to herself than to us.

Ben and I exchanged a knowing look. These *girls* were surely the same bitches George had been talking about the night before Abigail's funeral.

"Mrs. Turner," Ben started in a gentle voice. "Katherine and I don't really know that much about Abigail's problems, only that they began after she broke her jaw."

"It would really help us to hear more about what she went through," I added.

Mrs. Turner stared first at me and then at Ben before settling back in her chair. She let out a deep sigh. "I'd just assumed George had told you everything. My daughter's problems actually started a couple of years before the accident with her jaw. We didn't know it at the time, but she was being bullied. There were four girls, the same ones she'd known since kindergarten, making her life a living hell. They called her Abs Big Butt because of her weight."

"That's just cruel. What grade did all this happen in?" Ben asked.

Expert that I am on the behavior of adolescent girls, I answered for Mrs. Turner. "In middle school, right, Mrs. Turner? When girls are at their meanest."

Mrs. Turner nodded. "But these girls got even nastier as they got older. But I'm getting ahead of myself," she said, reaching for her glass of lemonade. "She lost a lot of weight . . . what with her jaw wired shut and all. Her new figure gave Abigail a confidence she'd never known before. She was so proud of that first bikini. I remember it well—red with little white polka dots."

Mrs. Turner set her lemonade down and picked a daisy from the bouquet in the center of the coffee table, plucking the petals off one by one. When all the petals were gone, she tied the stem in a knot and tossed it over the side of the porch. "The same girls who'd bullied her wanted to be her friend," she continued. "For Abigail, it was like being the new girl in their grade. Boys were calling and texting her all the time. It didn't take Abigail long, though, maybe a month or two, before she realized she didn't belong in their group. They were drinking and smoking marijuana, and Abigail wasn't ready for any of that. She wanted out almost as soon as she got in."

"Uh-oh," I said.

"Mm-hmm. These girls were not the type to be ignored." Mrs. Turner pulled a tissue from her pocket to wipe her tears. "As you know, Abigail was a very private girl. She never told us about the torture she endured, even when she started seeing her psychiatrist and was going for weekly weigh-ins at the pediatrician's office. I've asked myself time and again why wouldn't she have confided in us?"

"Pride," Ben answered.

"That's exactly what the doctors said, Ben." She reached over and squeezed his hand. "Knowing how close you are with your sister, I'm sure you can imagine the anger George feels toward these girls."

"Did George know these girls before?" I asked.

"Yes. Since preschool. One of the girls' brothers is actually a close friend of George's. He was at their house the night he—" Her voice caught on a sob, preventing her from continuing.

I gave her a moment to compose herself and then asked, "The night he what, Mrs. Turner?"

She stood and wandered over to the porch railing. "The night he punched the maple tree in our front yard and broke several bones in his hand. Only the good Lord knows what that girl said to set him off so."

Ben and I joined her at the railing. And for a long time, we watched the activity on the creek in silence, each lost in our own thoughts of Abby and George.

We left Mrs. Turner a little while later with our well-intentioned promises to come and visit her often. Instead of going home, we took the boat out into the river. We rode all the way to the mouth of the Chesapeake Bay and then back again to Urbana.

As much as I'd been trying to get my mind around it, my heart had refused to accept Abby's death. It was only now that I was beginning to understand she wasn't just off at Camp Mont Shenandoah or visiting her favorite cousin in Charleston. She wouldn't be coming home tomorrow, or even next week. I would never see her kind eyes again or watch the freckles spread across her nose when she smiled. From now on, if I wanted to connect with her, I'd have to come out here, in the river, where the sun glistened like diamonds across the water.

My heart ached for George and all he was going through. Learning to live without his sister was one thing, but having to face the girls who were indirectly responsible for her death was another matter. In the small community where the Turners lived, George no doubt frequently encountered those girls at parties or at the gas station or out in the boat on the weekends. And every time he saw them, he would have to face the brutal reality of Yabba's death all over again.

Why would those girls have chosen someone as kind and humble as Abby to destroy?

Fuck those bitches.

EIGHTEEN

Our parents were waiting for us at the table on the porch behind a mountain of steamed crabs. During the past two weeks, my parents had suggested one activity after another for us to do together, as if a round of twilight golf could make up for all the years we'd done very little as a family. Even though I thought their relentless pursuit impressive, I wasn't quite ready to trust that their intentions might last.

They surprised Ben and me by offering us a beer with dinner, a signal that they considered us on the pathway to adulthood. For the first time in as long as I could remember, if ever, we enjoyed each other's company. We talked about politics and about our lives at UVA, but mostly we fantasized about the new sailboat my father was considering buying. As much as it seemed like we were getting reacquainted after a long absence, it felt as though we'd just met our parents for the first time, Adele and Spalding Langley—only they no longer seemed like our parents but our friends.

When all the crabs were picked clean, I pushed back from the table and wiped the crab gunk off of my arms and face with a paper towel. "I feel gross. Are you game for a swim, Ben?"

He kicked back his chair and was already on his way to the pool when he called to me over his shoulder, "Last one there has to blow up the floats!"

I leapt off the end of the porch and sprinted across the lawn to the pool, managing to catch up and then bypassed Ben. I stripped down to my bathing suit and dove into the water before he even reached the gate.

"Be sure to toss me one of those floats when you have them ready," I yelled at him, backstroking the length of the pool. "And don't forget to turn on the pool lights."

We floated on our rafts under the glow of the full moon. The tree frogs croaked and the crickets chirped, competing every now and then with the putt-putt of an outboard motor as it made it's way past our property. Too much time had passed since I'd spent such an evening at the river. It was as lovely as it was bittersweet.

"Is it just me or is it impossible to be here and not think of Yabba?"

Ben rolled over onto his stomach, but when his float started to sink, he flipped back over again. "It would be easier for us to deal with her death if we lived down here all the time, but since we don't face the things that remind us of her on a daily basis, it'll take us longer to sort through our grief."

"It seems like all I've done this summer is think about her, but it's ten times worse being here now. Her death is so fresh, like it happened yesterday instead of four months ago."

"It sucks, doesn't it?" Ben climbed out of the pool. "I'll be back in a minute."

He grabbed a couple of towels out of the pool house, then tossed one on a nearby lounge chair for me and wrapped the other one around his waist. He snuck around the front of the house and down the hill toward the tackle room, returning a minute later with an armload of beers.

"Well, aren't you the boss?" I said, paddling over to the side of the pool nearest him.

He popped the top off two beers and handed one to me. "Cheers," he said, holding his bottle out to mine.

I tapped his bottle once and then again. "To new beginnings."

Ben set his bottle down on the edge of the pool and cannon-balled into the water. He swam back over to the side next to me. "George has every right to be pissed off at those girls for what they did to Yabba, but at least George had the sense to hit a tree instead of one of them. I have no excuse for what I did to you, Kitty, only that I let my anger get the best of me because of the drugs. I reached for whatever I could find to make me feel better, to help me forget. I wanted to be numb, to exist on planet oblivion. Alcohol was effective for a while, but then I needed something more, something stronger. And it snowballed from there."

"I understand, Ben, and I admire how hard you've worked to make amends and get your life back on-track."

He hung his head. "If you want to know the truth, I'm scared to death of what's going to happen when I go back to school."

"What do you mean?" I asked, bracing myself. In order for Ben and me to finally put everything behind us and start fresh, we needed to talk about Emma. Only I wasn't ready for it yet. Our new bond was way too fragile.

"I'm scared to death of what's going to happen when I leave Blessy."

"Your self-appointed sponsor?" I smiled, thinking about what a strong presence Blessy had been in our lives. "Where did she take you that day, the day after Lizzie's party?"

"She didn't tell you?" When I shook my head, he shrugged. "It's hard for her to talk about. She probably just assumed I would tell you."

"Okay, so now I'm really curious. What gives?"

"She took me to the James River Home for the Disabled to visit her daughter."

"Her daughter? What happened to Natasha?" I'd met Blessy's daughter several times over the years. She was only a few years older than me, in her midtwenties, with an adorable little girl of her own, Asia. As far as I knew Nat was healthy and working as a court reporter in the Richmond court systems.

"Not Nat. Her other daughter—"

"Wait a minute, what? Blessy has another daughter?"

He nodded.

"What's wrong with her that she has to live at this home?"

"If you'd zip your lips I'll tell you." Ben took a deep breath and exhaled it slowly. "Blessy has another daughter named Alice, who's about thirty years old. She has a big head and mangled legs and the most amazing positive attitude." Ben took a long drink from his beer and set the bottle back down. "You know how we've always suspected that there was more to Blessy's relationship with Dock and MayMay than we thought?"

I nodded.

"Well, that's because there is. Blessy grew up in a tiny little shack down the street from Dock's office. Even after she was married, she lived there with her parents, her four older brothers and sisters, and all their children, her nieces and nephews. Dock found Blessy on the front porch of his office during a thunderstorm late one July afternoon. She was nine months pregnant and going into labor, but she was also strung out on drugs."

My breath caught in my throat. "Blessy? No way."

"Yep. And she had never even been to a doctor before."

"Nuh-uh."

"It's hard to believe," Ben said, shaking his head. "Anyway, baby Alice was in such bad shape when she was born, Dock air ambulanced her to Richmond. In order for the baby to get the medical support she needed from the state, Dock had to report Blessy to child welfare services. About a week later, Blessy came to see Dock and begged him to help her. He gave her a job and a place to live, away from her abusive husband, but most importantly, he made sure she got clean. When she was strong enough, she asked Dock to help her move to Richmond where she could be close to Alice."

"And that's when Dad promised he'd give her a job and look out for her."

Ben nodded. "And she gets to see her daughter nearly every day. You wouldn't believe how much I've learned from Alice and all the other children at the home."

"How so?" I asked. It'd been a long time since I'd seen this empathetic side of my brother. If only he could find a girl who brought out that sensitive, caring side of him.

"I've been back to the home five times now, once a week since the Fourth of July. The kids always run up to me and hug me. They love it when I read to them or throw the ball with them or work a puzzle with them. I have to make myself go sometimes, because it's hard. It breaks my heart to watch them struggle with their various impairments."

I reached over and mussed his hair. "You should be proud of yourself, Ben. It takes a special kind of person to be around such challenged children."

He cocked an eyebrow at me. "You do it."

"True, but the kids I meet have broken bones that will heal or illnesses that can be treated. Mom wouldn't volunteer her time like that. Can you see her playing checkers with a mentally challenged child? Seriously, Ben, you've given those children a special gift."

"Maybe. But they've given me so much more. They've helped me stay clean."

His eyes welled with tears and I gave him a moment to compose himself.

"We can wait until another time if you're not up to it, but I have some tough questions for you. That is . . . if you don't mind me asking."

He shrugged. "You have every right to ask."

"I've been wondering . . . is it safe for you to be drinking?"

"Truthfully? No. But I'm trying to limit myself. And I've sworn off hard liquor completely. That shit makes me a mean drunk."

"If your behavior at Thanksgiving is any indication, I agree." I climbed out of the pool, wrapped myself in a towel, and sat back down on the edge, dangling my feet in the water. "Okay, so let me ask you this. The next time you're feeling down about something, are you gonna be able to handle it without turning to drugs?"

"There are no guarantees, Kitty, but I feel more in control than I have in a long time. I'm focused, not just on finishing my business degree but on applying to culinary school as well." He'd been keeping that little tidbit of information to himself, waiting for just the right time to surprise me. He pointed at me, laughing. "Gotya!"

I kicked my feet in the water and moved my upper body in a victory dance. "Uh-huh. Oh, ye-ah. My brother's gonna be a chef."

We broke into a fit of laughter like we hadn't experienced together since Emma entered our lives. I ran over to the pool house and turned on the stereo to The Highway station on Sirius radio. I dropped my towel and slid back into the pool. "Remember what Dock used to say? 'Reach for the stars and strive to be great, because you only get one chance in life to fulfill your dreams.'"

Ben nodded. "I can hear him now. 'Missed opportunities become the might-have-beens that will plague you for the rest of your life.'"

We finished our beers and opened another, talking more about culinary school while I gathered the nerve to ask him the one question I needed an answer for.

"At the risk of spoiling the mood . . ." I took a deep breath and held it in for a long minute. "Before I begin my second year as her roommate, I need to know what's going on with you and Emma."

"Nada," he said, shaking his head. "I haven't spoken to her in six weeks."

"Whew-wee, that's a relief." I ran the back of my hand across my forehead, wiping fake sweat from my brow.

"Look. I understand if you don't believe this—and if you don't I'll keep trying until you do—but what happened on the Fourth of July scared the shit out of me, enough for me to make some changes in my life. I'm clean and I plan to stay that way, Emma or no Emma."

As much as I *wanted* to believe him, an uneasy feeling in my gut told me things were far from over between the two of them. I had no idea what any of it meant for me as her roommate, but I knew I needed to prepare myself for another turbulent year.

***

The next day, while Ben and Dad were out fishing, I made my way down to our small section of beach, wanting nothing more than to dig my toes in the sand and finish the last remaining chapters of *Cutting for Stone.* When my mother came down about an hour later, I knew my quiet time was about to be interrupted, but she surprised me. Instead of making her customary grand entrance, she set up her chair and settled quietly into her September *Vogue.*

When I reached the end, I closed the book and tilted my head back.

"Isn't it good?" my mother asked, peeking up from her magazine. "I heard Verghese speak a couple of years ago at the Junior League Book and Author Dinner. He's an interesting man."

I nodded. "Both a physician and a successful author. He makes me want to forget about nursing school and become a doctor."

She put her magazine in her bag and rummaged around for her sunscreen. "Speaking of nursing school, you'll be getting into the meat of your degree this fall, won't you?"

I shrugged. "For the most part—although I still have a few general ed requirements left."

"How *are* things for you at UVA, Katherine?" she asked in a genuine tone. "With the sorority and nursing school?"

I shifted in my beach chair and watched as she rubbed sunscreen on her face. The skin around her mouth and on her forehead was smooth, so smooth I wondered if she'd snuck off to a specialized clinic in Switzerland for some state-of-the art treatment while she was abroad.

A part of me didn't think she had the right to ask me about my life after the way she'd manipulated me into going to UVA, but I saw in her eyes a warmth I hadn't seen in a long time. And I was intrigued.

"Things are okay, I guess. Pledging Tri Beta was definitely the right decision for me. Nursing school is challenging, but I'm pretty sure my studies will mean more to me after having spent the summer working in the ER."

"Are you still planning to reapply to UNC?" she asked.

"I'm still thinking about it. Applications aren't due until January, so I still have plenty of time to decide."

"You know your father would be more than happy to use his connections." She reached over and squeezed my hand. "And this time, I promise not to interfere."

I smiled at my mom. "I appreciate the offer, but if I decide to reapply and I get accepted, I want it to happen on my own merit."

She cupped my chin in her hand. "I'm very proud of you, you know. I'll be the first to admit I misunderstood you. I underestimated your abilities, Katherine. You're a lovely, mature young woman and you will make a fine nurse. Or doctor, if you are so inclined." She pulled her hand away. "Now tell me about Emma. It seems as though I might have misjudged her as well."

I rolled my eyes. "Everyone misjudges her, Mom. It's all in the way she operates."

"How so?"

I sat up straighter in my chair. "Okay . . . well, here's a hypothetical situation to use as an example. It would be so like Emma to walk out on this beach right now and invite us to do something really fun and cool, and we'd go along with her because we wouldn't be able to resist her charm and coercion. Then, while we're doing this really awesome thing, she'd flatter us into thinking we're the only people on the planet, her best friends. And before we knew what had happened, we'd be tangled back up in her web."

Mom put her manicured hand over her mouth as she laughed. "Looks like you've got her number."

"Finally. But I fell under her spell many times before I was able to recognize the real Emma."

"And you're rooming with her again?"

"Yep. I'm stuck with her." I dug a shell out of the sand and hurled it into the water. "There's something I never told you about Emma." As gently as I could, I explained how Emma had lied to the sorority during rush and how her father was serving time for distributing heroin.

She scrunched her brow together. "That's unspeakable. So her father was never an English professor?"

"Nope. He was a janitor and his cleaning closet was his office."

Mom clenched her jaw, her eyes full of anger. "Do you think word got out about this? You know, throughout the Chi Delta house?"

"Not if Honey Mabry had anything to do with it. She is all about keeping this a secret to avoid tarnishing the reputation of the sorority."

"Honey Mabry knows about this?"

I thought back to my first night on campus when Emma and I met Honey in the women's bathroom at the KO house. "Look, Mom, Honey is not an innocent party in all this. She shunned Emma from the very beginning. She used her sources to dig around until she found something she could use against her."

My mother turned her head away from me and used the edge of her towel to blot away the tears. I reached over and gave her arm a squeezed. For the next few minutes, as she pulled herself together, we watched a father tow his young son and daughter tubing behind their boat. Their mother was riding in the passenger seat, holding on tight to her straw hat, while the father drove around in circles, doing donuts. Neither of us said as much, but we were both reminded of *our* family, once upon a time.

"I've been wrong about so many things. You must think I'm a fool," she said, sniffling.

"In some ways, Mom, I'm as much to blame as anyone. I should've told you right after rush about Emma. Even before, when I knew she was using you to get sorority recommendation letters."

"Only because you knew I wouldn't listen to you."

"Still, that's no excuse."

Mom pulled a tissue from her bag and blew her nose. "Since I've screwed everything else up in such a big way, I'm looking to you for guidance. We have to do something to help Ben get away from Emma. Maybe we can stage an intervention or something, with you and me and Daddy, maybe Spotty and Reed."

"It won't work. We've already tried."

Mom and I caught sight of Dad and Ben coming toward us in the boat. When Ben held up a string of flounder, we gave him a thumb's-up and cheered.

I turned back to my mother. "Anyway, Ben says it's over between them. He realizes how controlling and manipulative Emma is. He was obsessed with her, not in love with her."

"Do you think it would help if I had a talk with him?"

"You can try, but Ben is not a three-year-old boy. You can't smack his hand and tell him to stay away from Emma because he might get burned. She's a college kid in heat, not a hot burner on the stove."

I watched the tension drain from her body. "So we do nothing?"

I nodded. "And let him figure this out himself. He seems to have grown up a lot this summer. All we can do is hope he stays away from Emma when we go back to school. But if he starts seeing her again, we will stay close to him, keep our finger on his pulse."

"In other words, we sit and wait and hope disaster doesn't strike?"

I shrugged. "Welcome to my world."

NINETEEN

I loved the idea of Archer and Spotty as a couple, Ben's best friend and mine, two compassionate people who were always taking care of others—but he'd been monopolizing her time all summer. Archer and I agreed to a girls' night out, one last hurrah before we committed ourselves to round-the-clock studying. Unfortunately, the only time we were both available was two days before classes started at UVA. I sent Ben to Charlottesville ahead of me, and because second-year students are allowed to keep their cars on campus, I drove up the next day on my own.

By the time I got there, Ben and Emma were already back together.

I must admit, I was happy to see them. It was a hundred and ten degrees outside, I had a hangover, and the two of them were eager to help me unload my car. Even so, it brought back unpleasant memories of move-in day a year ago. I couldn't help but wonder if the situation were an omen of another bad year to come.

Emma and I had been assigned to an apartment-style suite we were to share with Phoebe and Carla in Bice House, a building designated for sophomores and juniors with all the modern conveniences the dorms for first-year students lacked. Our apartment had two bedrooms, two baths, a kitchenette, and a large living area. Like our old dorm, the bedrooms were small with cinderblock walls and a tiled floor, but Bice offered a fitness center and game room on the first floor, and playing fields and tennis courts on the grounds behind the building. Not to mention the most important feature of all—air conditioning.

It wasn't until Emma went to the bathroom that I had an op-portunity to be alone with Ben. "What in the hell are you doing with her? Are you insane?" I whispered.

"Relax, Kitty. I'm a changed man. I can handle it."

"No man can handle that," I said, gesturing toward the bath-room door. I started to walk away from him, but turned back around. "At least promise me you'll stay in touch this time."

"Deal," he said, holding his hand out to shake on it. "And to prove I mean it, if you want, we can go back to having brunch on Sundays."

I took his hand in mine and gave it a firm squeeze. "Fine, but I'm warning you, I have a bad feeling about this."

During the frequent trips to my car, Emma told me all about her summer in Texas. Apparently, her seven-and nine-year old-cousins, Sally and Lena, were total brats. But she'd earned a fortune driving them around to their friends' houses and to their country club for swim-team practice and tennis lessons. She'd even gone on a weeklong vacation with them to Hawaii and stayed at the Ritz Carlton on Maui.

Emma slammed the hatchback shut on my VW bug and waved to Ben as he drove off in my car, moving it from the unloading zone to a permanent parking space. "Life is sweet for my aunt and her family. Unlike my mother, she had the good sense to marry a smart man, a man who's made a fortune from drilling for oil in the Gulf. See that white Lexus over there?" She pointed to a small SUV, the kind I always thought looked like an egg on wheels. "My aunt gave it to me."

I glanced at the car and then did a double take. "Wait a min-ute. She *gave* it to you?"

"Yep. She decided to get a sedan, and knowing my parents can't afford to buy me a car, she gave me her Lexus. Can you believe that?"

I shielded my eyes from the sun so I could see the SUV. "It looks brand-new."

"It's not. It's five years old." Emma picked up two of my duffle bags and headed for our building. I grabbed the last of my things and followed her.

"What about insurance?" I asked, catching up with her. "It must cost a fortune on a car like that."

"Uncle Hollis is paying for it," Emma said, holding the door open for me.

An image of Emma providing sexual favors for Uncle Hollis popped into my mind. If Emma's aunt was her mother's *younger* sister, then Hollis could still be in his early forties, which meant he might be hot. But if the sister was older, he was probably pushing fifty or maybe even fifty-five like my parents. Ancient. Gross. Either way, it was not quite incest because they weren't biologically related. But still.

"Seriously?" I asked as I started up the stairs. "He's paying for your insurance?"

"Yep, but only if I promised to go back to Houston next summer to nanny for the girls. I mean, twist my arm. They're taking Sally and Lena to Australia and they asked me to go with them."

"Sounds like a sweet deal." I dumped my bags on my bed. "But back to the car thing. You know you've got to have it serviced, get the oil changed and all, and with gas prices as high as they are—"

"I can afford it, if that's what you're getting at. Hollis had the sixty-thousand-mile service done on the car before I left Texas, and I have plenty of money in the bank to pay for gas, even the premium kind I'm supposed to burn."

Plenty of money in the bank? Bingo. Sounded to me like someone had found herself a genie. All Emma had to do was rub her uncle's member and, magically, he granted her wishes. *But wait a minute. Where did Ben fit in the picture?*

Emma grabbed my hand and dragged me across the room to her closet. "Look at these clothes." She opened the door and ran her hand along a row of what appeared, even to my untrained eye, to be haute couture dresses.

"Did you buy all these?" I pulled out a tailored halter dress that crisscrossed in the back. It was made of fine white linen with beautiful lines, a dress that was way too sophisticated for a college student.

"No, silly." She took the dress from me, hung it back in the closet, and closed the door. "My aunt is ADD. She gets tired of everything after wearing it only once. I'm not too proud to accept hand-me-downs like those. Would you be?"

"I guess not," I said, turning my attention to my unpacking.

I once saw a movie where some poor guy was stuck in a nightmare—every day was Groundhog Day for him. With Ben and Emma back together, it appeared as though my second year at UVA would be a repeat of my first. That is, until the next day when I entered my anatomy lab to find Thompson McCray as the assistant.

"You've been assigned to the table over here," he said, greeting me at the door and guiding me to a setup across the room. "I saw your name on the list this morning, and I rearranged things so you'd be in my group. I hope you don't mind."

Mind? I wanted to dive into his deep-blue eyes and never come up for air. "How's your mother?" I asked instead.

True to his word, because he understood I needed time to recover from my Fourth of July ordeal, Thompson had waited at least a week before contacting me again. We'd limited our communications to texts, mostly guarded messages about nothing important. We were working out our plans for a date when he was called to Atlanta to be with his mother, who'd been diagnosed with breast cancer.

"On the mend. Or so it seems." He held both hands up for me to see his crossed fingers. "They were able to do a lumpectomy, followed by rounds of chemo and radiation. All the early reports are promising."

"I'm so glad, Thompson. When I didn't hear from you . . ."

"I meant to call," he said, lowering his voice when several students entered the lab. "I just got so wrapped up in her treatment."

"It must have been so hard for your family."

He nodded. "A lot of good came out of it, though. My sisters and I are closer because of all the time we spent together, either while Mom was in the hospital or during her daylong sessions at the infusion center." Thompson had two older sisters, one twenty-eight and the other thirty, both of them married and living in Atlanta. "I learned so much about cancer and chemotherapy and the patient side of doctoring."

"I can think of easier ways to gain experience, Dr. McCray."

A smile crept across his face, causing his dimple to appear and his eyes to twinkle. For the rest of the lab, I was acutely aware of his presence, even when he was down at the other end of the table. Anxious to see him again, I showed up ten minutes early for the next lab, two days later, on Wednesday.

I was making adjustments to my microscope when Thompson snuck up behind me and set two concert tickets down on the counter. "Care to analyze these under your scope?"

I glanced down at the fine writing on the tickets. "Dave Matthews?" I turned around to face him. "Are you kidding me?"

"Look at the date before you say yes." He pointed to the logistical information on the ticket. "The concert is on Labor Day Monday. You may already have plans to go out of town for the holiday weekend."

I shook my head. "Today is only the third day of classes and I already have a ton of work. I'm not going anywhere this weekend but the library—and the Dave Matthews concert, of course. I can totally take time out for him."

"Well then, I hope you'll also consider making time for dinner Friday night, because there's no way I can wait five whole days to see you again."

Thompson surprised me by preparing a picnic dinner, which we spread out on an old quilt on the lawn. It had been a hot, humid day, but once the sun dropped below the mountains, a gentle breeze stirred and caused the temperature to immediately drop ten degrees. We drank Chardonnay from red plastic Solo cups and nibbled on cold pasta and fried chicken. I felt the same connection with Thompson that I'd experienced at Lizzie's party, a bond deepened all the more by our passion for medicine.

We arranged our study sessions in the library so that we still had time for several weekend outings, which included the football game Saturday night and a long bike ride on Sunday morning—in addition to the Dave Matthews concert on Monday night. During the weeks that followed, Thompson and I spent as much time together as we could possibly manage. He'd already completed his undergraduate degree, and his fraternity days were in the past. He was sorely focused on his studies, and in no way resented the demands the sorority placed on my time. He was neither controlling nor clingy but patient and supportive of my other commitments. His gentle side would guarantee him success as a doctor; to be the recipient of such kindness touched me at my core. He grew to know me better than I knew myself. When I was grumpy, he insisted I go back to my dorm and get some sleep. He prepared healthy snacks of grapes and raisins and nuts when I got the hunger shakes, and he suggested we go down to the Corner for ice cream or watch a club football game when I grew tired of studying and needed a diversion. And just as his intuition was spot-on about my other needs, he sensed when I was ready to take our relationship to the next level.

Because I was committed to Thompson emotionally, the physical part came naturally. Not that I'd been consciously saving my virginity for marriage, I'd just never met anyone I wanted to have sex with. Unlike the girls I knew who hooked up with random guys for one-night stands, sex was personal to me. I needed someone who respected me enough to show me the way.

Thompson rented a one-bedroom garage apartment, two blocks from campus, from a chemistry professor, Dirk Campbell. Or Dirktor Doolittle as Thompson liked to call him. He wasn't married, but he had at least a dozen different types of animals— two miniature schnauzers, a Siamese cat, a turtle, a ferret, several different kinds of lizards, three hamsters, a snake, and an aquarium full of colorful saltwater fish. When Doolittle modernized his cottage several years ago, he'd added a kidney-shaped pool, complete with tropical plants, an outdoor bar, and a hot tub. In exchange for the use of his pool, Thompson minded the farm while Doolittle was gone, which he was most weekends to visit his lover up in DC.

On an unseasonably warm Friday afternoon in late September, Thompson sent me a text: *Bring your bikini and meet me at the oasis in half an hour.* When I arrived forty-five minutes later, around six thirty, I found Thompson floating on a raft with a Styrofoam cooler bobbing up and down beside him. He reached inside the cooler and produced a bottle of champagne, the good kind with the orange label my parents bought every year to toast their anniversary. The big grin on Thompson's face and the twinkle in his eyes told me we would wait no longer.

Dangling our feet in the water, we sipped champagne and ate slices of cheese with french bread until the sun was gone and the lights had come on in the pool. The tropical foliage provided protection from the rest of the world. We were alone on our island. Leaning down to kiss my neck, Thompson untied my bikini top and tossed it into the pool. When I slipped into the water away from him, he stepped out of his swimsuit and came in after me. I swam breaststroke laps around the pool until he caught me. As he brought me to him and kissed me hard I could feel his muscles firm against my body. The only thing separating me from his arousal was the thin fabric of my bikini bottoms. He yanked my bottoms off, lifted me out of the pool, and made love to me on the hard slate surface of the deck. The burning pain gave way to bliss as we moved together as one. Thompson made love to me with tender passion; during those moments, nothing mattered to me more than the man I loved. When it was over, we lay spent, side by side on the deck, holding hands while we stared at the stars.

"Are you okay?" Thompson asked, running his hand across my belly.

"Hmm-mm. Better than okay."

We slid back into the water and swam around for a while. Feeling the silkiness of the water against my naked body was delicious and erotic. The second time we had sex was even better. There was no pain, only the thrilling sensations as Thompson brought my body to life. He was my first, but whether or not he would be my only, I understood he would always be the best. The special thing about having sex with a medical student, at least my medical student—he appreciated the anatomy of a woman.

Sex with Thompson was hot. I felt like the molten lava erupting from a volcano when his hands were on my naked body but what I loved about it the most were the talks we shared afterward. Once our bodies came together as one, so did our minds. We talked about our past, the present, and our hopes for the future. We shared our innermost thoughts about everything. Except Ben. Out of respect for me, Thompson never mentioned Ben's behavior at the Rolands' Fourth of July party or the bruises he saw on my throat the following day. While I knew Thompson was capable of giving Ben a second chance, I also understood there would be no third.

Adding Emma to the mix only complicated the situation.

She and I were getting along as well as could be expected considering the friction between us. And it helped that I hardly ever saw her. I was spending as much time with Thompson as she was with Ben. We both slept in our room during the week, but our class schedules were so different that we rarely came or went at the same time. Our conversations, typically limited to five minutes, addressed only whose turn it was to clean the bathroom or stock up on cereal and juice for our kitchenette. I wasn't any happier about her relationship with my brother than I'd ever been—and I certainly didn't attribute it to Emma's involvement in his life—but Ben seemed steadier and more focused than he'd been in several years.

On the second Sunday in October, over pizza at the College Inn during our weekly lunch together, Ben announced it was time for me to introduce him to Thompson. When I reminded him they'd already met on the Fourth of July and that he had a lot of work to do to change Thompson's opinion of him, Ben promised to make nice. We agreed it would be best for the three of us to have dinner together alone, someplace off campus where we could talk without interruption. I set the date for the Thursday night of the following week, but when Archer decided to come in early for the Halloween weekend, my plans for a quiet dinner with my boyfriend and my brother turned into burgers and beer for a crowd at Brewster's on the Corner. Naturally, she included Spotty, who invited Reed, who texted at the last minute that he was bringing a date.

"I'm sorry our plans have gotten so out of control," I said to Thompson when I found him waiting for me on the steps leading up to his apartment. "I wouldn't blame you if you didn't want to go."

"In that case, text them now and tell them we can't make it." He began dragging me up the steps.

"Wait a minute." I snatched my arm away. "I said I don't *blame* you for not wanting to go. That doesn't mean you don't *have* to go. Are you chickening out on me?"

"Chicken, hell. If you're going to blame someone, blame yourself." He drew me in and nuzzled my neck. "You should never have worn those black boots with those tight jeans."

"Come on, you naughty boy." I grabbed his hand and led him back down the stairs. "We need to go if we wanna get a good table."

For our sacrifice, Brewster's gave us their biggest table by the window. With Halloween less than a week away, pumpkins glowed on the bar, black plastic spiders sprang from the ceiling, and ghosts illuminated the corners—all contributing to the restaurant's festive atmosphere. Every third person came dressed for the occasion with the most popular costumes of the year representing vampires and Mario Bros and Lady Gaga.

Archer and Spotty arrived twenty minutes later with Reed and his date, Maddie Maloney, the girl I once thought was so perfect for Ben. We settled in with a round of beers and an appetizer sampler. No one dared to talk about it, but I could tell by the sneaked peeks at their watches and quick glances toward the door that everyone was aware when Ben was almost an hour late.

"Who asked her to come?" Archer said, bringing the conversation at the table to a halt.

We watched Ben force his way through the crowd with Emma following on his heels, like an annoying fly. She tugged on his jacket hood and grabbed at his arm until she finally got his attention. He leaned down and she whispered in his ear, but whatever she said seemed to irritate him. He jerked his arm away from her and continued on toward our table. In one fluid motion, Emma slipped out of her coat and lowered herself to the empty seat next to Thompson, making a big show of crossing her long bare legs. She followed the introductions around the table until we reached Maddie. Her eyes narrowed, and her lips tightened, and her face drained of color. She turned her back on Ben and focused her attention on Thompson, cranking up the volume on her charm to a near-deafening level.

"If she gets any closer to your boyfriend, she'll be in his lap," Archer whispered in my ear.

Spotty leaned across Archer toward me. "Leave it to that bitch to show up uninvited. Ben specifically told me this afternoon that she wasn't coming."

"It's *my* bad," I mumbled. "When our group of three turned into a party of seven, I should have asked her to come. Prepare for battle, because if she thinks we excluded her on purpose, she'll make us all pay."

Sitting back in my chair, I pretended to talk to Archer and Spotty while I eavesdropped on Emma, who was describing in great detail to Thompson her costume for the Monster Bash on Saturday night. She was planning to dress like an angel in all white—bodysuit, see-through negligee, and go-go boots—for the *Hell on Earth* theme. The more she talked, the more it became apparent by her slurred speech that she'd already had a lot to drink. Thompson was making every effort to include Ben in the conversation, but my brother was too busy staring across the table at Maddie Maloney to notice.

"Guess what, Kitty?" Emma leaned further than was necessary across Thompson to get my attention. "I'm spending Thanksgiving with your family at the river. Isn't that cool?"

I glanced over at my brother in time to see the muscles tighten in his face. I could tell he was as happy as I was about the idea of spending Thanksgiving with Emma.

"It's so cute that your friends call you Kitty," Thompson said, mussing my hair.

I rolled my eyes and reached in my purse for my phone. I sent a quick text message to my mother: *Book rooms at homstead asap unless u want to feed emma turkey for thnxsgiving.*

During the months since I'd returned to school, my relationship with my mother had improved significantly. The silent communication of texting and emailing had given us not only the opportunity to say the things we didn't know how to say to one another in person but also the chance to think about our responses before we replied.

She must've been sitting by her phone because she texted me back within a couple of minutes: *Done.*

I called Ben's name three times before I got his attention away from Maddie Maloney. "Didn't Mom tell you about Thanksgiving?"

"What do you mean?" he asked, casting a nervous glance at Emma. "I assumed we were going to the river."

"Nope. Mom and Dad booked rooms for us at The Homestead. You know how obsessed they've been about family time lately."

His face brightened, but he tried not to smile. "That's cool," he said, ignoring his girlfriend's gaze. "I haven't been to The Homestead since we went for my twelfth birthday."

Emma shifted in her seat to face Ben. "What does that mean for me?"

Ben shrugged. "Didn't you say you needed to go home to see your mother? Now the decision has been made for you."

"I was talking about going home over Christmas break, not Thanksgiving, you bastard," Emma said, pushing back from the table. She kicked her chair out of the way and stumbled toward the door.

Somewhat reluctantly, Ben stood up and followed. Our window offered us front-row viewing for the scene that unfolded on the sidewalk outside. Ben caught up with Emma and grabbed her arm. She swung around and slapped him hard across the cheek. The glass was thick and her voice was muffled but we could still hear her scream—"That bitch of a sister of yours is such a fucking

skank!"—for the benefit of everyone gathered around on the street
and at our table.

A student, dressed in a hippie costume with a tie-dyed band
around his head and a peace sign on his neck, stepped between Ben
and Emma and tried to break them apart.

"Hey, dude, mind your own fucking business!" Ben got in the
man's face, towering over him until he ran away.

With the hippie out of the way, Emma attacked Ben, pounding his chest with her fists and clawing at his face with her nails.
My brother finally managed to wrap his arms around her body and
immobilize her until she calmed down. Then he turned his back
on the gaping crowd and ushered Emma in the opposite direction.

Thirty seconds later Ben appeared at our table, alone, to gather
their coats. "I'm sorry things had to end like this, man," he said to
Thompson, shaking hands with him before turning his back on
everyone else.

Reed, the great avoider of conflict, signaled to his date that it
was time for them to leave. "Sorry to cut out on y'all like this," he
said, tossing a twenty-dollar bill on the table, "but Maddie made
plans with some of her sorority sisters for dinner."

With only the four of us left at the table, we looked around at
one another, unsure how to proceed. "I don't know about y'all, but
I'm ready to order some dinner," Thompson said, rubbing his belly.
"And I'm pretty sure that large crowd waiting at the bar over there
would appreciate it if we moved to a smaller table."

The hostess showed us to a booth in a cozy corner at the back
of the restaurant. "I'm sorry, Thompson," I said when we were settled. "I should have told you about her sooner."

Archer dropped her jaw. "What the heck, Kitty? You mean to
tell me you haven't told Thompson about Emma? After everything
she put you through last year?"

"And there's a reason for that, Arch, if you'll let me explain.
Remember Lizzie's party and what a mess Ben was that night?" Archer nodded. "Well, that was Thompson's first impression of him."
I turned to Thompson. "I wanted you to have a chance to get to
know the real Ben"—I bit my lip to hold back my tears—"before

I introduced you to his girl-thing. It's embarrassing that a guy like my brother, who has so much going for him, would fall for someone like her."

Spotty slapped Thompson on the back. "You'll like Ben once you get to know him. I promise. He's a good guy. He's just been in a really bad place for a really long time. I must say, though, I was encouraged by his behavior tonight."

Archer raised an eyebrow at Spotty. "How can you say that after what we just witnessed?"

"Because I know Ben," Spotty said. "And I was watching him tonight. Unlike his girlfriend, it didn't appear like he'd been drinking before he arrived, and he didn't have much while he was here."

"I noticed that too," I mumbled.

Spotty looked pointedly at me. "We are not in the same place we were in last year. Ben was mad as hell at Emma tonight, and jealous that Reed was out with Maddie, but he was not drunk."

"By the way, what's up with Ben and Maddie?" Thompson asked. "Did they used to be together?"

"Yep, and guess who broke them up?" Archer asked. "Emma."

Thompson rubbed his eyes with his balled fist. "I'm no psych major, but Emma is clearly not firing on all cylinders."

Spotty sat back in his chair and guzzled half of his beer. "It makes me crazy to think about what she's put poor Ben through," he said. And for the next half hour, we relived the past twelve months for Thompson, stopping only long enough to order dinner. We told him about the disaster with the sorority and the drugs and the spring break trip to Florida. By the time our food came, we'd convinced Thompson that Emma was suffering from some sort of mental disorder.

"I can tell how much the three of you care about Ben," Thompson said, studying each of our faces in turn. "If I had to render an unqualified diagnosis, I'd say that Ben is addicted and Emma is his drug. Obsessive-compulsive disorder meets psychopath. A dangerous, if not a deadly, combination."

"Seriously, Thompson?" Archer asked with her mouth full of food. "A psychopath?"

Thompson nodded. "The superficial charm, promiscuous sexual behavior, and pathological lying—it's textbook Psych 101."

At a sudden loss for appetite, I set my half-eaten hamburger down on my plate. "And just what the hell are we supposed to do about that?"

"Get some professional help, for starters." Thompson reached for my hand. "In the meantime, you need to keep them apart as much as you can."

"That's exactly what Kitty and I have been trying to do," Spotty explained to Thompson.

"Then keep it up," Thompson said. "Get creative like Katherine did earlier when she texted her mother under the table to book those rooms for Thanksgiving."

Archer laughed, spitting beer all over the place. "You sneaky little bitch."

"It worked, didn't it?" I handed her a napkin and turned my attention back to Thompson. "Do you really think Emma is dangerous?"

Thompson put his arm around my shoulders and pulled me close. "Let's just say I'd feel a lot better about the situation if you didn't have to sleep in the same room with her."

TWENTY

No doubt my roommate was a twisted sort, untrustworthy and egotistical, but labeling her a psychopath seemed extreme. Thompson's diagnosis prompted me to do some additional online research. It creeped me out to discover how much she fit the mold—a manipulator with complete lack of empathy toward others and total absence of remorse for one's actions.

There were few nights over the course of the next seven weeks that I didn't sleep with one eye open. The tension between Emma and me had reached an all-time high. She'd crossed a line with the things she'd screamed about me outside of Brewster's. The battle had escalated with the stakes now higher than ever.

When it became increasingly more difficult for me to focus and exams were on the horizon, I turned once again to my campus psychiatrist friend. This time Elise Withers was of little comfort. She advised me to keep my valuables locked away and to be careful of what I said when Emma was in the room. Being forced to live with someone I didn't trust with my favorite T-shirt, let alone my life, wore on my nerves in a huge way. I was grateful for the short Thanksgiving break, and counting the hours until Christmas. Although I knew Emma's influence had the power to reach across a thousand miles, I was relieved when she announced she was traveling to Texas to spend the break with her aunt and uncle.

We'd had such a good time at The Homestead over Thanksgiving, our parents surprised Ben and me with a trip to New York to see the Rockettes in the days leading up to Christmas. We appreciated their attempts to grant us more independence and treat us with more respect, and although we knew they were only alleviating their guilt over their acceptance of an invitation to the mountains with friends, we did not turn them down when they insisted we take a group to the river for New Year's.

The only bachelor amongst three other couples, Ben appointed himself chef and went about planning a feast fit for visiting royalty. When we became bored with the party scene in Richmond, Ben and I headed for the river early, on the thirtieth, to shop for food and freshen up the house.

We unpacked the car and moved all the wicker furniture out of the living room and back onto the porch. Then, with a mushroom pizza and a six-pack of Natty Light between us, we settled into the leather club chairs in front of the fire to make out our grocery list. My buzz gained me the confidence I needed to ask my brother how he felt about our guests sharing rooms with their dates.

He raised an eyebrow at me. "What you really want is my blessing to shack up with your boyfriend."

I shrugged. "Pretty much so, yes. But I'm not the only one worried about how you might feel. Archer also wanted me to talk to you."

"I'm not worried about Archer and Spotty. She is in his very capable hands. You and Thompson are a different story. Tell me the truth. Does he treat you well?"

"He's a good guy, Ben, but you'd already know that for yourself if you hadn't blown your chance to get to know him."

Ben looked away from me, hiding his face in shame. "Do you think Thompson will give me a chance to redeem myself?"

"Yes, because that's the kind of guy he is. But this time don't screw it up. Thank God, Emma isn't around to sabotage our weekend," I added under my breath.

Ben got up to stoke the fire. "I won't screw it up. I promise. Anyway, all that unpleasantness with Emma is gone from my life." He placed the poker back in the rack and turned around. "She and I broke up," he said, laughing at my expression, my mouth hanging open like a baby drooling on its bib. "Gee, Kitty, don't look so surprised. I'm sure deep down you're thrilled."

I uncrossed my legs and sat up straighter in my chair. "Thrilled doesn't begin to touch it. I'm euphoric and ecstatic and exhilarated all at once. Damn, Ben, that's the best news ever." I offered my hand up for a fist bump.

"Let's just hope it's over for good this time."

"Wait a minute. What do you mean?" I jumped up out of my chair to face him. "Either you *are* or you're *not* broken up. Unless the two of you have decided to be friends with benefits, in which case I'm doing a nosedive from delighted to devastated. Don't jerk me around."

"Actually, *I'm* the one who's being jerked around." He reached in the cooler for two more beers, popping the top off of one and handing it to me. "What would you say if I told you Emma is stalking me?"

"I'd say I'm not surprised." I eased myself back down in my chair and patted his seat for him to sit. "Talk to me. What's going on?"

He took a long swill from his beer and sank back into the down cushions of his chair. "It started a few months ago. Probably that night at Brewster's, if I had to pinpoint a date. By the way, I never invited Emma to come with me. I don't even know how she found out about it."

For weeks after that horrible night in October, I'd waited for an apology from Ben. When one never came, I let him slide, but only because I could see how hard he was working to get his life back on-track.

I leaned back in my chair and kicked my feet up on the ottoman. "Well *I* certainly didn't tell her. How *did* she find out about it, if not from you or from me?"

"Cell phone maybe," he said, shrugging. "Either yours or mine. It's not like she didn't have access to both."

Chills traveled my spine. "That's pretty scary."

He nodded. "Seeing Maddie and Reed together that night made me realize how much I'd screwed up my life. Don't get me wrong, I think they're perfect for one another, but I couldn't help but compare her with Emma. Emma in her unattractive state of drunkenness and Maddie so polished and articulate, so put-together."

"You'll find someone like that, Ben." I peeled off part of my label, wadded it up, and flicked it at him. "But you can't move on with your life until you get rid of psycho-bitch, once and for all."

"She's changed so much since I first met her. I know you don't want to hear about it, so this is the only thing I'll say. Emma has gotten so perverted about sex. She likes it rough." Ben's eyes narrowed and zeroed in on my neck. "Regardless of everything that happened last summer, that's not who I am."

"That's all behind us now. You don't need to bring it up again."

He hesitated for a minute before he nodded. "Okay." He flipped open his phone and showed me his missed call log. "Check this out."

I took the phone from him and scrolled down the list. "Damn. She's called you at least eight times since we've been sitting here."

"She sends me twice that number of texts."

"Isn't she supposed to be in Texas?"

"She was in Texas for Christmas, but now she's skiing in Aspen with her aunt and uncle and their kids."

"What're you gonna do if she keeps harassing you like this?"

"I only have one semester left before I get the hell out of UVA. I'll have my business degree and then I can finally apply to culinary school," he said with a mischievous smirk.

"Good for you, Ben." I tapped his bottle when he held it out to me. "I'm really proud of you for chasing your dreams. Where will you go, New York?"

"Yes, if everything works out the way I hope it will. New York is close enough to home, but far enough away from psycho-bitch."

"You know . . . the last time I spoke to George he mentioned he was applying for an internship on Wall Street. Has he said anything to you about it?"

Ben shook his head.

"Maybe you guys could get an apartment together or something." I reached for my cell phone in my purse on the floor next to me. "Let's call him and see if he wants to come over."

Ben got up to put another log on the fire. "I don't know, Kitty. We have a ton of stuff to do tomorrow. Do you really want to deal with a hangover?"

I looked up from my phone. "Who said anything about a hangover? George has only been out of rehab for a few months."

"Apparently that doesn't mean anything to George. Every time I've talked to him recently, it's been late at night and he's been weeping in his whiskey."

"Really? I've spoken to him a few times myself. Sounded to me like he was doing better." I abandoned the idea of calling George and dropped my phone into my purse. "Sucks, doesn't it? The thought of losing a sibling? Which in my case would mean you. Don't let this go to your head or anything, but I'd be crushed."

"Right back at you, little sis." He grinned at me for a minute and then his face turned serious again. "What if George is just using his grief as an excuse to cover up his addiction?"

"Or what if he's using alcohol as a crutch to relieve the pain in his heart? I can't imagine how hard it must be for the Turners during these first holidays without Yabba."

TWENTY-ONE

We were so busy with buying groceries and putting fresh sheets on the beds and stacking firewood on the back porch that we never had time to eat lunch the following day. It was five o'clock before I had a chance to sit down and relax with a bowl of popcorn and a Diet Coke. I had just settled in at the bar in the kitchen to watch Ben create his masterpiece dessert when Thompson arrived at the front door with two bottles of red wine and a ginormous box of fireworks.

"Here, let me help you with that." Ben took the box from Thompson, set it on the floor, and began digging through the fireworks like a dog digging for a bone. "Damn, man. I'm no expert on pyrotechnics, but these are not your average fireworks."

Thompson gave me a quick peck on the cheek. "They are the real deal," he said to Ben. "Straight from South Carolina where the law is lenient about explosives."

"Which would make them illegal in the state of Virginia." I placed my hands on my hips and tapped my foot, pretending to be mad. I wanted nothing more than for my brother and my boyfriend to be friends, and in a stroke of brilliance, Thompson had found just the right spark to light Ben's fuse. Boys will be boys with their toys, and all that junk.

"Doesn't concern me any." Ben smiled up at Thompson. "Does it bother you?"

Thompson shrugged. "We're way out in the country. Who's gonna know?"

The doctor had given Thompson's family the best Christmas present they could've hoped for. His mother's cancer was in remission. I sensed a renewed energy in him, and for the first time in months, the worry lines were gone from his face.

Ben stood and greeted Thompson. "How'd you get these, anyway? Please tell me you didn't drive all the way down to South Carolina yourself."

Thompson shook Ben's outstretched hand. "If I'd known they were gonna be such a big hit, I would've gladly driven to California to get them. But the truth is a friend of mine brought them back from Charleston, where he was visiting his grandmother for the holiday."

I clapped my hands together. "Okay boys, let's put the toys away for now." I opened the door to the front-hall closet and kicked the box inside. "Ben, just a friendly reminder that you have chocolate melting on the stove."

"Oh shit!" he said, making a dash toward the kitchen.

"Do you need any help with that?" Thompson, my brother's new best friend, called after him.

"Sure," Ben yelled from down the hall, "if you know anything about white chocolate mousse."

As it turned out, Thompson knew nothing about baking except how to stick his finger in the bowl for a taste. Nevertheless, the two of them worked together for the next hour like a couple of experienced chefs, beating eggs and whipping cream and straining raspberries. When they were finished, they had the three separate parts that made up dessert—white chocolate mousse in chocolate meringue shells with raspberry coulis.

Loaded down with beer and champagne and Krispy Kreme Doughnuts, the rest of our gang—Spotty and Archer, Maddie and Reed—arrived a little after six in the same car from Richmond. We were all comfortable together without the tension of having Emma around.

Once the groceries were stored away and coolers of beer placed strategically around the house for easy access, we gathered downstairs in the game room. For the next hour, the girls watched the highlights of the upcoming New Year's celebrations on television while the guys—with the exception of Ben who was busy running back and forth between the kitchen and the grill—played pool.

The doorbell rang as *Entertainment Tonight* was ending. I heard the thumping of Ben's feet in the hall above me, and then the sound of George's voice in the foyer.

"George!" I dropped my magazine on the coffee table and rushed up the stairs to greet him. "OMG, I'm so glad to see you." I jumped on him, wrapping my legs around his waist like I was eight years old, begging him not to go home at the end of a really great day. "Please say you'll stay for dinner. Ben's cooking."

"Yeah, dude," Ben said, slapping George on the back. "You can be *my* date. I'm flying solo."

"You? Stud-man? Since when can't you get a date?" George asked, doubling over in fake agony when Ben play-punched him in the gut. Despite his attempt at humor, George's face was pale and his eyes were dull, as though his mind was clouded with turmoil.

"Seriously, though," he said, straightening up, "I just came by for a drink. I have another party later."

At the mention of a drink, the issue of George's visit to rehab crowded the room like an uninvited guest. We glanced around at each other, none of us knowing what to say next.

"Come meet Thompson first." I grabbed George's hand and dragged him downstairs to the game room. He barely had a chance to greet everyone before Spotty was shoving a pool stick at him.

George waved him away. "Chillax, man. I just got here."

"Sorry, dude," Spotty said, "but you're the first real competition we've seen all night."

"What're you talking about, Spotty?" George said. "You of all people should know that Kitty is your real competition. Have you forgotten that she's the champion of the Northern Neck?"

"She won't play with us," Reed said, sounding like a three-year-old whose best friend refused to help him build a sandcastle.

"You've been holding out on me." Thompson wrapped his arms around my waist from behind. "A female pool shark. That kind of turns me on."

Spotty ran his hand down the rack of cues until he came to mine. "Check this out, Thompson—she even has her own Hello Kitty cue."

Thompson and I reached for the stick at once, but he beat me to it. "There is no Hello Kitty brand on my cue," I said.

"Still . . . it's pink," Reed said. "A feminine weapon if ever I've seen one."

"The question is, do you know how to use it?" Thompson asked, examining the cue.

"I'll let you be the judge of that." I snatched the stick away from Thompson and looked pointedly at George. "You game?"

He held the stick over his head and stretched. "Yep. Time to realign some egos."

Ben arrived on the scene just as Reed was making the break. "Who let her out of the cage?" he asked Thompson.

Thompson laughed. "Is she really that good?"

He nodded. "Our grandfather taught us both to play on this very table when we were little. But because Kitty was his pet, pun intended, he shared all his secret strategies with her." Ben nodded his head toward the table. "Just watch."

Reed was successful in putting away the solid six in the far corner pocket off the break, but when he missed his next shot, the game turned to me. I sunk numbers ten and fourteen in one shot with little effort, and then followed up with number eleven in the corner pocket. Spotty screwed his turn up so badly we all laughed, leaving George several options. For the remainder of the game, aside from the occasional lucky shot by one of our opponents, the table belonged to George and me.

"Maybe next time I'll let you borrow Hello Kitty," I said to Spotty and Reed when the game was over.

In search of their dignity, Spotty and Reed challenged George and Thompson to the next game while the rest of us went upstairs to work on dinner. Archer and Maddie set the table with white linens and white china and every size and shape of candle they could find while Ben and I dug through three pounds of crabmeat for shell.

"I'm glad you remembered to call George," I said to Ben.

He froze. "I thought you were the one who called him," he said, looking up at me.

I shook my head. "He must've seen the lights on. He looks like shit, like a vampire, with those dark circles under his eyes."

Ben began adding the ingredients—Saltine cracker crumbs, a beaten egg, mustard, mayo, and Worcestershire sauce—to the crabmeat to make crab cakes. He was using his hands to work it all together when the doorbell rang. He looked up at me and grinned. "Your turn."

"Surprise!" Emma shouted when I opened the door for her. She looked ridiculous, like a little girl playing dress up in her mother's leopard-skin fur coat.

"What the hell are you doing here?" Ben said, arriving on the scene with crab gunk still on his hands. "You're supposed to be in Aspen."

She pushed past me and planted a noisy kiss on Ben's lips. "One of the brats got the flu," she said, slipping out of her coat. "I had no idea a real fur could be so warm." She folded it over her arm, and held it out to me. "Wanna feel it?"

I ran my fingers quickly over the fur and then snatched my hand back. "Is this your Christmas bonus from Uncle Hollis?" I asked her.

"Something like that," she said, making a start toward the stairs. "I need to freshen up after driving all the way from Texas. Where should I put my things?"

I held my breath, waiting for Ben to respond. "In my room," he said. When she smiled her conceited smile, the one that made me want to smack it right off her lips, he added, "You'll have it all to yourself, because I'm sleeping in my parents' room on the top floor."

Emma stomped up the stairs, and Ben and I returned to the kitchen. "What the fuck is she even doing here? I didn't tell her we were coming to the river, did you?" Ben whispered.

"Are you kidding me? This is déjà vu from that night back in October. She must've read one of our texts."

He washed the crab goo off his hands and dried them, pacing back and forth. "Duh, Kitty. Use your head. We didn't even decide to come down here until last week."

A chill traveled my spine. "Oh my god, you're right. She did not have access to our computers or our phones. Okay, so now I'm a little creeped out. Should we call someone?"

"And say what? My brother's ex-girlfriend is stalking him and she just showed up at our door looking like Cruella de Vil wrapped in one-hundred-and-one Dalmatians?"

I shrugged. "Maybe not the police but Mom or Dad or someone. Just in case we wake up dead."

"Okay, so now you're overreacting." He stuck his hands back in the mixture and began patting out a crab cake. "Archer or Maddie probably posted something on their Facebook page. Let's just be cool, and with a little luck, she'll get bored with us and go away peacefully in the morning."

"Sure, I'll be cool," I said, heading toward the hallway. "Just as soon as I go upstairs to see what's taking her so long."

"Don't provoke her, Kitty," Ben called after me. "I'm warning you."

I stuck my head back in the kitchen. "She's our houseguest. I just want to make sure she has all the towels and pillows she needs. Oh, and FYI, Maddie and Archer are not friends with Emma on Facebook."

As expected, Emma was nowhere to be found, in or around Ben's room. By the time I climbed the stairs to my parents' room I was furious, and when I found her laying out a sexy teddy on their bed, I was blinded by anger. I'd never been in a physical fight before, but my rage took total control over my body. I grabbed her arm and jerked her around. "You black widow bitch! Ben specifically told you to put your things in his room."

My first fist missed her nose by inches, but the second one connected with the side of her head just above her ear. Her face registered surprise for a split second and then she latched onto me, pulling me backward to the bed. We clawed and slapped at each other but she eventually gained control by wrapping her legs around my waist and grasping a huge chunk of my hair. While I was fighting to get loose, Emma screamed over and over for help.

We heard the pounding of feet, like a galloping herd of horses, coming up the first set of stairs and then the second. Emma yanked my head toward her and snarled, "Watch this, bitch. Your beloved brother is so dumb he falls for it every time." She relaxed her legs from around my waist and let go of my hair. "Get her off of me." She made a great show of pushing me out of the way just as Maddie, Archer, and Ben entered the room.

I stumbled backward, landing on my butt in the rocking chair on the other side of the room. I jumped up and went after her again, grabbing a handful of her hair and hauling her from the bed. Tightening my grip, I brought Emma's face close to mine. "You're gonna pay for everything you've done to my family."

I jerked her head one last time before shoving her out of my way. I raced down both flights of stairs and went straight to the bar where I poured two fingers of Jack Daniels in a crystal tumbler. I kicked it back and felt the liquid burn my throat, the only sensation in my otherwise numb body. I was going for the decanter again when Ben stopped me.

"That's not the answer, Kitty. Come with me." He took my hand and led me out onto the porch.

The frigid air slapped me in the face and slowed my racing heart. Inhaling huge gulps of salty air, I made my way over to the railing. Lights beamed in the black night from the homes up and down the Irvington side of the creek, but without even a sliver of moon for illumination, our less-populated side was pitch dark. Which meant we couldn't go next door to borrow a cup of sugar or to ask for help if a deranged psycho-bitch suddenly attacked us with an ax.

"What happened up there?" Ben asked, coming to stand beside me at the railing. "I told you not to provoke her, but the two of you were going at each other like roosters in a cockfight."

"It was so freaky, Ben. For the first time in my life, I lost total control of myself." I told him about the negligee and how Emma had staged the fight to look like I was doing the beating. "I may have started it, but . . ."

"I understand," Ben said, shaking his head in disgust. "She really got you here." He pointed at my cheek.

"What do you mean?" I ran my fingers along my cheek, feeling the puckered skin and the stickiness of blood. "Is it bad?"

"Bad enough it needs to be cleaned."

"You mean sterilized. I may have to go through a series of rabies shots." I elbowed Ben in the ribs. "So are you ready to call Mom and Dad now?"

"They're all the way up in the mountains, remember? Probably well into their fourth or fifth martini by now."

"Believe me, Ben, she does not have your best interest at heart. You need to stay way the hell away from her. She is dangerous."

Ben's face beamed dark red in anger. "After tonight I'm gonna run that little bitch out of town if I have to drive her to Norfolk myself and load her up on an aircraft carrier headed for the Persian Gulf."

"That's a pie-in-the-sky dream if ever I heard one. You can avoid her, Ben, but I have to live with her."

"No way I'm gonna let you live with that whack job."

"And just what the hell do you think we can do about it in the middle of the school year?" I asked, hearing the desperation in my voice.

"Students are always flunking out after the first semester, Kitty. And others transfer to different schools. They'll have an opening somewhere, maybe not a single and it might not be your first choice . . ."

Something that resembled hope stirred in my belly. "Maybe."

Thompson stuck his head out of the door. "Brr, it's cold out here," he said, stepping onto the porch. "Is everything okay with you two? Archer said I should come and check on Kitty, that she and Emma got in a fight." When he saw my face, he grabbed my arm and pulled me toward him. "What the hell happened to you? We need to get that cleaned up."

Thompson whisked me off to my room for some first aid and much-needed psychotherapy. Forty-five minutes later, we came back downstairs feeling slightly rejuvenated and hungry for dinner.

Maddie and Archer had found place cards amongst my mother's party supplies, and arranged them so Emma and I were across from each other but at opposite ends of the table. Illuminated by the dozen votive candles that separated us, I could see the scratches on her forearm when she raised her fork to her mouth for a bite of salad. Unlike my battle wounds, the skin did not appear to have been broken, just a series of red lines crisscrossing her arm. Cat scratches.

As usual, Emma monopolized the conversation during dinner. A discussion about our generation's lack of ethics led to a debate over whether it was equally acceptable for a woman to satisfy her sexual needs with random pickups in the same way some men do. Whether to get a rise out of Ben or whether she simply enjoyed watching the rest of us squirm, she cited instance after instance of her more spontaneous encounters. Every time an attempt was made to change the subject, Emma maneuvered the conversation back to sex. We all sprang from our chairs with relief when Archer announced we were only thirty minutes away from midnight.

With all the leftovers stored in the refrigerator and the dishes placed in the dishwasher, we gathered in the living room to watch the ball drop on television.

"I could only find two flutes," Emma said, offering the tray of champagne to Ben and me before anyone else. "And since you're the host and hostess, the privilege belongs to you."

Ben and I sipped the champagne with the same sense of obligation we had to wear the silly hats and blow the noisemakers Reed and Maddie brought. The strain of having Emma in the house had placed a damper on our evening. While the others participated in the traditional round of kisses and best wishes for the New Year, Ben and I stood together at the edge of the crowd.

"Get your coat, man," Thompson said, slapping Ben on the back. "Time for fireworks. We need your great pyrotechnics expertise."

"I think I'll sit this one out," Ben said to Thompson. "But Spotty and Reed are both Eagle Scouts. You're in good hands with them."

While the guys separated their fireworks into piles on the dormant winter grass, the rest of us gathered along the porch railing. With the exception of our voices, and those echoing from a party across the creek, the night was quiet, so much so I almost hated to disturb it with the blasts from our rockets.

"It's snowing," Archer said, sticking her hand out to catch a flake. "Maybe we'll get snowed in and have to spend another night."

I cringed at the thought of being trapped with a psychopath. I watched Emma rub her body all over Ben's, cozying up to him against the cold. Sensing she had an audience, she wrapped her arms around his neck and pulled his face down, making certain I could see her stick her tongue in his mouth. Irritated, he pushed her away, and whispering loud enough for everyone to hear, reminded her they were no longer in a relationship.

Things got a little fuzzy for me after those first few explosions of color. The only thing I remember—other than at the end when Spotty lit a whole package of firecrackers and I mistook them for gangsters shooting at us with machine guns—was Ben slamming Emma up against a porch column. I'd never blacked out before. It was as if my mind had fallen off a cliff into an abyss. A bottomless pit of nothingness.

TWENTY-TWO

Ben and I did a quick search of the house. When we didn't find Emma in any of the obvious places—sleeping on the sofa in the game room or drinking coffee in the kitchen—and when she didn't answer any of our texts or calls, we woke the others and combed the place, looking under beds and in closets. One by one, we gathered beside the window in the kitchen to stare at the lone set of footprints in the snow.

Thompson grabbed the coffee pot and began filling it with water. "Okay, so let's try to piece this thing together. Who was the last person to see Emma?"

Maddie rolled her eyes. "That's a stupid question. We were all on the porch when Ben banged Emma's head up against the column, and we all saw him follow her inside and up the stairs afterwards."

Reed dropped his arm from around Maddie's shoulders. "Let's not be so quick to jump to conclusions," he said, moving away from her and closer to Ben.

Maddie glared at me. "I'm guessing *you* don't remember anything since Thompson had to literally carry you upstairs to bed."

"Retract the fangs, Maddie," Spotty said, laying a hand on my shoulder for support. "Being nasty isn't going to help anything."

"She's right, though." I rubbed my eyes as if clearing them would restore my memory. "I remember very little about being out on the porch. And nothing from when we came inside."

"That's not like you, Kitty," Archer said. "You've never been one to drink too much."

"And I didn't last night. I had a few beers, spaced out during the evening, and a glass of wine with dinner." I locked eyes with Ben. "Oh, and that shot of bourbon to calm my nerves after the fight with Emma."

"Are you sure you only had one shot?" Maddie asked, her lip curled up in distaste. Maddie had gone to bed as one of my favorite friends and woken up a prima donna bitch.

"Okay, that's enough. Everybody stop arguing." Reed wrapped his fingers through the handles of six coffee mugs and carried them over to the table. "Let's all sit down and try to figure this thing out together."

Spotty poured everyone coffee while Thompson passed out the glazed doughnuts.

"The reality is that none of us should have been drunk after all we had to eat," Ben said, hanging his head. "Myself included."

Maddie tore off a tiny piece of doughnut and pointed it at my brother. "Exactly, Ben. None of us *were* drunk except you and your sister."

Thompson folded the top back on the box of doughnuts and placed them on the kitchen counter. "Maddie, your blame and sarcasm are counterproductive. If you can't offer anything constructive, maybe you should leave the room." He turned his back on her. "Katherine, you were only a little buzzed before dinner, and you had plenty to eat, including two helpings of white chocolate mousse. I had no idea you were in such bad shape until I came up to the porch after setting off the fireworks. Did you have only the one glass of champagne?"

"Wait a minute," Archer said, sliding her chair back from the table. "Ben didn't seem wasted to me either until after the champagne." She picked up one of the flutes from the tray of empty glasses on the counter and sniffed it.

"Don't waste your time," Maddie said to Archer, nodding toward the glasses. "We washed those last night."

Archer set the glass back down on the tray and ran her hand on the counter and behind the sink. "What're you looking for?" I asked her when she dropped to her knees and began crawling around on the floor.

"My ring, the sapphire my parents gave me for graduation. I took it off when I was doing the dishes, but I must've put it back on. It's probably upstairs." She stood and wiped her hair out of her face. "Anyway, remember how Emma insisted that Ben and Kitty drink from the only two flutes? I'll bet she drugged them."

Reed nodded. "Which would definitely explain why they both got so hammered so quickly. It was probably Liquid X, easy enough to find if you're into that kind of thing."

Maddie shook her head in disbelief. "Give me a break. Nobody drugged anybody. Why can't you just admit it, Ben? You had too much to drink, lost your temper, and now a girl has gone missing."

I set my coffee mug down and stared across the table at her. "Why are you being such a bitch? Despite all of your insinuations, nobody in this room did anything to hurt Emma. There's a single set of footprints leading down to the dock. Single means one, Maddie. If those footprints belong to Emma, she probably got in a boat with somebody and went somewhere."

No one dared speculate on the other possible scenarios. Emma was way too narcissistic to commit suicide, but I would not have ruled out the likelihood of an accident.

"And if we're planning to call the police," Ben added, "we better do it soon, before the sun comes out and melts the snow."

"What should we tell them?" Spotty asked.

Ben set his eyes on Maddie. "The truth. We need to tell the police everything about what happened last night so they can help us find Emma. I'm convinced this is just another one of her stunts, and I can't wait to see her in person so I can kick her ass out of our lives for good. But if something did happen to her, I want the police to see those footprints."

Two patrol officers arrived in less than thirty minutes. With bloodshot eyes and breath that reeked of whiskey, they dragged their dumpy bodies up our front steps. With one quick glance at the footprints, interested only in wrapping up the case in time for an early lunch, Officers Collins and Hathaway jumped to the conclusion of suicide. It took a fair amount of psychological profiling from Thompson to convince them that, while she might be a troubled young woman, Emma was way too self-centered to be suicidal.

"With all due respect, young man," Collins said to Thompson, "if you know this woman so well, why don't you tell us where she is?"

Ben stepped in front of Thompson. "Listen, Officer, until about a month ago, Emma was my girlfriend. So I know her well enough to be fairly certain she went off somewhere to party and is crashed on someone's sofa, or in their bed, as we speak."

The other officer, Hathaway, placed his hands on his hips. "Well, if that's the case, son, why the hell did you call us?"

"Because of the footprints," I said, speaking up for the first time. "*If,* for some reason, Emma does not show up, and it turns out that something did in fact happen to her, the footprints are evidence—evidence that will be gone by noon."

"Besides, we don't even know for sure that they're Emma's footprints," Archer added.

I nodded. "The one thing that doesn't make any sense to me in all of this is that Emma's things are gone. She either put them in her car or she took them with her. But why would she do that if she was just going to have a drink with a friend?"

"What friend?" Collins asked. "She's not from around here, is she?"

"No, but she does know *someone.*" I walked over to the window. "George Turner. He lives right over there." I pointed across the creek. "He was here last night. For about an hour. But that was early, around seven or so."

Collins furrowed his eyebrows. "George Turner? As in Holden Turner, the commonwealth attorney's son?"

"He's the one," I answered.

"Have you had any communication with him this morning?" Hathaway asked.

"No, but it's not even ten o'clock." When Ben saw the stern look on Hathaway's face, he whipped his phone out of his pocket. "I'll send him a text now."

"Don't send him a text, boy," Collins said to Ben. "Call him. And if he doesn't answer his cell phone, try his house line."

We all held our breath while Ben dialed both numbers and left messages on each line.

"Holden Turner is an important man around these parts. Looks like we have no choice but to call in the big guns on this one," Collins said to his partner, who nodded in agreement.

While Hathaway paced up and down in front of the fireplace in the living room, snapping orders at dispatch to call in the detectives, Collins went outside to his patrol car for supplies. From the kitchen window, we watched him take pictures with a digital camera and spray something out of an aerosol can onto various footprints along the line from the house to Emma's car and down to the dock.

Reed and Maddie disappeared to their room and returned a little while later with their overnight bags strung across their shoulders. I could see the tension in Reed's face when he pulled Ben and me aside. "I'm sorry about all this. I guess a person's true character really shows itself during a crisis."

"Don't sweat it, buddy," Ben said, squeezing Reed's shoulder. "Maddie doesn't know us that well. I can only imagine what she thinks. If you don't mind, though, will you check with the police to see if they have any questions for you before you leave?"

Reed nodded. "I'm gonna drive Maddie to Richmond and come straight back."

Ben smiled at his friend. "With any luck, by the time the police are through with you, Emma will be back and we can all go home to Richmond together."

"Yeah dude, wouldn't that be nice?" Reed said, offering Ben a high five. "We should auction off the opportunity to be the first to slug her when she shows. I can promise you I'll be the highest bidder."

***

Detectives Bonnie Breton and Eric Erikson stepped from their unmarked car and took command of the scene with the experience and confidence the patrol officers lacked. Right away, Detective Breton honed in on the most obvious detail that Humpty and Dumpty failed to notice. "What happened to your face?"

"I had a fight with my roommate," I said to her, running my fingers along the welt on my cheek.

Gently, in a way that reminded me of my grandmother, the detective lifted my chin toward the light. I lowered my eyes and watched her as she examined the scratch. With her crooked teeth and double chin, there was nothing pretty about the female detective, but I found her slate-blue eyes warm and full of compassion, a sentiment her partner seemed to lack.

Detective Ericson curled his lip up as if he'd gotten a whiff of rotting fish. "Now let me guess. Your roommate and the missing person are one and the same?"

I shrugged. "Naturally."

To make certain the detectives understood the whole scope of the situation, Ben and I described our relationship with Emma, and for the second time that day, Thompson presented his theory about Emma's psychopathic behavior. Both Breton and Ericson seemed to believe our stories, although they cautioned us that their opinions might change if Emma didn't show up in a couple of days.

"You did the right thing in calling us," Detective Breton assured Ben and me. "Typically we don't respond so quickly to missing-person calls, but having only one set of footprints leading to the dock complicates the situation. There are several things that concern me here, enough to do a little more digging before I'm willing to assume Emma got in a boat and took off with her lover."

"I'd be willing to bet my next pay she's just shacking up with some lucky bastard she met along the way." Ericson's chuckle was awkward in the midst of our silence. He cleared his throat. "But maybe she just went down to the dock to get some fresh air, fell and hit her head, and knocked herself out on the way overboard."

Detective Breton turned to Ben and me. "Although it's too late to test for it now, judging from the way the two of you described your experiences last night, I believe there's a good chance you were drugged. And yes, probably with Liquid X or a similar substance. Do you think it's possible Emma took some herself?"

I thought back to the night, during rush last year, when I found Emma and Ben with their noses in a mountain of cocaine. "It wouldn't be the first time she used drugs," I said to the detectives, avoiding my brother's gaze.

"Then I can think of a hundred scenarios that might have happened to a drugged person stumbling around on a dock on a night as pitch-dark as last night." Breton looked pointedly at Ericson. "Why don't you and I have a look around outside while these kids keep trying to get in touch with George Turner?"

I glanced toward Maddie who'd been sitting on the edge of the sofa, during our chat with the detectives, waiting to pounce on the first opportunity to get the hell out of our lives. "Detective Breton, do you think it's possible to get whatever statement you need from my friends before you go down to the dock? Maddie and Reed have to get back to Richmond for a family commitment this afternoon," I lied, anything to get the hostile bitch out of our house.

"Of course." She handed a form to both Maddie and Reed. "If you would please write down whatever information you think might be pertinent, including your contact information, then you're free to leave." She started for the door, but then turned back around. "This might sound a little strange, but given the circumstances, it would be helpful if you could leave the shoes you were wearing last night so we can make prints. We'll get them back to you as soon as we can."

It took a lot for Reed to convince Maddie to loosen her grip on her Tory Burch boots. He wrapped his arms around her and whispered in her ear, and whether he told her he'd buy her a new pair of boots or whether he promised her a weekend by the fire in his parents' mountain ski lodge, his proposition seemed to placate her. Maddie smiled up at her lover, nodding her head, but she glared at Ben and me as she dropped her boots beside the front door on her way out.

Ben and I walked them to their car.

"Look, man," Reed said to Ben, "I'm counting on you to be in the taproom at the club for the six o'clock football game tonight. That's how sure I am this bitch will show up any second with some lame explanation."

"It's a beautiful thought, bro," Ben said, leaning back against the hood of the car. "But don't hold your breath."

While Ben and Reed said their goodbyes, I wandered over to Emma's car and lifted the door handle, surprised to find it unlocked. Once Reed and Maddie had driven off, I called Ben over. "Look at this shit," I said, removing an oversized Michael Kors tote bag from the passenger seat. "Do you have any idea how much the bag alone costs?"

Ben opened the back door and pulled out a large Louis Vuitton duffle. "No, but I'm pretty sure this one costs at least a grand. It looks like the little poor girl has found herself some rich bastard to wrap around her pinky finger." Ben stuck his head inside the car. "Do you see her keys anywhere? Or her cell phone?"

I found her keys in the cup holder and held them up, jingling them. "But I don't see her phone, unless it's in one of these bags." I dumped the contents of the tote on the driver's seat, and searched through the tubes of lipstick and tampons and other assorted bottom-of-pocketbook junk until I found a small satin satchel. I shook a pair of diamond studs and a sapphire ring out into my hand. "That little thief."

"Are those *your* earrings?" Ben asked, his eyes wide with horror. "The one's MayMay left you?"

"Yep, and this is Archer's ring." I slid the sapphire ring on my middle finger and looked up at my brother. "Ben, when Thompson and I came upstairs after my fight with Emma last night, I hid these earrings way back in the back of my bedside table drawer. Unless she snuck upstairs sometime during dinner or while we were watching the ball drop—and I seriously doubt that happened because I don't remember her leaving the group—Emma took these earrings while Thompson and I were asleep."

Ben slumped against the car. "This is almost more than I can handle." He placed the LV duffle on the hood of the car and ripped it open. "Holy shit," he said, thumbing through a rubber-banded wad of cash. "All hundred-dollar bills." He put the cash back and removed a small zippered case. "What the heck? Did she rob a jewelry store?" He reached inside the case and pulled out a handful of designer jewelry—David Yurman and Roberto Coin and the likes.

I went around to the passenger's side and began searching the glove compartment and down on the floorboard. "I'm guessing you want this back," I said, handing him Emma's computer. "Is the serial number registered in your name?"

He shrugged. "I paid for it with my credit card, but I gave it to her as a gift. It's not going to matter much if she's dead, now is it?"

"How dare her!" I screamed, slamming the car door shut. "That bitch came into our house as a guest, an unwanted one maybe but still a guest, and she stole from us. Not only did she rob us of our dignity by drugging us and putting us in this embarrassing situation, but she also took our most treasured possessions. If she were here now, I'd kill her myself."

"What's going on here?" Detective Ericson called to us as he rounded the corner of the house. "The two of you may have saved us the many hours it would've taken to get a search warrant, but you've compromised the investigation. Whatever you found in there will not be allowed into evidence."

"This car is parked on my property, Detective," I said. "Which in my book makes it fair game. This is an emergency. We were hoping to find her cell phone."

"And did you?" Breton asked, joining us.

I shook my head. "No such luck."

She peered over our shoulders at the loot. "Did you find *anything* useful?"

Ben and I stepped aside so the detectives could examine the contents of Emma's bags. "She's been babysitting for her aunt and uncle's children out in Texas over the holidays," Ben explained.

"My guess is, Emma took these things from them, because she certainly couldn't afford them herself."

"Is that her computer?" Detective Erickson asked, eyeing the MacBook Air that Ben was holding.

"I'm not sure who it technically belongs to," Ben said, "but I bought it for her last spring. It's been in her possession ever since."

"Then I suggest we take it inside and see what we can find," Erickson said. "Maybe a telephone number for her mother or her relatives in Texas."

As it turned out, Ben had already stored in his phone the number to Emma's home in Altoona when she visited her mother at Christmas a year ago. While the two detectives disappeared into the living room to make the call, I took the computer to the kitchen where the rest of our guests were scrambling eggs and making yet another pot of coffee.

I settled at the bar and flipped open the computer. "Knowing Emma, her password has something to do with money."

"Good guess," Ben said, nodding. "Try *gold*."

Archer raised her eyebrow. "As in, *digger*? How'd you know?"

Ben shrugged. "She told me."

I typed in the keys and waited. "That's it. I can't believe Emma actually set her password as gold."

Spotty glanced at us over his shoulder from the stove where he was scooping up eggs. "Seriously? After all she has put us through? Nothing would surprise me, even if we learned she was on a flight headed to Las Vegas right now."

"Except she wouldn't have boarded a flight to Sin City without this." I pulled the bundle of money out of Emma's bag and held it up to show the others.

Archer's eyes grew wide. "Holy Moley! That's a lot of cash."

Detective Ericson entered the room with his pocket-size notebook in his hand and his partner on his heels. "We were able to reach the girl's mother, one Joyce Stone, but she hasn't seen or heard from her daughter since Thanksgiving, during which time they had some sort of altercation. According to the police reports, when the mother called the daughter out for coming home stumbling drunk, the daughter came after her with a serrated kitchen knife of some sort. Fortunately, a nosy neighbor happened to be walking his dog by the kitchen window at the time and called 911.

We glanced around the room at one another, our shocked expressions saying what are mouths were unable to speak.

"The good news is that she was able to put us in touch with her aunt out in Texas," Detective Breton said. "The bad news is that there's more bad news."

Ericson cleared his throat and consulted his notebook. "Apparently, the aunt, one Claire Dennison, walked in on Emma and her husband in bed together." Ignoring his partner's scornful stare, the detective nodded his head enthusiastically in response to the gasps from our group. "How do you like that? Try to give the girl a break by offering her a job and look what happens. She sleeps with her husband and then robs her blind."

I held up the wad of money. "Did you ask them about this? Do they make a habit of leaving wads of hundred-dollar bills lying around? There's at least five thousand dollars here."

Detective Breton took the bundle of money from me and placed it back in Emma's bag. "I talked to Mrs. Dennison for a while. It's actually very sad the way it all played out. Her daughters, Sally and Lena, worshipped their cousin Emma. These two little girls, neither of them older than ten, are the ones who walked in on their father and Emma in bed together. Naturally they were upset. So, while the mother and father were in another part of the house consoling their hysterical daughters, their niece broke into their wall safe and cleaned it out before she took off."

"And she just happened to have the combination?" Ben asked what everyone else was wondering.

Detective Breton pointed her finger at Ben. "That's the interesting part. Neither Hollis Dennison nor his wife ever showed the safe to Emma, but she was in and out of it in less than ten minutes."

"That makes me want to throw up," I said to the detectives. "I'm sure she's searched all through this house and the one in Richmond. Talk about feeling violated. I hope you told them we would have their things sent right back to them."

Ericson nodded. "Only they said something about a leopard-skin fur coat. I don't remember seeing it in the car."

"That's because she's wearing it," Ben said.

When both detectives looked at Ben suspiciously, I explained, "She had it on when she got here. She made a big deal about it."

"And she was wearing it during the fireworks," Archer added.

Breton walked over and stood behind me, looking over my shoulder. "Have you discovered anything useful on her computer?"

I'd been skimming through Emma's emails while we were talking. "Actually I have. For the past few days, Emma has been exchanging emails with her old boyfriend. His name is Peter Packham, and he goes to school in Florida—at Flagler, I think. Apparently he's down there now, working during the Christmas break at some seafood restaurant." I scrolled down, looking for a particular e-mail. "It says right here, dated yesterday, that she was planning to leave our house after midnight and drive down to see him. She even mentions stopping along the way in Savannah to get a few hours' sleep."

"Now that's disturbing," Breton said, her face pinched and her lips puckered. "It's evidence that Emma had concrete plans, which she's probably missed out on. Can you find his contact information anywhere? The name or phone number where he works?"

I checked her contacts folder and then scrolled back through the e-mails. "All I see is the name of the restaurant, the Crazy Lobster."

Detective Breton scribbled the name of the restaurant on an index card and stuffed it in her back pocket. "We'll do our best to get in touch with him, but other than paying a visit to the Turners, there's not much more we can do for the time being except wait."

"What can we do to help?" I asked the detectives.

"You can pray that your friend makes it back safely." Breton looked first at Ben and then me. "Because if she doesn't, the two of you are going to have some explaining to do."

TWENTY-THREE

A coin toss awarded Ben the privilege of calling our parents, who assured us they were on their way but that it would take them the better part of the afternoon to drive down from the mountains. Keeping one eye on the clock and the other on the dock, we stripped beds and washed sheets and moved our things around so the guys were now downstairs and the girls up, with the exception of Ben who returned to his own room down the hall from mine. After nibbling on leftover tenderloin for lunch, we broke into mini-search parties and combed the grounds looking for clues. As anticipated, the snow had melted, taking with it the only valuable evidence in the case. Our search succeeded only in killing time, at least an hour and a half of it. When George's phone lines continued to go unanswered, I positioned myself by the french doors for the remainder of the afternoon. Focusing the binoculars across the creek at the yellow farmhouse on the hill, I watched and waited for any signs of life—a shadowy figure moving around inside the house, a car pulling into the driveway, the kitchen light coming on a dusk.

Our parents arrived prepared for an emergency—a hurricane or a snowstorm or the crisis of a missing person—with a grocery bag full of junk food and a stack of old movies. Thompson poured a stiff bourbon for my father and an ample glass of Merlot for my mother, and waited with them on the sofa in the living room while the rest of us unloaded groceries and carried their bags to their room. My parents listened with patience and concern, asking pertinent questions and drawing their own conclusions without casting judgment. Their reaction was not at all what I had expected from them, but if ever there was a time for my parents to finally grow up, the night of this dismal New Year's Day was it.

For the rest of the evening, we ate hot wings and meatballs and chips covered in dip while watching one bowl game after another. Although no one mentioned it, everyone was aware of the seconds ticking away and the bell ringing the half hour on the ship's clock on the mantle. Every minute we drifted further away from the alleged time of Emma's disappearance, and every hour it became less likely she'd return.

I slept very little that night, although I tried not to toss and turn for fear of waking Archer, who snored softly beside me. As light began to creep through the blinds, I finally dozed off, only to be startled awake again by the sound of a car coming down the gravel driveway. The events of the day before came back to me, flooding me with fear, paralyzing every part of my body except my eyes as they came to rest on the alarm clock beside me. It was already nine thirty, and the house was still silent. Eerily silent. No one banging pots and pans around in the kitchen. No coffee aromas were drifting up the stairs.

A car door slammed outside followed by footsteps crunching the gravel and shuffling up the brick steps. The doorbell rang, a ring-a-ling-a-ling like the old-timey telephone that once hung on the tackle-room wall, followed by the sound of my parents' hushed voices as they made their way down the stairs from their bedroom. My heart pounded against my chest, and my pulse throbbed in my ear.

I stepped into my slippers, grabbed my robe, and joined Ben who was already in position on the top step, elbows propped on knees, face buried in hands, waiting to hear what we both knew was coming. I pulled him close and hugged him tight as Detective Breton broke the news. I tried to wrap my mind around the details—the haunted boathouse; Emma's skull bashed against a metal cleat; Ben, Thompson, and myself wanted at the station for questioning.

Ben ran to his room and I followed him, holding him as he sobbed for the girl he once loved. My mother joined us a little while later and we sandwiched Ben between us, smothering him with kisses and cooing our sympathies in his ear. When the appropriate amount of time had passed and Ben's tormented sobs had subsided, my mother repeated what she'd learned from the detectives.

"Why Thompson?" I asked when she told me the detectives only needed to question the three of us, not Archer or Spotty.

"Because apparently he's your alibi," my mother said to me. There was no need for her to state the obvious. Thompson could vouch for me during the overnight hours since he'd been sleeping beside me in my bed.

"Did the detective say whether they'd gotten in touch with the Turners?" I asked.

Lying flat on his back between us, Ben glanced at me and then quickly shifted his attention to Mom, waiting for her response.

She nodded. "George has an alibi as well. His parents."

I swung my feet over the side of the bed and went to the window. An image of the footprints was burned in my mind, Emma's last walk on earth. I wondered if she'd been in a hurry or taking her time, moving her hips back and forth in her sexy way.

"There was only one set of footprints in the snow," I said, turning back around to face my mother and my brother. "I don't understand why that evidence doesn't prove the innocence of everyone who slept in this house that night."

My mother stood to face me. "It's the best evidence in your favor, no doubt about it. But according to the detectives, they still have some concerns about the two of you." She ran her finger down the angry red scratch on my face. "But listen, I have some good news as well. Your father called Max Robinson yesterday and put him on notice. He's on his way down here now, so let's get moving. We need to get dressed and find something to eat."

Even though Ben and I had known Max Robinson for most of our lives, we'd only seen him once a year, on Christmas Eve, when we were dressed in our party clothes. He was unprepared for the sight of our disheveled appearance in our jeans and sweatshirts.

"Ben, you and Katherine need to go back upstairs and change." Max pointed at Thompson, who was wearing nice corduroy pants and a cashmere sweater. "Put something on like this young man is wearing. And, Katherine, a dress please, maybe some tights, something that makes you look sweet."

Ben and I stared at him incredulously.

As if reading our minds, Mr. Robinson said, "I know it may seem disrespectful to your friend to be worried about how you're dressed after just learning of her death. But you need to put those thoughts aside for now. This will likely be the most important first impression you'll ever make."

"But we've already met both detectives," Ben argued.

"And you'll likely meet some more today." When Ben turned reluctantly toward the stairs, Robinson added, "And don't forget to shave."

I'd never given much thought to the difference in age between Thompson and me, but when he climbed in the front passenger seat of Mr. Robinson's Yukon and began talking to him, man to man, about his concerns for our case, I felt like Ben and I were the children, relegated to the back seat for being naughty.

We reached the main road and made a left-hand turn towards White Stone. "Tell me about the haunted boathouse," Mr. Robinson said to Ben and me through his rearview mirror.

Ben nodded at me, his sad eyes pleading for me to do the talking.

"Well . . . "—I thought back to the legend I'd heard dozens of times during my life—"a long time ago, way before we were born, a local fisherman's wife lost her husband to a storm out in the Chesapeake Bay. For years afterward, the neighbors reported hearing sobbing coming from the boathouse on stormy nights. Which of course was the wife calling to him to come home. Tragically, the woman was killed when her house was struck by lightning and burned to the ground while she was sleeping."

"Let me guess," Robinson said. "The neighbors still claim to hear the woman crying in the boathouse during storms."

"Exactly. But believe me when I tell you, we've spent many a stormy night camped out in that boathouse waiting for the woman's ghost to appear." I smiled gently at Ben. "And the only thing we ever saw was our first buzz off of a mason jar of vodka stolen from our parents' liquor cabinet."

Robinson chuckled, then turned serious again. "Here are the obstacles as I see them. In addition to your extensive knowledge of this boathouse and your close relationship with the victim, the biggest problem we are facing is that you were both seen fighting with this girl on the night she was killed. All of the above pretty much makes y'all murder suspects numero uno and numero dos."

"But the foot—" Ben started to protest.

"Forget about the footprints," Robinson said, tightening his grip on the steering wheel. Mr. Robinson was small in size, but his commanding voice made his presence known in any crowd. I'd never seen him perform in a courtroom, but I was glad he was on my side. "The two of you are the logical suspects, and you can bet every investigator on this case is going to try to pin this on you."

I gazed out of the window, wondering how we'd gone from celebrating New Year's to being questioned for murder. The bare trees along the side of the road reminded me of soldiers, sentries standing guard along the way to the prison. I glanced at my brother, who stared at the back of Thompson's head and looked miserable, a man lost in his grief. Despite everything he'd told me, and all he'd tried to convince himself, he had never stopped loving her.

My grandfather's words rang out in my ears—*If you are strong for Ben, he will be strong too.*

"What do you know about George Turner?" I asked Mr. Robinson.

He waited for the car in front of him to make a left-hand turn at the stoplight in Kilmarnock before answering me. "Only that he has a very strong alibi: his father, the commonwealth's attorney."

"Trust me, George is somehow involved in this mess. I mean, think about it. A. He lives right across the creek. B. His boat is actually in the water instead of in dry storage like ours. C. He knew my roommate. He was at our house on New Year's Eve when Emma arrived so unexpectedly." I paused, debating whether or not to use my trump card and sacrifice my friend's future to protect my brother's. "And then there was the matter of his recent visit to rehab for anger management and alcohol abuse."

Ben jerked his head toward me.

I shrugged. *What else could I do?*

Ben nodded. *You did the right thing.*

"Now that, Katherine, is some very useful information," Mr. Robinson said, nodding his head with enthusiasm. "Let me ask you this. Have the two of you told the police the truth about everything so far?"

"Yes, sir," we answered in unison.

"Then let's make a pact. I'll get to the bottom of this mess, but the two of you, in turn, must continue to tell the truth."

We spent the next two hours answering the same questions over and over again. Finally, after assuring the detectives we wouldn't leave town, we drove back to White Stone in silence. When we got to the house, we discovered that, in our absence, Archer and Spotty had taken Ben's car home to Richmond.

"I don't understand. Why'd they leave?" I asked my mother.

Mom placed a cheese-and-meat sandwich platter in front of Thompson and me. "They just have some things they need to take care of before they go back to school. Archer wanted me to be sure to tell you she loves you and to call her as soon as you can."

"Translated—they felt like they were in the way," Thompson said. "I've been wondering if maybe *I* should head on back to Charlottesville as well. I have plenty of work to do to get ready for next semester, and you have enough to deal with without having to worry about a houseguest."

Mom handed Thompson a hoagie roll and a jar of mayonnaise. "I know we've only just met, but as far as I'm concerned, this murder investigation has moved us beyond the point of being guests to one another. From now on, I'll expect you to make your bed and do your own laundry."

This seemed to put Thompson at ease for the moment. But fifteen minutes later, when we were stretched out on the dock with our backs against a piling, enjoying the warmth of the sun on a rare fifty-degree January day, he raised the subject again.

"I wouldn't blame you if you needed some space," he said, taking a bite of his sandwich.

"Go back to Charlottesville if you need to, Thompson, but don't do it because you think it's what I want. Ben is in a bad place right now. He's counting on me to give him strength, which is strength I get from you."

"Say no more." Thompson nodded and looked up toward the house. "Speaking of Ben, where'd he go?"

"Upstairs, to take a nap." I took a gulp from my water bottle and wiped my lips with a napkin. "Listen, the police are too busy protecting the commonwealth's attorney's son to worry about finding the real killer. If we're going to find anything that'll help us get out of hot water, we're going to have to do it ourselves."

"That's my girl," he said, winking at me. "What's your plan?"

"You know me so well," I said, wadding up my napkin and throwing it at him. "I haven't gotten beyond this first part, but before the police decide to impound Emma's car, we're going to search it until we find something that will lead us to the real killer."

TWENTY-FOUR

And we found that something tucked under the visor on the driver's side of Emma's car—an old-fashioned room key from the Shady Oaks Motel in White Stone.

I flipped the plastic key chain over in my hand. "Room number one-fifteen. I know your bedside manner is impeccable, but how do your investigative skills rate?" I asked Thompson.

"Yet to be tested." Thompson removed his car key from his coat pocket and dangled it in front of me. "But hey, I'm game."

Thompson and I agreed to take the legitimate approach and speak to the manager first, but when we pulled into the parking lot of the one-story motel and saw no sign of life in the front office, we decided to have a look around on our own. We parked on the opposite side of a late-model Chevy pickup truck, the only other vehicle in the lot. Holding our bodies flush against the wall, we peeped inside room 115, making sure it was empty before letting ourselves in with the key. We searched everything quickly and thoroughly, under the bed and in the drawers and on top of the shelves in the closet. Despite the outdated décor, the room was clean and ready for the next couple to spend an hour of their afternoon hidden away from the world.

"There's nothing here," I said, plopping down on the bed. "What was I thinking? Did I seriously believe we would find a handwritten letter from Emma pointing us to her killer?"

"Hold on a minute, now. Let's think about this before we give up so easily." Thompson lowered himself to the bed opposite me.

"Why would Emma have rented this room in the first place if she was planning to spend the night with you?"

I lay back flat and stared at the ceiling. "Who knows? The drive from Texas to Virginia is over twenty hours. Maybe she needed a nap before she crashed our party."

"Your house is not that easy to find through all the winding country roads. I know she's visited you a couple of times, but would she have known how to get to your house without directions?" It irritated me when Thompson made me come to my own conclusions instead of giving me the answers right away.

"Well duh." I rolled over on my side and propped myself up on one elbow. "She used her GPS. She probably got our address from the telephone book."

Our eyes drifted to the bedside table. "It's all yours," Thompson said, handing me the phone book.

I opened it to the *L*'s and ran my finger down the page. "My father's name is underlined," I said, flipping through the pages to the *T*'s. "And so is Holden Turner's. That goddamn little bitch." I heaved the phone book across the room. "Would this information still be stored on her GPS?"

Thompson shrugged. "At least, on mine, you can pull up previous destinations." He stood and pulled me to my feet. "Shall we go check it out?"

I held the door open for Thompson. "Do you think there's any point in talking to the manager?" I asked, jiggling the knob to make sure it was locked.

"Whether we want to or not, here he comes." Thompson nodded toward a man—probably in his mid-thirties, and wearing blue-jeaned overalls and a camouflaged hunting coat—heading our way from the motel office.

"Just what'd y'all think you're doing?" he called out to us.

I took a step towards him. "Coming to talk to you, actually. We need your help."

He remembered Emma right away from the picture I showed him on my iPhone, although he was reluctant to release any information until I shed a few tears and mentioned murder.

The manager held his giant hands up to me. "I don't want no trouble now, little lady. The local law is my kin. My grandpappy, God rest his soul, was once the sheriff of Lancaster County. His son, my uncle, is a senior patrolman. Whatever I tell you, I'm gonna have to tell them too."

I nodded my head in enthusiasm. "And we want you to. All I'm trying to do is save my brother from going to jail for something he didn't do," I said, shivering against a sudden gust of wind.

The manager's lips parted in a gentle smile that gave us a glimpse of rotting teeth. "Then let's go inside where it's warm. Feels like that cold front has decided to come on through."

We followed him down the sidewalk, with a trail of body odor and stale cigarettes in his wake. His office was more than warm. It was hot and stuffy, suffocating. He removed a box from under the counter, a wooden card file that resembled my grandmother's old recipe box. He flipped through slowly, taking his time until he found the card he wanted.

"She checked in around noon on New Year's Eve day. If I remember right, she's the one who drove in from Texas?" His eyes scanned down the card. "Yup, white Lexus SUV with Texas tags."

Thompson leaned over the counter to look at the card. "How'd she pay for her room?"

The man pointed a nicotine-stained finger at the card. "Says here, cash."

"Did you get an imprint of a credit card?" Thompson asked. "You know, for incidentals?"

"No need for that. We don't offer room service or fancy movie channels."

I pointed to a sign above the counter. "Did she rent by the hour or by the day?"

"Says here, daily." The manager stuffed the card back in the box. "But I remember she had a hard time deciding. She wanted to take a nap and get cleaned up, but she thought she might be staying with friends overnight." He walked over to the door, watching a middle-aged couple spill out of one of the rooms and climb into the Chevy truck. "Things got kind of busy that afternoon, it being

New Year's Eve and all. But I remember your friend left sometime around four o'clock and was gone for over an hour."

"Do you have any idea where she might've gone?" Thompson asked.

"Nah." The manager turned back around to face us. "I figured she'd gone out to get some hair thingamajig or sparkly makeup to doll herself up for the big night. She left for good around seven, and I ain't seen her since."

"Well, thank you for your help," I said, jotting my number down on one of his reservation cards.

After making the manager promise to call me if he thought of anything else, Thompson and I jumped into the car and sped back to the house.

"Both addresses are right there, see?" Thompson pointed at the navigation screen in Emma's Lexus. "The memory doesn't record the date or time, but she went to the Turners' address on Creekside Drive at some point before she came here. I'm guessing around four o'clock when she left the motel for an hour."

My mind was spinning with unanswered questions. Were George's parents at home at the time of her visit? Did Emma call George first to let him know she was coming, or did she just show up out of the blue? Had she been communicating with George since they first met over Labor Day weekend last year?

I shifted in my seat toward Thompson. "I need to borrow your car."

"I'm sorry, Katherine," he said, shaking his head. "No way I'm letting you go over there alone. It's best to let the police handle this."

"Because they're doing such a good job of it?" I got out of the car, slammed the door, and headed toward the house for Dad's keys.

Thompson caught up with me. "Wait a minute, stop," he said, grabbing the hood of my coat. "If you insist on going, then I'm going with you." His deep-blue eyes bored into mine.

"It's not that I don't want you to go with me." I glanced over at the Turners' farmhouse across the water. "It's just that Mr. and Mrs.

Turner are like my second parents. I have a comfortable relationship with them, and I'm not sure they'll be able to speak freely in front of a stranger. Anyway, I need you to stay here with Ben. I'm worried about him."

Reluctantly, he handed me the keys to his Land Rover. "I don't like it, but all right."

Sliding the keys from his fingertips, I stood on my tiptoes and kissed his cheek. "You're the best. You know that, don't you?" He pointed at his lips, and I planted one there too, a passionate kiss that expressed my gratitude for his support.

He followed me to his car. "Remember, to start it, you put your foot on the brake, not the gas, and then push the button," he said, explaining the keyless ignition system that confused me every time I drove his car.

When the car started right up, I closed the door and rolled down the window. "Don't worry. Everything will be fine. I'm going to look them in the eye and dare them to lie to me. I'll be back here with a confession in my hand in less than an hour."

He bent over and stuck his head through the open window. "It's that cocky attitude of yours that worries me. I don't think you realize the danger in this situation. Emma is dead, Katherine. And if what we believe is true, George is the one who killed her. You need to watch your back."

"The Turners are not going to hurt me, Thompson," I said with more conviction than I felt. "They're like family."

"Maybe once upon a time, you had that kind of relationship with them, Katherine. But they have made it abundantly clear their allegiance no longer extends beyond their immediate family. Not to you and certainly not to Ben. I want you to text me when you get there, before you go inside, and then again as soon as you leave to head back here. Okay?"

"Fine." I puckered my lips and kissed the air. "Stop worrying."

As I drove away, I caught a glimpse of Thompson's concerned face in the rearview mirror. I remembered his warning—*Watch your back.* I dismissed the idea as paranoid, which would prove to be the biggest in a long list of mistakes I'd make that day.

TWENTY-FIVE

Mrs. Turner was wearing the same flannel robe with the faded blue flowers she'd been wearing when Ben and I visited her in August. But instead of the warm smile I remembered from that day, her mouth was set in a thin line. "Katherine, I'm surprised to see you," she managed in a shaky voice. Instead of inviting me in, she closed the door a little against the cold. Against me.

Mr. Turner appeared behind her. I was shocked at how much he'd aged in the few months since Abigail's funeral. His hair was all the way gray, nearly white, and the lines around the corners of his eyes were etched deep with worry. In a George Clooney kind of way, he was still a handsome man, but life had taken its toll, the grief over the loss of his daughter too much for him to bear. "Considering the circumstances," he said, "I'm not sure it's such a good idea for you to be here. It's unfortunate your brother had to drag us into this mess."

His nasty tone stunned me. And to think I'd been feeling guilty for bringing more hardship on his family. "My brother?" I asked, taking a step toward them. "You mean Ben? The boy you taught to water ski? The one who used to wait all week long to go sailing with you on the weekends? The guy who thinks of you as his second father? Is that the brother you're talking about?"

Mr. Turner's shoulders slumped as he stepped out of the way to let me in. I should have left the Turners' house at that point. I'd already gotten what I'd come for. Their guilt was evident in their glazed eyes and pinched faces. They were covering for their son.

And the need to find out how George was involved in Emma's murder propelled me inside like an outboard motor on a boat.

"I understand Emma came over here for a visit on New Year's Eve," I blurted once we were seated in their living room. "Was that the first time you met her?"

The Turners exchanged a concerned look. "That girl was never in this house," Mr. Turner said, as if delivering the closing arguments to a jury.

George bounded up the stairs from their basement playroom. "Why would your roommate come to see me when she was so in love with your brother?" he asked, plopping down on the sofa next to me.

Here we go with the brother thing again.

I took a closer look at George and I didn't like what I saw. His eyes were wild, black and shiny like pinballs bouncing off the ceiling and the walls. His smile was bright, too bright considering the circumstances. Afraid of pushing him over the edge, I opted for a more gentle approach. "How're you holding up, George, in the midst of all this craziness?"

"I have nothing to hide." His quick response made me wonder whether he'd been rehearsing with his father all afternoon.

Mr. Turner moved to the edge of his leather recliner, the same chair he napped in on Saturday afternoons while watching NAS-CAR. "George, I caution you to be careful about what you say."

I didn't blame Mr. Turner his hostility, but I resented it. The way he'd so easily dismissed our relationship was like a knife to the heart for me. When he noticed me staring at him, I lowered my eyes to the floor at his feet and caught the shimmer of a shiny object beneath his chair. It was hard to tell from where I was sitting, but the object appeared to be a piece of silver jewelry, oddly familiar to me in some way.

"Stop worrying, Dad." George leaned back against the cushions and propped his legs up on the coffee table. "I have an alibi, remember?"

His father nodded. "But *you* need to remember that Katherine is desperate. She'll do anything to protect her brother, to take the suspicion off of Ben, even if that means pointing the finger at you."

I shifted on the sofa to face George, shutting Mr. Turner out of the conversation. "What time did you leave our house on New Year's Eve?"

"Hmm, let's see." His eyes darted around the room as he tried to remember. "You were out on the porch with Ben at the time. Must've been about twenty minutes after your fight with Emma. You really kicked her ass good, didn't you, Kitty?" George's expression was smug, just as I imagined it was when he told this story to the detectives.

I leaned back against the sofa cushions and took a deep breath. "It wasn't like that at all, George."

"Then what was it like, Katherine?" His use of my given name was pointed. His message was clear. We were no longer close enough for him to call me by my nickname.

George's father glared at me as though I was on the witness stand and he was waiting the opportunity to question me. "I'm not sure you'd understand," I said under my breath to George.

"Try me," George said.

"Can I still trust you?" I asked and he nodded. "Like I trusted you that night when we pricked our fingers and promised to always be friends?" I stared at him, hard, daring him to violate the pact we'd made that night. I didn't know where our conversation was headed, but I knew I desperately needed to connect with the George of old, to remind him of what we'd once meant to one another. "Remember, Porgie? In the haunted boathouse?"

Mentioning the boathouse was a risk, and I held my breath hoping it would have the right effect on him. George smiled and his features softened as his mind wandered back to that night. I was all set to remind him of a dozen other stories when my cell phone rang and ruined the moment. I excused myself and walked over to the window.

Thompson's voice was panicked. "Katherine, you need to come home. Ben's been arrested."

I stared across the creek at our house and watched the patrol car pull out of our driveway. I'd been so engrossed in waiting for one of the Turners to make a slip that I missed the whole event. "Where are my parents?" I asked, trying not to sound alarmed.

"Here, with Mr. Robinson, but they're getting ready to leave for the police station."

"You ride with them, and I'll meet you there." Without giving Thompson a chance to protest, I hung up and turned around to face three sets of inquiring eyes.

"In all the time I spent in this house as a child, I never noticed you have such a clear view of our place. Much more unobstructed than we have of yours." I sounded both sarcastic and accusatory, just as I intended. "With a pair of binoculars, you can see what's on my plate while I'm eating breakfast at the kitchen counter. I'll be sure to close my blinds at night from now on."

"Is there a problem at home?" Mrs. Turner nodded at the cell phone in my hand.

"What?" I asked as though I'd forgotten about the devastating call. "No, everything's fine. My family wants me to meet them at the Sand Piper for an early dinner."

"The Sand Piper is closed for the holidays," Mr. Turner said.

"Really? I don't think my parents realized that. Oh well." I shrugged and started toward the door. "We'll figure something out when we get there."

All three Turners stood at once, anxious for me to leave. As I passed in front of Mr. Turner, I dropped my phone on the carpet in front of him. When I bent over to pick it up, I reached under the chair for the mysterious object. No wonder the silver and leather bracelet looked familiar.

"Interesting." I held it up for inspection. "I gave this bracelet to Emma for Christmas a year ago. I can't imagine how it got under your chair, unless of course Emma dropped it when she was here for a visit. I'm certain I don't need to tell you, Mr. Commonwealth's Attorney, that perjury is considered a felony, punishable with jail time. A considerable amount of jail time if I'm not mistaken."

I'd seen his face turn red like that only once, many years ago when he caught George sneaking a five-dollar bill from his wallet.

"Nice to see you all." I sauntered toward the door, but quickened my pace the moment I was outside.

"Hey, Kitty, wait up," George called, following me out into the driveway. He caught up with me at the car and reached for the handle to open the door for me. "You seem upset. Was that phone call bad news?"

"Truthfully?" I looked up at George from the driver's seat. "The police just arrested Ben." Eager to get out of there, I didn't wait for his response. I placed my foot on the brake and pushed the start button just as Thompson had instructed me, but after several frustrated attempts, I couldn't get the engine to fire. "I need to get to Lancaster. Will you please start this car for me?"

He nodded and we switched places. "Whose truck is this anyway? Your *boy*friend's?" he asked, running his hand over the wood paneling on the dash. He pushed the start button and the engine fired right up. "So what's the big rush to get to the sheriff's department? Can't wait to show them the bracelet you found now, can you?"

I stared down at George, looking for any trace of the kind-hearted boy who used to be my friend. Whether it had started with Abigail's death or whether this mean streak had always been a part of him, hidden away beneath his outgoing personality, his good nature had succumbed to anger and hatred.

Ignoring the warning from deep within my subconscious, I asked, "How does it make you feel, George, to know one of your *best* friends may go to jail for a crime *you* committed?"

"So we're going to play it that way, are we?" He jerked the car door with such strength I was forced to let it go or risk losing four of my fingers. I grabbed at the door handle, but with a demented grin on his face, George pushed the lock button and lowered the window just a crack. "I've always wanted to test-drive a Land Rover to see if they really handle like everyone says they do. You know, climbing up the sides of hills and jumping over ditches, shit like that."

He slammed the car in forward and then reverse and then into forward again as he executed a three-point turn in the driveway. He drove up beside me and motioned for me to get in. Even though every fiber of my being warned me that Thompson's new car was not worth my life, that he would not want me to sacrifice my safety for something that could so easily be replaced, I got in anyway.

George raced to the end of his driveway and then peeled off down the street toward White Stone. "Maybe it's time I come clean with the sheriff and tell him everything I know about what happened that night."

I glanced over at him expectantly. "Really?" I asked.

"Duh," he said, clucking his tongue at me. "Now why would I want to do that when Ben is doing such a fine job of taking the rap for me?"

"Because it's only a matter of time before the detectives realize they can no longer cover for you. I mean seriously, George? You're the one with access to a boat. And once I show them this bracelet"—I twirled the bracelet around on my finger—"and tell them what I found in her room at the Shady Oaks Motel . . ."

He cut his eyes at me. "You're bluffing," he said, a hint of doubt in his otherwise confident expression.

I *was* bluffing of course. The only thing two underlined names in a phone book proved was that Emma had tried to get in touch with us. "Funny thing—the motel manager is related to one of the patrolmen. Unlike the detectives who are so eager to protect your family, this patrolman likes to play by the rules. He promised me he'd make certain this evidence falls into the right hands."

George made a sudden, sharp, right-hand turn down a long dirt driveway. Although I'd never driven there in a car before, my sense of direction told me we were headed toward the haunted boathouse. The driveway was bumpy, pitted from years of rain and snow, but Thompson's truck handled it with ease.

"Gee, this is fun." George glanced over at me and I could see his eyes were on fire. "Let's test out the four-wheel drive." He turned the knob beside the gearshift, switching into four-wheel drive. "You know, I like this ride so much, maybe I'll ditch you here and take off for California or Seattle or Montana."

"Right, George," I said, rolling my eyes, pretending that I wasn't scared out of my mind. "The police will catch you before you cross the state line."

George pointed at me. "You see, Kitty, that's where you're wrong. They won't know to be on the lookout for me without you to tell them." He put the truck in park and nodded toward the water. "And you will be floating at the bottom of Carter's Creek with all the other little fishies."

A chill raced down my spine. How could I have been so foolish? George was never going to turn himself in. He was a desperate man, a murderer intent on covering his crime to save himself from a life in prison. Or the death penalty. My best chance was to escape the car.

"Look, George. This is no big deal." I held the bracelet in the air, making sure he was watching as I lowered it to my bag. "I'm going to put this in here for now." I dropped the bracelet and quickly removed my cell phone from the side pocket, cupping it in my hand so George couldn't see it. "We'll figure out a way to get Ben off without having to drag you into it. Just let me drive you back to your house so I can get to the sheriff's office."

"Not a chance, you dumb bitch." George reached down and snatched the bracelet up in one quick swoop. "All this time I thought you were smarter than the rest."

I opened my eyes wide and faked like I was seeing someone outside George's window, a childish game Ben and I still play on occasion. Lucky for me he fell for it, at least long enough for me to unlock the door and sprint away.

It was cloudy and drizzly and close to sunset. I stumbled down toward the boathouse, ducking under vines and dodging trees and jumping over downed tree limbs. When I got close to the burned-out foundation of the house, I stepped on an old brick and twisted my ankle. I fell to the ground and, despite my best efforts to silence my sobs, I cried out in pain.

I managed to dial 911 on my phone as I crawled on my belly toward the old chimney, the only part of the house not destroyed by the fire that killed the old widow. Crouched in the fire pit, I whispered to the operator, "Please help me. My name is Katherine Langley and I'm on the property of the haunted boathouse off of Tarpon Road. Send the police. Hurry. George Turner is trying to kill me."

"You're damn straight I am," George said, towering over me. He grabbed me by the wrist and yanked me to my feet, pinning me back against the chimney. I was reminded of the night Ben tried to choke me, the night I vowed never to be that vulnerable again. With all my strength, I rammed my knee in George's groin. Despite the immense pain in my ankle, I limped as fast as I could toward the boathouse, aware of George's cries of agony behind me. I hid in the corner behind the door and waited for him to come after me. Minutes later he swung open the door, but I pushed it back on him, causing him to lose his balance. He stumbled but managed to catch himself on a piling to keep from falling into the water.

He came after me with all the fury I imagined he used to kill Emma. As he grabbed a handful of my hair and wrestled me to the dock, I caught sight of a large brown stain, the dried blood from Emma's head wound. As much as I disliked her, I never wanted her to die. Was it like this for her? Was she as terrified as me?

"Why couldn't you have just left it alone, Kitty?" George said, sitting on top of my chest, pinning my arms to the dock with his knees. "Now I'm gonna have to kill you just like I killed Emma."

"Why *did* you kill her, George?" I struggled to breathe beneath his weight. "The George Turner I know is not a murderer."

"The bitch deserved to die." He wiped a line of drool off his mouth with the back of his hand. "She lured me out here with the promise of sex, but then the little tease turned on me. When I got mad at her for holding out on me, she started saying all these horrible things about Abigail."

"Tell me what she said to you, Porgie. Talk to me." As much as I was buying time for the police to arrive, I felt the need to comfort

George. I could see *my* George, buried beneath his crazed state, crying out for help.

"She said it was better for Abigail to be dead than for her to have to look at herself in the mirror every day and know she would never be beautiful."

Tears filled my eyes at the cruelty of my dead roommate's final words. And to think I was responsible for bringing Emma into George's life. So much of what'd happened to Emma, she'd brought on herself. I had the scratch—healing now but still visible—on my face to prove how easily she could get under someone's skin.

"I'm sure Abigail is proud of you for defending her. She loved you, George." I sniffled, unable to wipe my nose with my arms pinned. "But she loved me too. And Ben. Just as we loved her."

His expression confused, George gently ran a finger down my cheek, tracing the track of my tears.

"Think about what you're doing, George. Our Yabba-Dabba-Abigail would not have wanted you to hurt us, under any circumstances."

He opened his eyes wide as if he'd just woken from a bad dream. Slowly and evenly, he let out a deep breath, relaxing his body. He looked down at me, as if seeing me for the first time. "That's right, Porgie. It's me, Cat," I said softly. We stared at one another as all of his anger and my fear washed away. We were friends again, taken back in time to the night before Abigail's funeral.

George brushed a stray strand of hair from my forehead and then he rolled off of me and leaned back against a piling. "How'd my life get so screwed up, Kitty?" He rubbed his eyes with his balled fists. "Things are so fucked, right now. Nothing seems real."

I sat up and wrapped my arms around my knees. "People handle grief in different ways."

"Most days I feel like just giving up. I want to die and go to heaven so I can see Abigail and know she's safe. Except now, because of Emma, I won't be going to heaven."

I certainly wasn't one to cast judgment at the pearly gates of heaven, but I wanted to give my friend whatever smidgeon of hope I could summon. "Emma was evil, George, pure and simple. We found a car full of jewelry and cash she'd stolen from her aunt and uncle. That is, *after* she'd broken up their marriage by sleeping with her uncle."

"Nice." George rolled his eyes. "Your roommate was twisted, Kitty, but then you already knew that, didn't you? What a waste of such beauty. I can still hear my mother saying to Yabba, 'Beauty is as beauty does.'"

We fell silent for a minute, and I could hear a dog barking off in the distance. When the sirens of the rescue vehicles pierced the quiet, I locked eyes with George.

"Here they come," he said. "My life is over now."

"I wouldn't say that. Don't forget your father is the common-wealth's attorney."

"Yeah, boy. I did him proud, didn't I?"

"My grandmother used to say that parents always love their children no matter what." I reached for George's hand and squeezed it. "Your father is well respected throughout this county. He's done a ton of favors over the years, favors that will now be returned. This is a tight-knit community. These people are your family. They will take care of you."

He nodded, although I couldn't help but wonder it he was thinking about those horrible girls who'd driven Abby to a slow suicide, those bitches that belonged to this same community.

"Anyway, if you ask me, you have the perfect temporary insan-ity case. You were out of your mind with grief for Abby and tor-mented by Emma's cruel comments about her. I'll vouch for you."

"You mean that? After everything that's happened?"

"*Particularly* after everything that's happened. Remember, I'm to blame for introducing you to Emma." I squeezed his hand again and released it. "You'll have to work hard, though, George. I mean really hard. And quit drinking. You need to have a clear head in order to get a handle on your grief."

"I don't deserve your friendship, Cat." George buried his face in his hands. "Yours or Ben's."

With his back to the doorway, George couldn't see the single-file line of people making their way down the path. Two policemen followed by Thompson and then Ben and my parents. I held up my hand to stop them from entering the boathouse, nodding once to signal that everything was okay.

"I thought we settled this years ago, Porgie. We swapped blood over it. Our friendship is unconditional."

"I remember." When George raised his head, I detected a hint of a smile on his lips at the bittersweet memory. He burst into tears, and the two of us cried together for all we'd lost. Friendship. Youth. Love.

The policemen huddled in the doorway, granting us our privacy for several long moments before growing impatient. They cleared their throats and shuffled their feet to let us know our time was up.

I kissed George on the cheek and whispered in his ear, promising him that everything would be okay. It was a lie, but it was one we both needed to hear.

So as not to startle George, I got up gradually and walked toward the others. With each step I took, time slowed a fraction of a second more, as if I were crossing the threshold into another era. Then, smiles of relief gave way to looks of horror—mouths dropped open and eyes grew wide. One officer stepped behind me, using his body to shield mine. I tried to turn and see what was happening behind me, but Thompson quickly pulled me toward him and held me tight.

Over Thompson's shoulder, I saw my father and read his lips, "No, son, no." The sound of his words was muted by the gunshot report echoing throughout the boathouse and across the water. I buried my face in Thompson's chest and waited for the pain—ten seconds, twenty, a minute—but it never came. I felt the thumping of my heart against Thompson's and the movement of our chests as we inhaled and exhaled in unison. Just to be sure, I blinked my eyes and cleared my throat. I was still alive. But if not me, who? I squirmed to free myself from Thompson's arms, but he only tightened his grip more to prevent me from seeing George's body lying in a crumpled heap in the same spot where we'd been sitting only moments earlier.

TWENTY-SIX

The detectives found a suicide note in George's pocket, smeared and wrinkled and dated November 15, Yabba's birthday. It was of little consolation to me that George had been planning his suicide for weeks, maybe even for months. I was the one who'd been with him during those last moments. If only I'd done or said something different. If only I'd known about the gun hidden in the corner of the boathouse behind the door.

Every painful step on my sprained ankle brought back the crazed look in George's eyes while every beat of my broken heart reminded me of how much I'd loved him.

My father drove to Richmond the following morning and returned shortly after lunch with two armloads of funeral clothes and Blessy. She wrapped her big arms around Ben and me and held us tight throughout the bitter cold, rainy afternoon. When we finally loosened our grip on her, she went to work, doing laundry and straightening up and making a meal out of the leftover contents of our refrigerator.

I was grateful to have Blessy around for the order she restored to our world, but it was my mother I turned to for comfort when I woke from my nightmares. I craved the warmth of her body like a newborn baby; and to make up for all the years she'd deprived me, she gave her affection freely. I relinquished my pain to her and she handled it like a tower of strength.

Blessy recognized the new bond developing between Mom and me and gave us the necessary room to explore it. When Thompson announced on Wednesday morning that he was heading back to Charlottesville to prepare for the new semester, Blessy begged a ride to Richmond, claiming she was needed at home to help with her sick grandchild.

On Thursday morning at eleven o'clock, we entered the Presbyterian Church in Irvington to attend our second funeral in less than a year. George's was much the same as Abby's. Same hymns, same minister presiding over the same tearful congregation, same multitudes packed together in the same pews. Same blue-sky day on the river.

What wasn't the same was Mr. and Mrs. Turner's attitude toward us. I expected awkward—I was surprised at hostile. I felt their blame when they avoided my hug and turned their backs on me to greet another friend.

"Right back at you," I wanted to say to them. I wanted to remind them that I was merely the friend, but they were George's parents. His problems had started well before New Year's Eve. Hell, I'd seen the change in him even before that Labor Day weekend when he'd first met Emma. The fun-loving boy I'd known for most of my life had become too serious, too sarcastic, too intense. George's anger had been festering for years. Emma was merely his victim, the last in a long line of bitches to torment the sister he adored.

So maybe I *was* the one who introduced George to Emma— I'm certainly capable of bearing my share of the responsibility—but let's be reasonable here. Mr. Turner took an oath in a court of law, with his hand on a Bible no less, to uphold the truth in the Commonwealth of Virginia. Not only did he betray me, he betrayed his countrymen. Worst of all, he betrayed his family. If he'd done his job, both as a parent and as the commonwealth's attorney, with Mr. Turner's connections, his son would be serving a reduced sentence at a minimum-security facility for temporary insanity. Instead, George was lying in front of me, cold and alone in a mahogany box every bit as shiny and lovely as Abby's.

Despite all the beautiful music in that church that day, the only song I heard was in my head—the sound of geese honking and waves lapping along the shores of a calm river.

There was no way Mr. and Mrs. Turner would ever share George's last words, his suicide note, with me. I would have to be satisfied with the comfort of knowing I'd had the opportunity to tell him, during his last moments on earth, how much his friendship had meant to me.

Friday's funeral was altogether different. Gray snowbanks lined the streets of Altoona, Pennsylvania, on our way to the Blessed Heart Catholic Church. Including our family and Emma's mother, there were exactly fourteen people in the church, easy enough to count. The hymns were solemn and the priest spoke only a few kinds words about a girl he clearly did not know well.

I met Emma's mother for the first time at the cemetery after the brief graveside service. Mrs. Stone was a tiny little woman, soft-spoken and socially awkward. She had been no match for her daughter's strong will while she was alive, nor would she be for the grief that would follow Emma's death.

Ben and I expressed our condolences and offered our apologies, and she, in turn, assured us we were not to blame. "Bad genes," she said, dabbing at her eyes with a tissue. "Like father, like daughter."

Our parents made a spur-of-the-moment decision to spend the weekend in Washington, DC on our way home to Virginia. Fine by me. I was certainly in no hurry to get back to school. All I had to look forward to in Charlottesville, with the exception of Thompson, was an empty apartment full of my dead roommate's things.

On Saturday, on their way to the Air and Space Museum, Ben and Dad dropped Mom and me in Georgetown for an afternoon of shopping in the boutiques. Our outing turned out to be the most enjoyable excursion, shopping or otherwise, we'd ever made together. We'd never done the mother/daughter thing well, but the events of the past week had delivered us to a new place, one where trust and love are accepted and returned. Murder and suicide are grown-up issues, deserving of the respect of everyone involved.

Ben and I ditched our parents after dinner on Saturday night and caught a cab over to the K Street Lounge to explore some of Washington's nightlife. We settled in at the bar and order shooters, a lemon drop for me and tequila for him, but only one for each. We discussed the terms for a codicil to the pact we'd made all those years ago on the day we ran away to the country club. Not only would we hold true to our promise to always be there for one another when one of us felt sad or needed help, we agreed to never again let anyone or anything come between us. No man. No woman. No drugs.

ACKNOWLEDGEMENTS

I would like to thank the following:

My children, Cameron and Ned, for being patient and understanding. I love you both with my whole heart.

My husband, Ted, for putting up with all the hours I spend with my face stuck in my computer.

My mother, Joanne Herring, who has always believed in me and whose courage and beauty inspire me.

My editor, Patricia Peters, for her amazing attention to detail.

Constance Costas for her time and patience.

I've had many critique partners over the years, but I'd like to thank Laura Rocha, Jaqui Hopson, and Lauren Davis in particular.

Gotham Writers' Workshop for helping me learn the craft.

Made in the USA
Charleston, SC
11 February 2013